D0908918

Soultown

Also by Mercedes Lambert

Dogtown

Soultown

MERCEDES
LAMBERT

VIKING

VIKING
Published by the Penguin Group
Penguin Books USA Inc., 375 Hudson Street, New York,
New York 10014, U.S.A.
Penguin Books Ltd, 27 Wrights Lane, London W8 5TZ, England
Penguin Books Australia Ltd, Ringwood, Victoria, Australia
Penguin Books Canada Ltd, 10 Alcorn Avenue, Toronto, Ontario,
Canada M4V 3B2
Penguin Books (N.Z.) Ltd, 182–190 Wairau Road, Auckland 10,
New Zealand

Penguin Books Ltd, Registered Offices:
Harmondsworth, Middlesex, England

First published in 1996 by Viking Penguin,
a division of Penguin Books USA Inc.

10 9 8 7 6 5 4 3 2 1

PUBLISHER'S NOTE
This is a work of fiction. Names, characters, places, and incidents either are the products of the author's imagination or are used fictitiously, and any resemblance to actual persons, living or dead, events, or locales is entirely coincidental.

Library of Congress Cataloging in Publication Data
Lambert, Mercedes.
Soultown / Mercedes Lambert.
p. cm.
ISBN 0-670-86684-9 (alk. paper)
I. Title.
PS3562.A454S66 1996
813'.54—dc20 95-26233

This book is printed on acid-free paper.

Printed in the United States of America
Set in Plantin
Designed by Junie Lee
Korean calligraphy by Haing Soon Lee

모든 여인이 스스로 자기운명을
주장하는 날을 바라보며
이 책을 정신대 여인들에게 드립니다

"She went up Noon Street," Pete Anglich said.
"A bad street for a white girl."

—from *Pickup on Noon Street,* by Raymond Chandler

Soultown

The moon slipped behind the eucalyptus trees. I sat up, stretched. It was nearly three in the morning. I must have knocked off. I'd been waiting and watching in my car for nearly five hours. A breeze began to blow from the west, and it made the leaves of the eucalyptus dance and chatter. From the other side of the trees came the persistent rumble of the 10 Freeway as crazy night riders raced into the dark.

I turned the radio dial. Oldies, black fuck music. Mexican love songs: "I suffer without you, my heart, my soul." I could make out some of the words because I've been studying Spanish at night school. "I suffer, I . . ."

I turned back to the oldies. It was a night for oldies. For "Earth Angel." For "Stagger Lee." "Only the Lonely." I twisted the rearview mirror. My hair was longer and still light from the summer. Nearly platinum. I'd started to wear makeup, and there was a line of black mascara smudged under my eyes. I swore as I used spit to wipe off the mascara. It would fucking figure I'd nod after waiting all this time.

It had been seven months since I'd seen Lupe.

I was probably the last person she'd want to see tonight.

The last time I'd seen her had been in court in February. For prostitution. And it had been six months before that when she'd vanished. In an instant I remembered everything again from that squalid August I wanted to forget. My office on Hollywood Boulevard. Lupe. My first dead person. Lupe. The gun. Lupe grabbing the gun from my hand. The explosion. Blood. The man on the ground bleeding to death. I'd promised Lupe she was safe, but she hadn't been. I hadn't been able to stop thinking about the enormity of my betrayal of her in Dogtown. She had good reason not to want to see me.

When Lupe disappeared that night at the end of August last year, she didn't come back to work the corner outside my office. She never called me. I looked for her on other blocks where women hustled. I looked on Western. I asked some of the girls I'd seen her talking to where she was, but all I got was a lot of attitude and more exposure to bad clothing.

The last I'd seen of her was in Division 40 in February. Just a few days after my twenty-seventh birthday. A Tuesday. The skies gray and unpredictable. Lupe wore the county blues and a pair of wrecked-looking K Mart brand tennis shoes. She had pulled her hair back into a tight ponytail, and I saw lines around her eyes that I had never noticed before. Her hands were shoved angrily into the pockets of the shapeless jumper that she had belted tightly around her slender waist.

Lupe shook her head almost imperceptibly as I started excitedly toward her in the jury box, where the defendants stand while awaiting arraignment. There are so many in and out of Division 40 that they don't even bother anymore to walk them in front of the judge's bench. She stood at the end of a line of six girls, three latinas and three blacks. The girls looked drained but restless, like they'd been up all night.

By then I had appeared many times in Division 40 on court-appointed burglaries, GTAs, and possession for sales. The bailiffs and clerks knew me. No one would stop me if I walked up to the box. A chicano bailiff stood between the latinas and the blacks per Sheriff's Department memo to keep them separated. The girl next to Lupe shivered and scratched at her arm. Lupe, her eyes rimmed in black liner, gave me the quick once-over.

I was wearing a new Anne Klein II suit, black, with a pale ivory silk blouse, and my pearls. Bally spectators. Black and white. I sat down in the first row with the other lawyers. I smiled at her, but she only stared back impassively. Someone called me by name.

Burt Schaefer, a lawyer I'd done some work for, said in a stage whisper, "A good morning, my little Miss Due Process. Ready to continue your battle for truth and justice today?"

I didn't answer Burt. I watched Lupe. I wanted to tell her how much I'd changed. I had to convince her I'd never tell anyone what had happened that freakish August in Dogtown.

"Très bien," Burt continued. "The PD's declaring unavailable on the broads. We'll all get one today."

I might get Lupe as a client! I nodded in Burt's direction as I continued to study Lupe. She was twenty-three now. Five feet four with long black hair that was curly from a new perm. She'd lost a little weight since I'd last seen her. Her eyes narrowed into hard dark slits as if she was thinking of something she didn't want to think about, but there was no further acknowledgment that she knew me. She turned away from me as the judge, who'd been in a side bar conference, laughed loudly and the City Attorney strutted back to his place at the counsel table, followed by an overweight and overworked looking PD.

"All right, ladies, just stand up when your name is called and we'll appoint a lawyer for you. You'll have time to talk later after we get everyone assigned."

My hands shook as I opened my briefcase on the chair beside me. I busied myself finding a pen so she couldn't see the flush I felt spreading across my face. The judge straightened the papers in front of him. With a flourish he called names. I saw Burt go forward to one of the black girls with Jheri curls and porcelain Wizard of Oz nails which curved at the end and were painted purple.

"Guadalupe Virginia Ramos."

Lupe stood and threw me a quick defiant look.

"Mr. Peralta, please."

Steve Peralta, a skinny weasel I've seen a million times in the court building high fiving with White Fence boys and taking cash from their grandmas, stood up. He walked over to Lupe and slipped her an oily card.

". . . Miss Logan, please."

I went forward when the judge called my name. The PD leaned back in his chair and handed me a copy of a complaint and an arrest report on a Velma Roberts. A bloated black woman in her early thirties waited for me. Her hair was bleached nearly the color of mine. I glanced down at the papers. A 647. Solicitation. I nodded at the woman and gave her my card.

"Whitney Logan? What kind of name is that?" With a disappointed sigh, she stuffed the card in her pocket.

I glanced over at Lupe. Up close I saw she had an old bruise on her right cheek.

"You ever done this before?" asked the black woman. "You look like a social worker."

A grin lit up Lupe's face.

"Yes, Ms. Roberts, about a dozen times so far this year. I can take care of business as well as any lawyer here." I tried to erase the hostility I heard in my voice. "Don't worry, I know what to do."

She still looked skeptical.

Lupe dropped her gaze and examined Steve Peralta's card with exaggerated attention.

"All right, everyone, we're going to hear that motion now. Counsel, please get these cases ready. I'd like to resume the arraignments in about half an hour," ordered the judge.

The chicano sheriff and the other bailiff, Harley, a big white boy who likes to work out, took the women out of the jury box back into the lockup.

I asked the clerk to show me Lupe's file. I got my yellow legal pad and uncapped my pen.

Guadalupe Virginia Ramos.

Good. She had told me her real name. I flipped to the back of the papers to check her CII computer printout. No aliases. Good. Had she told me the truth about her record? No. Two prior arrests and convictions for prostitution. One in the end of '89 and the other the middle of last year. She'd lied. She'd said she'd only been arrested once. Third offense. She was looking at a county lid. A year. Ray Charles could see that coming.

I turned to the arrest report. February 17, 10:45 P.M. Approximate location Gardner just south of Sunset. I read quickly. Basically it came down to Lupe soliciting an undercover officer. I handed the file back to the clerk.

At the end of the jury box lounged Steve Peralta telling a loud story to Harley and the other bailiff. He hadn't looked at Lupe's file yet.

"Hey, Steve," I interrupted. "You think we could trade cases?"

Steve looked at his audience. "They give you one that's too tough for you, Logan? Maybe you want to go back to the office and do a nice little divorce."

The chicano bailiff laughed politely with Steve. Harley looked uncomfortable, divided in his loyalties. Harley has asked me out in the past. He wanted to know if we could go pump iron together sometime. Only Harley seems to be aware of what is under this black Anne Klein II suit.

The hours at Gold's Gym. The repetitions. The cuts across my back that most people can't achieve without steroids. I can run twelve miles now. And do three times a week. Tae Kwon Do three times a week with Master Sun Lee out in North Hollywood. I am never going to be afraid again. That's what I've wanted to tell Lupe. That I will never again have the failure of nerve I had when she grabbed that gun from my hand and had to pull the trigger. That she is safe with me. That I am worthy of her respect. Of her confidence. That I am her friend.

"Fuck you, Steve."

I asked Harley to let me into the lockup. Steve followed, still grinning. Except for the low drone of Burt Schaefer's voice as he read the police report to his client, the holding cell was quiet. The women probably had a dismal sense of déjà vu. The light was yellow and unappetizing. The walls smeared with the bold but graceful *placas* of Sad Eyes, Mousie, and La Donna. I hung back slightly, watching. Steve called Lupe's name.

Lupe rose from the concrete bench, tilted her chin grandly, then cast her magnificent brown eyes in his direction. She strutted forward.

"Save it, sweetheart," sneered Steve. "I'm going to try to fix it so you don't have to put that thing on ice for a long time."

I saw the muscles tighten around Lupe's mouth, but then

she formed a slow, beautiful, gracious smile for him. He opened the police report, which he read quickly to himself. He snapped it shut.

"Anyone who can bail you out?" he asked her.

Lupe's eyes flickered toward me.

"*¿La fianza?*" he repeated when she didn't answer. "Five hundred bucks."

I started forward.

"Hey, you, Logan, ain't you here to help me?" Velma Roberts lumbered forward to the bars.

Lupe turned toward Steve Peralta and shook her head. She moved so that her back was to me. She said something to him in a voice I couldn't hear.

"I don't got all day," Velma Roberts insisted.

I smiled professionally at her and nodded, trying to overhear what Peralta was telling Lupe.

Velma Roberts banged on the bars. "I got to get out of here. I got two little babies. The county'll take 'em away from me if you don't get me out of here."

I went to work. Velma Roberts was a strawberry. A strung-out pro. She grabbed the bars of the cell impatiently as I did my introductory schmooze, explained the arraignment, and talked about her constitutional right to a jury trial. I mentioned her prior. I glanced quickly toward Lupe again, but her back was still to me as she talked with Steve Peralta. Forcing myself to concentrate on Velma Roberts, I cited statistics and told her I'd find out what kind of deal I could cut with the City Attorney. Velma Robert's eyes were bloodshot. She was fat the way some women are when they're on the pipe. Smoke for two or three days, don't eat or sleep, then crash, come to and eat everything. The stop-me-before-I-kill-again kind of eating.

Steve and Burt were gone by the time I finished. Lupe lounged against the back wall talking with one of the other latinas. I walked down to the end of the cell until I was opposite her. Velma Roberts and the black girls stopped humming. The latina nodded toward me as she asked Lupe a question. Lupe looked at me without replying. She pushed herself away from the wall and strolled toward me.

"You like?" Lupe placed her hands on her hips so the coarse blue dress clung to her. "It's Susan Hayward. *I Want to Live*."

"I been looking for you, Lupe. For months. I didn't want to see you here." I sighed wearily. "A defendant."

"Citizen accused," she bristled.

"Right, soliciting a vice cop. I thought you were too smart for that."

"Pigs were trippin'. Another one of those fucking sweeps. It's keeping you busy, though, isn't it? New suit?"

"I've been worried about you. I wanted to find you and"—I lowered my voice—"tell you I'd never tell anyone what—"

"I ain't gonna talk about it."

Had she been able to forget Dogtown? "It's just . . . I thought we were . . . after everything that happened . . . friends."

"You still think I'm Myrna Loy? Forget it. I ain't interested in no *Thin Man* shit."

"I can bail you out." I'd never let Lupe know how broke I was. How little work I had. All the money I owed on my credit cards for silk and gabardine suits for work, an Hermès purse, so I'd look as if I was really making it as an attorney. Sometimes I had to use the cards to buy my groceries. I could come up with five hundred bucks for Lupe in a couple of hours—even if it meant asking my folks for the money.

Lupe leaned against the bars so her face was inches from mine. She smelled like cinnamon gum and Chanel No. 5. "My boyfriend'll bail me out."

"Yeah? Which one? One of your tricks? Where is he? Where's your brother, Hector? I don't see them here waving wads of cash."

"I didn't call yet." She snapped her gum like she was bored.

"You're not going to call. Not Hector. I was there when he told you he was going to kick your butt and take your boy Joey from you if you didn't quit prostituting. You're always talking about what a good mother you are—so what happened to Joey last August anyway?"

Lupe stood up straighter and shifted uneasily from one foot to the other. "He's with my mother."

"That's where he was all along?"

She sighed. "Yeah. When I went home that night after . . . He was asleep at my mom's. I promised her she'd never have to worry about Joey. Or about me. We was sitting at the kitchen table. She started to cry. Then Hector came in and he told me that if I fucked up again he'd have Joey taken away from me for good." She looked away. Was she going to cry?

"Let me help you. I'll pay your bail."

"*¿Qué pasa,* Lupe?" called the latina from the back of the cell. *"Hay un problema?"*

Lupe turned and shook her head. *"No, no. Un momento, 'mana."* She leaned toward me again with a hard look on her face. "I'm going to take care of myself. My way. My boyfriend'll bail me out. I'll give Steve Peralta a blowjob. I'm not doing any time. I'm going home, I'll get Joey, and I'll enroll him in Montessori school."

"Yo te ayudo."

"You speak Spanish now?" She looked amused.

I nodded. "LA's forty percent latino now. A lot of my clients—"

"Sí, sí. Alta California. La tierra de mi raza."

"Not too fast. I've only had one semester."

"*Alta California.* The land white people stole from *México.* That's what's wrong with you. White guilt. That's why you try to hang out with me. I got my own homegirls"—she jerked her thumb toward the *chola* leaning against the wall —"and I don't want your help. Leave me alone. Forget you ever knew me. And nobody's ever going to take Joey away from me again. Not Hector, not my mother. Not the *pinchi Departamento* of Social Services. I'll be out of this hole in a couple hours." She let go of the bars and pointed at my Bally spectators as she backed away from me. "Nice kicks. That's one thing I'll say about you. You always got nice kicks." Then she turned to her friend and resumed the conversation I'd interrupted.

I walked to the door that led back into the courtroom and knocked. Behind me I heard Lupe's voice and that of the other woman, tropical and light like breezes stirring the palms. I knocked again. I heard them laugh. Finally Harley opened the door and let me out into Division 40, where this time the jury box was full of men being shuffled through their arraignments.

That was seven months ago. Lupe had drawn a county lid and had done six months good time. She'd gone down a lot faster than Velma Roberts, who held out for a jury trial—a real circus with Velma testifying against my advice. Before the trial I'd been to Sybil Brand Institute for Women to see Velma on a last-ditch effort to get her to cop a plea; while I was there I sent Lupe a visit-request form from the attorney conference room, but she refused to see me. I sent her two letters and they came back unopened. Now Lupe's six months were up.

Was I an idiot to be waiting in my car in the middle of the night for her? I finished wiping the mascara off. I opened my purse for more and for my Chanel Tempting Red lipstick. They were at the bottom of my purse. Under the snub-nosed .38 two-inch detective special I bought in my local shopping mall last fall. I have a license. The gun is legal, but carrying it concealed is not. If I'm ever stopped I will say I'm coming from the range and forgot to put it back in the trunk of my car. I've spent many hours at the range. I can load this .38 in the dark and I can take a man's head off at twenty-five yards. At least on paper targets. Lupe never believed I was competent at anything.

In front of me, drenched in cinematic moonlight, stretched the uninspired and poorly landscaped facade of Sybil Brand Institute for Women. At SBI they like to process the women out after midnight.

I put on more mascara and some lipstick. A gate on the south end of the building began to open. There was activity in the sheriff's office at that entrance. I heard an intercom being activated and voices I couldn't understand. A woman appeared in Sybil's open doorway, then stepped without hesitation into the passage between the jail and the fence separating the two worlds.

It was Lupe. Even thinner than when I saw her arraigned. Dressed in a tight red skirt and a purple spandex bustier. Her red stilettos clicked across the pavement. The moonlight danced between us. A sluggish female sheriff stepped out of the guard box and unlocked the gate for Lupe.

I opened my car door and got out.

Los Angeles was a dream on the other side of the freeway. The damp breeze blew again from the west and Lupe raised her arms above her head triumphantly embracing the sky like Judy Garland striding onto the stage of the Palladium.

"*Nuestra Señora Reina de Los Angeles*, this is your daughter." Lupe threw back her head and laughed.

I walked to the front of the car. Lupe walked toward me.

"Thought you might need a ride." I pointed at my old car.

"You have a hard time minding your own business, don't you?"

"It's impossible to get a cab up here. The buses aren't running for another couple hours."

Lupe shook her head. She had a tiny black tear painted under her left eye. "Every time I see you there's trouble. I don't want any trouble. Today's the first day of the rest of my life."

"Want me to drive you to the bus stop? Down on Eastern? You can wait till the sun comes up."

"Ten days I knew you. Less than ten days," she said angrily. "And two people got killed." Lupe frowned and looked away into the distance. I knew then that she thought about what happened in Dogtown as much as I did.

"That's why I've been chasing after you, to tell you I'll never tell anyone. Why can't you believe that? I think you got busted this last time because you wanted to get caught. You wanted to be punished."

Lupe stared at me in disbelief. "You are a real piece of work, you know that? Wanted to get caught! Fucking pig was wearing a Brooks Brothers suit and a hearing aid."

I got in and started the engine. "Fine. Do whatever makes you happy. Wait for the bus. I'm leaving." I gunned the engine as I switched on the lights.

The headlights illuminated the front of the jail. In front of them Lupe stood cast in dramatic shadows. She kissed her fingertips and blew the kiss into the wind. She took one last look at the jail, then walked over and opened the passenger door. She got into my car. I pulled it in a U and headed out of the parking lot.

"Take me to get something to eat," Lupe said. "Then over to get Joey. My mom don't get up till around six."

I nodded. I would take Lupe to the Pantry on Figueroa and 9th. It's open twenty-four hours. They have giant breakfasts, steak, eggs, and pancakes. She'd like a good meal. Maybe she wouldn't notice it was only a few blocks from the garment district where we had found a dead body that dangerous August.

"Just breakfast. And go get Joey. That's it, *¿entiendes?*"

I nodded again. I had wanted her to mention my makeup, to notice how I'd changed, but she stared out the window at the dark hills. I heard her heave a sigh of relief as I pulled onto the freeway.

The old Pantry restaurant was crowded at four-thirty in the morning. Working men in jeans and construction boots. Drunks speaking loudly above the clatter of silverware falling on the floor. Rockers in black leather. Waiters in long white aprons hurried from the grill to the tables carrying big plates with eggs, ham, and pancakes hanging over the edges. We took a table in the back. Men stared at Lupe as she strolled down the sawdust-covered aisle. She seemed to grow taller under their inspection, but she took a chair so her back was to the room. I pulled out my chair, a bit miffed. I have a better body than Lupe. I work hard on it.

A waiter with a coffeepot appeared at our table as soon as we sat down. These are real waiters. Men who do it for a living. Not the ones who tell you their names. "Hi, my name is Ted. I'll be back with your burger unless my agent calls."

Lupe glanced over her shoulder to inspect the menu written on a blackboard attached to the wall. "Bacon, extra done, two eggs over easy, rye toast, dry. A large oj. Short stack. This comes with potatoes, doesn't it?"

A girl can work up a real appetite in jail.

The waiter took my order and left. Lupe reached for her coffee. "Man, I'm beat. Been up since five yesterday morning."

I touched Lupe's wrist. "What's this?" The name "Joan" was tattooed on the pale brown skin of her inner wrist.

She put the cup down and laid her arm on the table. Her skin was warm. My fingers jumped away from it.

"Someone you met in jail?" I didn't want to look her in the face. I kept staring at her wrist. I could see the smeared letters were written with black eyeliner pencil.

Lupe's laugh sounded like one of those snooty-talking cats on tv commercials. "Jealous?"

"Why do you want to mark yourself up like that?"

"You got a boyfriend yet?"

I didn't say anything. The last one, if you could call him that, had been the commodities broker nearly two years ago. I guess some people would think two years is a long time to go without a date.

The waiter interrupted with the food.

Lupe spooned fried egg onto toast and smiled smugly. "No one?" She popped the toast into her mouth and chewed noisily. "Tell you what I'm going to do for you. Since you're giving me a ride and all. I'm going to help you get laid. We're going to find you some nice *vato*. Maybe a lawyer."

"I don't like lawyers!"

"Nobody does. But it's someplace to start." She prodded the other egg so the yolk ran.

"So who's Joan?"

Lupe shook her head as if I was hopeless. "Crawford. Of course. *Rain. Above Suspicion. Mildred Pierce.*"

I dumped more tabasco sauce on my scrambled eggs. "Haven't you given that old movie star stuff up yet? Take a look at your life. You're twenty-three years old . . ."

"Twenty-two."

". . . still standing on street corners, three-time loser in the county system." I shook my head. "The old Hollywood. It's just a dream. Always has been."

Lupe shook her head. "Joan? A dream? A star! She never took shit from anyone. And I'm sure she didn't have any trouble getting laid."

I put my fork down with finality. Lots of men look at me. Every day. They'd love it if I'd talk to them. "I don't have any trouble. I can get as many men as I want. Whenever I want."

"It's been at least a year, hasn't it?" Lupe inquired knowingly.

I stood and picked up the check. "Let's go. Your mom'll be up soon."

Lupe checked her makeup and put on dark lipstick before she rose to face the room. I heard the click of her heels behind me and the excited murmuring of stockbrokers and construction workers in her wake.

The sun was just coming up as we pulled in front of the house she shared with her mother on Floral in East LA. It was a small wooden place painted yellow. There were black bars on all the windows, and the wrought-iron screen door looked like something out of a medieval dungeon. Red hibiscus flanked the front door. An ineffectual-looking fence separated the property from the neighboring similarly fortressed residences.

"Where's my car?" Lupe wondered.

I looked up and down the block. Lupe's red Fiat with the primer gray passenger door was nowhere to be seen.

"They're keeping it in the garage for you."

"These houses don't have garages," she snapped impatiently. "If they did, everyone's cousin from Michoacán would be living in them."

"Maybe Hector's driving it," I offered.

She shook her head. "He's got a Camaro. Real cherry."

It didn't look as if anyone was up in Lupe's house. None of the lights was on. I heard radio music coming from the other houses. Juan Gabriel was singing. I'd been listening to his records on the border radio all summer long. A guy walked out of a faded green house across the street and began to water the parched lawn.

"Thanks for the ride." Lupe got out of the car.

"I'll wait to make sure things are ok."

"Of course they are. My mom expects me. I called her from jail yesterday and told her I was getting out. She'll be making *huevos rancheros* for me and hot chocolate. Joey will be there in the kitchen all dressed up for me in a new shirt." Lupe opened the gate to the house. *"Adiós."*

Lupe walked up the sidewalk to the front door. She took a key from her cheap black vinyl purse, opened the door, and went inside without looking back. I sat in the car. Everything I'd wanted to tell her, that I'd been rehearsing for months, and I hadn't been able to say a word. I'd practiced over and over in front of my bathroom mirror. *Lupe, I'm sorry. It was my fault. I should never have gotten you involved. I'll never tell your secret.* That's the way I wanted to tell her. One long breakneck confession and it would be over forever. We would be free. The smell of her drugstore perfume permeated the car.

I turned the ignition on. It was Tuesday. I didn't have any court appearances to do. Although I was getting at least two or three appointments per month from the Superior Court and was still doing some of Burt Schaefer's overflow, I was barely making ends meet. Harvey Kaplan, my office landlord, had raised my rent at the beginning of the summer to $650. Not an unfair price considering the size of the office and the use of Harvey's library, but it was on one of the worst stretches of Hollywood Boulevard, a block and a half west of Western Avenue, Le Sex Shoppe, and a group of video arcades populated by crack dealers and Vietnamese street gangs. The sun was rising. It would be another hot day. I took my sunglasses from the glove compartment. I should go down to the Torrance courthouse and try again to get on their list to pick up some cases. I was aware I was moving slowly.

I looked at Lupe's house again. It was probably built in the forties. That's ancient for Los Angeles. She'd never told me what her mother did. Or anything about her father. Did they own the house or rent? Was there a father? Was he like my father? I pushed that thought out of my head. I do not like to think about my father. Three neatly trimmed rosebushes struggled for recognition at the south end of the building beneath an open window I presumed to be the kitchen. A woman in her early fifties appeared in the window.

It had to be Lupe's mother. I let the car idle. The woman stepped nearly out of view as though retreating from someone. An angry Lupe appeared in the window. She was yelling at her mother in Spanish.

"¿. . . por qué?"

"Cálmate, hija . . . ," her mother entreated.

They moved away from the window, but the yelling continued. I heard a dish break. I was wondering whether to go up to the house when the front door was flung open and an irate Lupe came flying down the steps with her purse in one hand and a scrap of paper clutched in the other. She threw the gate open, and it slammed shut behind her.

"Hector came a few nights ago and took Joey from my

mom! He says I ain't fit to raise him 'cause I was in jail!" Lupe exclaimed angrily as she climbed into my car. "He's got a new girlfriend. Some slant. A waitress. My mom thinks they're in Koreatown. It's a fucking miracle she even knows the name of the dive where this muff works, but the girl gave Hector a crummy calendar to give my mom as a present. Look, it's got the name and address on it." Lupe dangled the torn piece of paper in front of me. "Girl's named Kim. How fucking typical. Kim."

I put the car into drive. "I presume this means you'd like me to take you to Koreatown."

Lupe nodded unhappily. "Hector took my car and gave it to his slutty girlfriend to use."

I grinned to myself. Now I'd have time to tell Lupe everything and let her see how well things were going with me. I drove down her street to Brooklyn Avenue, hung a right and pointed the car toward the Civic Center. I didn't know exactly where Koreatown was, although I'd seen an exit sign for it on the Santa Monica freeway. I had no idea then how big Koreatown was and how crooked the streets.

Lupe fidgeted restlessly next to me as I headed west. We crossed the bridge from East Los to the edge of JTown and then through downtown past the courthouse and up over the hill into *Varrio Loco Nuevo*. She turned on the radio. I had it set to a rock station that spins the same kind of hard-driving bass-heavy hysteria played at Gold's Gym. Good music for working out. Massages the adrenals. It is good music for driving.

"Goddamn it. I hate that noise." Impatiently Lupe switched stations. The soothing soft guitar sounds of some Mexican troubador filled the air and she relaxed slightly. "How could I be friends with someone who listens to that crap? I know you like me, Whitney. I know it would please your commie red heart to be friends with an actual brown person from a lower socioeconomic group, but your shit gives me a headache."

I made another turn and we rolled down to 8th Street. There were no signs for Koreatown. It was all one big Central American refugee camp with dingy laundry hanging out of open apartment windows.

"We can't be friends because we have different taste in music? That seems pretty superficial." Didn't she care about the deeper values I could bring to a friendship? Loyalty, honesty . . .

Lupe nodded. "Gotta draw the line somewhere." She examined the torn piece of paper. "Cafe James Dean."

"Doesn't sound very Korean," I said knowledgeably as I made the turn down to Olympic Boulevard.

Ahead of us stretched the boulevard, waves of heat shimmering and shaking above the blacktop. Lupe shifted restlessly in her seat. The sun, a silent marauding disk of orange and gold, licked at the locked windows of the buildings lining the street.

"5757 Olympic. Hope they're open." She stared out the car window at the changing languages of signs above businesses as we neared Vermont. Spanish. Broken English. Then dense incomprehensible Korean. "What do Koreans eat for breakfast?"

I thought it was a joke and waited for the punch line, but Lupe lapsed into her own thoughts.

This area was once a series of fashionable suburban streets of single-family white upper-middle-class homes built between 1890 and 1910. Now everything was Korean. Hanmi Bank. Amorean Cosmetics. Banners lettered with black square self-contained characters of an imposing secret language. Office buildings, computer stores, dozens of small restaurants, beauty salons with pictures of white women with stiff permanents in the front windows. Small groups of Central American men hung out in front of a building supply store hoping to be hired as day laborers.

Last spring Koreatown was in flames; today only a warm breeze up from the Sea of Cortez whispered through the streets.

"There it is," Lupe announced.

I slowed the car down, but all I saw was a couple of Salvadoran schoolgirls in blue plaid Catholic school uniforms, rolled into miniskirts, at a bus stop.

"Over there," Lupe insisted. In a minimall at the end of the block on the north side of the street, I spotted Cafe James Dean.

Lupe yanked down the sun visor and checked herself in the mirror. She did a quick number again with her dark red lipstick. She tugged the purple spandex bustier up so slightly less cleavage showed.

I pulled into the driveway of the minimall and parked two doors away from the cafe in front of a bakery. There was a CLOSED sign on the restaurant, but the bakery was open.

"Let's go in," I said, indicating the bakery. "We'll buy something. Act like we have some purpose for being here, then we'll look around."

Sullenly Lupe followed me in. Three large glass counters were filled with red, green, and brown things in plastic bags. A Korean woman in a white smock stood behind the counter. A flicker of suspicion flashed in her eyes; she quickly replaced the look with one of attentive but guarded shopkeeper courtesy. I picked up the nearest bag of red things. Honey rice cakes. It was labeled in Korean and English.

"Made out of rice?" I asked.

"Everything made out of rice."

With the bag of red things still in my hand I looked

around the bakery. Pale cookies. Ladyfingers. Five-layer wedding cakes decorated with doves and white sugar bells. "Are these sweet?"

A disdainful look flashed across the woman's face. I wondered if she was suspicious because I was white or because Lupe looked Mexican. Maybe she just didn't like having a woman dressed like a hooker in her store. She snatched the bag from me and replaced it with a bag of the brown things. "Three dollar."

I paid. "When does the restaurant next door open?"

The money disappeared into the cash register. "Don't know."

I heard Lupe slam out the door behind me.

"You think this is a goddamn sightseeing tour?" she said angrily when I came out of the bakery. It was nearly eight. The street was full now of cars headed downtown. The door of a video store plastered with posters of martial arts movies opened. A middle-aged man came out to sweep the sidewalk in front of his business. I wanted to point out the posters and tell Lupe I was studying Tae Kwon Do, but she'd already walked away toward the west end of the building. I hurried after her to the entrance of Cafe James Dean.

The front door was red. There were no windows. A red sign above the door spelled out the name in stiff black script. There was no sign about the hours it was open, no menu posted. I tried the door, but it was locked. Lupe rounded the corner of the building. An alley ran behind the businesses.

A fairly new blue Toyota van with more of the ubiquitous black Korean characters painted on the side was parked outside the back door of the restaurant. The van was closed up, but I imagined it was a supplier of some kind of food product. Lupe stepped in front of the van and peered in its illegally tinted window.

The back door of Cafe James Dean was slightly open. Lupe turned from the van to the door. She put one hand on the door.

"Are you sure it's ok?" I asked. "It's awful early."

She gave me the look that said I was hopeless and pushed open the door.

Three men with big knives stared back at us. With fingers wrapped loosely and familiarly around knives flying like flashes of silver lightning, they hacked at a bloody carcass.

"*¿Quienes son?*" one of the men demanded. Blood dripped from the knife he held in front of him.

Because they were short, deep caramel colored, and Indian looking, I guessed they were Salvadoran or Guatemalan. Boxes of unfamiliar vegetables and roots were piled between them where they sat in the anteroom of the restaurant's kitchen. The other two men stopped their savage chopping, their knives hovering in the air.

"*¿Dónde está la mujer Kim?*" Lupe asked. I glanced at the oozing carcass. Was it a pig?

The boldest of the Salvadorans pointed his knife into the kitchen. A large commercial stove and refrigerator took up one wall and in the center of the room was a large wooden prep counter covered with chickens' feet. A middle-aged Korean man prodded another animal carcass in a huge stainless steel cauldron of boiling water. A white-clad woman, her apron smeared with blood, looked up from the other end of the counter where she was making dumplings.

"I want to see Kim," Lupe announced loudly to the chefs.

"Kim John Oh?" the man asked. They looked questioningly at each other over the cans of food, bottles of oil, jars of spices. A glossy calendar with a generic beautiful Korean woman posed uncomfortably but proudly in front of a painted backdrop of craggy mountains hung on the wall.

"I know she's here," Lupe insisted as the man and

woman drew closer to the door that led into the dining area. "Kim. Kim," Lupe yelled.

The dumpling woman started toward Lupe. "You go now!"

The man said something to the woman before turning away to gather a large handful of crushed dried herb, which he threw into the boiling water he tended.

"Kim. Kim," Lupe cried out again.

The door to the dining area swung open, and into the kitchen strode a gorgeous woman in her late twenties. Her black hair was tied loosely back with a shiny gold-colored ornament and fell nearly to her waist. Her complexion was flawless and pale. She had on complete eye makeup although it was early in the day. She had a fine shape, slender but with tits that looked too good to be true. She wore a pair of skintight black Levi 501s, a cheap-looking pair of red high-heeled sandals, and a USC t-shirt. Even in the cheap heels she was only about five feet three.

"You Kim?" Lupe said aggressively. I saw she too was surprised by the woman's beauty. "You with Hector?"

I remembered Lupe's brother, Hector "Manos" Ramos. Bullet head. Punch-drunk. Fucked-up nose from being broken so many times. What would a fox like this be doing with Hector?

The woman folded her arms and nodded her head. "Are you Hector's sister?" Her English was perfect. "Hector said you were in jail and wouldn't be back until the end of the year."

"Jail!" Lupe exclaimed. "I was in the navy. The S.S. *Sybil.* We just docked. I hear you been taking care of my little boy for me, and I came to get him."

"I can't give Joey to anyone except Hector."

"This is my lawyer." Lupe jerked her thumb in my direction. I tried to look professional. "Let's not have any problems."

"You don't have any guardianship papers or anything giving you temporary custody, do you?" I asked. "A power of attorney signed by Ms. Ramos perhaps?"

Kim shook her head.

"I thought not. It is the legally correct thing for you to turn the boy over now. Hector doesn't have any legal claim to him either."

"But Hector said—"

"Where's Joey? Is he here?" Lupe pushed open the swinging door into the dining room.

The dining room was paneled with pale pine, and black vinyl booths lined the perimeter. Six tables of the same pale wood were placed in the center of the room. A painted seascape mural of a port giving off to a huge vista of ocean covered one wall. There was no one in the room.

Lupe looked back in anger and confusion. "Where is he?"

Kim stood leaning against one of the booths. "At my godmother's. I go to bed late and get up early." I had a sudden hideous vision of Hector on top of the beautiful Kim. What could she see in him? How had they met? Weren't latinos supposed to have the smallest dicks in the world?

"Let's go get him," I heard myself say. "I'll drive."

Kim hesitated.

"Don't make me call the police. You don't have any papers," said Lupe. "We want to be friends. Particularly if you're my brother's squeeze."

Kim swung open the door to the kitchen again and we followed her. She said something in rapid high-pitched Korean to the man and woman who worked in the kitchen. I wondered if they were relatives of hers. I'd heard the Koreans all worked together in family businesses. The woman sputtered with annoyance as Kim took a navy Chanel purse that looked real down from a shelf and led us out.

Kim looked at my old Datsun with displeasure. She and Lupe stood by the passenger door glaring at each other until Lupe finally opened the door and climbed into the backseat.

"Where to?" I asked.

"My godmother lives nearby, over on San Lorenzo," said Kim.

"Hmm," Lupe snorted from the backseat. "Ever notice the majority of the streets in LA are named after Spanish saints?"

I told Kim I didn't know where it was and I needed directions. She told me to go around the block and back toward Vermont. Past Jack's Liquor, past a Lutheran church, past Raul's Barbershop—"*Se habla español*—We specialize in flattops." Behind the commercial din of Olympic it was all residential. Apartment buildings and small boxy stuccos. This area west of downtown was once a desirable place for middle-class dwellings. Today it is all immigrants. People who have arrived here within the last ten years. Two or three families in one house. The northern boundary, Wilshire Boulevard—"the Champs-Elysées of Los Angeles" as it was known in the twenties—is just another strip of minimalls.

Bamboo and squatty palms grew in front of the desperate stuccos. Birds of paradise fluttered in yards of dull-looking grass and gravel. A garden was terraced with green and white stones. Some of the trees and shrubs were severely clipped like bonsai.

"That's it," said Kim. "3333. She lives upstairs in the back. Number 4."

It was a streamline "moderne" apartment building of not more than ten units. I parked in front and we all got out of the car. Kim led the way down the sidewalk and into the building. We climbed the stairs. It was quiet, as if everybody had gone off to work.

Lupe touched her hair nervously, trying to rearrange it. It was six months since she'd seen Joey.

We walked to the back of the building. I heard the murmur of a man's voice speaking a language I couldn't make out but assumed was Korean. Kim stopped abruptly outside the door to number four. A woman's voice said something back to the man, shrill, urgent. Kim shook her head as though it would help her to understand. A noise like a piece of furniture being pushed across the floor snuffed out their voices.

"What's going on in there?" Lupe demanded.

Kim quickly unlocked the door. Lupe pushed her aside and stepped into the small foyer. I was right behind her. Two elderly Korean women dressed in long, full, fuchsia-colored skirts and short black jackets were bound together with extension cords in front of a white couch. The younger one had blood running down her cheek from a cut made by the cord's plug. We heard the squeak of another piece of furniture being pushed aside in the next room.

"Godmother!" Kim said in a low voice.

The old woman saw Kim and replied quickly in a whisper.

Kim bit her lip and nodded. She shoved Lupe toward an open door to the left of the foyer. It led into the kitchen.

"What the fuck is this?" Lupe snarled.

I heard soft footsteps coming from the back of the apartment into the living room. Had we been heard? I grabbed Lupe by the arm and pulled her into the kitchen to try to get us out of sight of whoever else was in the apartment. There was another door connecting the kitchen to a dining area that adjoined the living room. The dining area had no windows and was crowded with china cabinets lining the walls.

Within the partial shadows I hoped the cabinets blocked us from view. We pressed against the wall and held our breath as we peered into the living room.

A man in a sharp black two-button suit and a black hat, his face hidden by a pink mask painted with black eyes and a garish mouth, dragged a crying boy into the room. It was Joey! The man held a huge ugly 9mm Browning automatic with a silencer on it. He said something angrily to the godmother and jerked the boy by the arm for emphasis.

Lupe edged forward, but I grabbed her around the waist, pulling her back, and clamped my other hand over her mouth. Kim sank silently down against the wall.

"Ahnee, ahnee," cried the other woman, who had been silent. She kicked wildly at the man, trying to get him in the nuts.

The man threw Joey aside so that he hit the floor. Lupe bit into my hand. I saw the man's finger squeeze the trigger. The left side of the crying woman's face exploded and splattered the couch with blood, tissue, and something gray I knew was brain.

The man pointed the gun at Kim's godmother, who sprawled weeping across the other woman's body. Her face and gown were speckled as though with confetti by the moist but dead remains. I wondered if she was in shock. My stomach swirled. I felt like throwing up. Joey howled. The man asked the godmother a question, then slapped her several times when she didn't answer. Kim clenched her hands together as if she was going to pray. The godmother nodded wearily toward the southeast corner of the room, where a rosewood cabinet with a Sony tv on top of it stood.

The man crossed the room toward the dining area. I tightened my grip on Lupe. The room was still spinning in front of me, and I could taste bile and other dark things in my throat. If he saw us he'd probably kill us too. I needed to get my gun, but it was at the bottom of my purse. I noticed he was wearing Bally loafers. His suit was good gabardine, and he wore an incongruous Brit public-school-type tie that contrasted bizarrely with his hideous mask. For a lunatic instant it made me think of Richard Nixon, and I nearly laughed out loud.

He pulled the cabinet drawers open and messed the contents around noisily with one hand. He was less than fifteen feet from us. Grunting with approval he pulled out a small black-and-gold chest inlaid with mother of pearl. He unfastened the clasp and looked inside with satisfaction.

Kim sighed unhappily. I glanced at her to tell her to shut up. How much longer before he heard us? I had to act before he found us. Another wave of nausea swept through me. Lupe moved impatiently against me. I let go of her waist. My hand brushed against her ass as I opened my black purse. Her hair smelled like gardenias. I forced my hand as quietly as I could to the bottom of my purse. I gripped my .38 and brought it out. Six shots. I could blow him away from where I was. It wouldn't be hard to explain why I'd shot him in the back. Lupe and Kim would verify my story. The man stopped. The gun was in his right hand. He cocked his head and looked around the room.

Kim looked at me curiously. I'd been on the range at least twice a week, sometimes three or four times if I'd had a bad time in court. If some ball-heavy moronic cop lied to me on the stand. If some shithead cut me off on the freeway. My intentions were not always good.

I drew the gun up and aimed. Kim nodded. "Do it," she mouthed. "Kill him." I felt Lupe's hot tears on my left hand, which still clamped her mouth. I knew why she was crying. She didn't think I could make the shot. She thought I'd hit Joey.

Joey howled again, still trying to get to his feet, but the masked man pushed him down as he strode toward the toppled old women. The man spat out a nasty triumphant phrase. The godmother raised her head. She was pale and creased by time, but I saw hatred in her eyes. He stuck the gun in her face so that it was almost up her nose. My heart stopped beating. I steadied my arm against Lupe and had him dead in my sights. I felt the cold edge of steel. Lupe moaned, shaking her head no. I fingered the trigger, ready to pull.

The man put his gun back into a shoulder holster and buttoned his jacket neatly into place. I glanced at Kim, who was crying silently. A bead of sweat rolled down my cheek. I let my finger ease away from the trigger. Clutching the black-and-gold chest, the man bowed condescendingly to the old woman. Kim nudged the kitchen door closed with her foot as the man turned toward the hall and the kitchen. I heard his footsteps pass by us, then the front door open.

I pushed Lupe away and stepped into the foyer in time to see him starting down the steps. I pulled the trigger, but missed him as he turned down the stairs to the landing on the first floor. He spun around. Seeing his hand come up with the gun I threw myself on the floor. A silent shot slammed into the wall behind me. Then he was gone.

Kim ran sobbing from the kitchen to her godmother.

"Joey!" Lupe rushed for her son.

I got up and shakily shoved the gun into the waistband of my jeans. I'd shot at someone! It seemed to me that it had happened fast, without thinking. Like losing your virginity on a clumsy summer night. I always imagined that if I ever had to shoot at a real person I'd feel something large, mysterious, and existential. But all I'd felt was scared and angry. I closed the front door. None of the neighbors had come out to see what was happening. That's how it is now: you hear gunshots and you mind your own business. Turn up the television. I looked to the living room. Kim held her godmother and murmured to her in Korean while struggling with the knots in the extension cords that bound the two old women.

I went over and knelt by the couch. The dead woman was chubby and brightly made up. She looked as if she'd been fun while she was alive. The broken cavity where the left side of her face had been continued to ooze slowly onto the couch. I'd done a voluntary manslaughter case with Burt Schaefer earlier in the year. Some poor dumb chicano in his early thirties from Montebello who'd clubbed in his girlfriend's head with a wrench while he was dead drunk. I'd had to study the autopsy photos and go to the UCLA medical library to look at more pictures of skull injuries, but nothing had prepared me for the pink and gray mess slithering down the dead woman's face and across her black silk bodice. My hands moved as in a dream, flying flying flying like a swarm of swallows across a wretched red sunset as I pulled at the knots.

I untied the women. Kim pulled her godmother away from the dead body and cradled her in her arms. The old woman went limp. She closed her eyes for what seemed like a long time. Kim continued murmuring in Korean. Finally the old woman's eyes fluttered open and she noticed me. She stared into my face for a few seconds before glancing down at my gun.

"You should have killed him."

I stared back at her in surprise. She spoke heavily accented but perfect English.

She struggled to her feet. "I must get a blanket." She motioned toward the body.

"I'll get it, Dorothy," Kim interjected, but the old woman shook her head and shuffled across the room toward a hall leading to her bedroom. Dorothy seemed like a weird name for a Korean. On the floor Lupe hugged the strangely silent Joey, shielding him so he couldn't see the dead body.

"Who's this?" I whispered to Kim across the body between us.

"Come on, Whitney, skip the small talk," Lupe growled. "Let's get the hell out of here."

Kim ignored her. "Jin."

"Jin Oh." The old woman reentered the living room carrying a sky blue coverlet. She started to cry again. "My sister."

"Why'd that guy kill her?" I asked, but the old woman called Dorothy seemed unable to speak anymore.

Joey got up from the floor where Lupe was holding him on her lap. He tried to totter toward the old woman, but Lupe grabbed him and covered his eyes so he wouldn't see the sprawling body beyond Dorothy. I wondered if Joey knew what death was. He was probably too young.

The dead woman's hand twitched violently. The dead don't just drop the way they do in the movies. The muscles keep contorting. Kim's godmother knelt near me on the floor by the couch. She took her sister's hand in both of hers and kissed it before wrapping the quilt around Jin Oh.

Lupe broke the silence. "How long's Joey been here? Did that guy do anything to him?"

The old woman shook her head.

"Just since last night," Kim said. "I already told you that."

The old woman nodded in agreement as she rose to her feet again. "You must be Joey's mother. Kim told me about you. He's a good boy. Jin and I took him to McDonald's last night." Tears ran down her face again.

"Who's that guy? Why'd he kill your sister? You didn't answer my question." Lupe got to her feet clutching Joey, who started to whine.

"What were they saying to each other?" I asked. "Did he kill her because of that box he took?"

Kim's godmother looked quizzically at me, then at Kim.

"I'm Whitney Logan. A friend of Lupe's." I jerked my

thumb in the direction of Lupe, who didn't contradict me.

"Why are you carrying a gun?" the old woman wondered.

"Yeah, why are you carrying a gun?" Lupe asked.

I shrugged. "Protection."

"Are you a detective?" asked the old lady.

"Not exactly, but in the past I have helped—"

Lupe shook her head in disbelief. "You're a lawyer. With an office on Hollywood Boulevard."

"Dorothy, I'm going to call the police," Kim announced.

The old woman shook her head angrily. "Didn't you hear what he said? That he'd kill me if I go to the police. Besides, do you think after last spring I trust the police?"

She meant the Uprising last April. She meant Koreatown burning. She meant the police standing by with their thumbs up their butts as the flames roared through the streets. Then the looters came. By the thousands. Mexicans, Central Americans, blacks joined together to rip off tvs, vcrs, cd players, furniture, and clothing as well as Pampers and food. There may have been whites, but I didn't see them on television.

"No. No police. They don't protect. Maybe this woman, Miss Logan, the detective, can help me." The old woman turned away from Kim and toward me. "Will you help me?"

Lupe laughed. "Hey, excuse me, I don't mean to disrespect the dead, but you got it all wrong. She's a lawyer. She does drunk driving cases. Burglaries. She can't help you. Or anyone."

I glared at Lupe. She did think I was a total fuckup. "I found one woman who was missing."

Lupe stared back at me angrily. "That woman got killed. It was a bad scene. *Vamos*, Whitney."

I dropped my gaze. Ashamed of my bravado. "Kim's right. Call the police. You can't just take the law into your own hands."

The old lady looked over at the blue coverlet on the couch. "I can pay you. What do you want? Five hundred dollars a day?"

"Whatever was in the box was so valuable the man killed for it," I mused.

"Yes, that's what Jin said to him. She said, 'This is too important to us. Take something else. We'll give you something else.' " The old woman faltered. "Then he called her a stupid old bitch and he shot her."

"Tell me what was in the box," I said.

"Kye," said Dorothy.

"What?" Lupe and I asked in unison.

This time the old woman spoke more slowly. "In our community we have *kye*. A group of friends put their money together and each person has a turn receiving the money."

"Didn't you ever wonder why so many Koreans own liquor stores and minimarts?" said Kim. "There was seventy-five thousand dollars in that chest. Dorothy, my godmother, was responsible for it."

Dorothy cast her eyes down, ashamed. She explained that five women pooled their money together every year. Yesterday she had gone to the bank to withdraw the group's money, and later this evening was to be the party to give away the money.

"Two years ago I received the money," said Dorothy. "I gave most of it to Kim. That's how she was able to buy the restaurant." Kim nodded in agreement and hugged her godmother. Dorothy added that four years ago Jin had received the *kye* money. "She took me to Italy for a month. We stayed in a villa outside of Florence."

I asked her who knew she had the money.

"The people at the bank, the women in our group, our relatives . . ."

Lupe looked surprised. "You think someone you know

did this?" She wouldn't look toward the couch. She kept jiggling Joey, who'd stopped whining and become catatonic.

Dorothy didn't say anything.

"What do you think, Dorothy?" Kim said impatiently.

"Someone from your own family? Your own *barrio* would do this?" Lupe shook her head in disbelief.

I noticed a gold-framed photo of the two old women on the small marble table at the end of the couch. They were smiling on a green hillside. They stood so close together there was no space between them. "You're going to have to notify the police, Dorothy. Just to get her buried. The mortuary's going to ask questions. Some kind of a report will have to be made."

The old woman shook her head stubbornly. "I'll get her buried. Tell me how much money you want. Seven hundred fifty dollars a day?"

I put my hands up to stop her. Wouldn't I be breaking the law? I'm not licensed as an investigator. "No, really. I can't."

"Find this man."

I shook my head. It had to be reported to the police or it would look as if we had something to hide. Could I be disbarred? What exactly was a crime of moral turpitude as defined by the State Bar? What could there be to hide?

"You tried to protect us," insisted the old lady. "You took a shot at him."

Yeah. It's a crime to be firing a gun within the city limits. Let alone taking potshots at someone.

"Maybe he'll be looking for you too now."

I'd take another shot at any SOB who tried to hurt me. Or Lupe.

The old lady grasped my hand. "Just find out who he is. Then I'll go to the police."

How well had he seen me? Would he look for me? He might still be outside. "Is that a promise?" I asked.

The old woman nodded. Kim looked angry.

"Ok. Seven hundred and fifty dollars a day."

"Plus expenses," chimed Lupe.

"If I can't find him by the end of the week, you go to the cops." Everything would be fine. It had happened too fast. He hadn't had a good look at me. The money would pay the rent at my office and get Harvey Kaplan off my back. The premium was due on my malpractice insurance. I extended my hand to the old woman. "Isn't Dorothy an unusual Korean name?"

"When I came to this country I saw *The Wizard of Oz*."

I remember the movie from when I was a kid. How surprised I'd been to discover the Wizard was just a little man.

"Are you going to cancel the party tonight?" I asked.

"No. They're going to have to be told about the money."

I asked her if she was going to tell them about Jin. My voice trailed off. I am not accustomed to speaking of the dead.

She nodded her head.

"Don't," I said. "We'll wait and see if anyone acts suspiciously. Who asks about her. Who acts worried."

Dorothy crossed the room to a dining alcove next to the kitchen. A mahogany table with four black chairs whose seat cushions were padded with red and gold silk patterned with flying cranes stood under a dusty chandelier. Peaches and nectarines in a fake gold mesh basket were placed on the table. I recognized the old blue-and-gold Wedgwood pattern "Rhapsody" in the china cabinet because one of my mother's friends had the same pattern when I was a kid. How beautiful I'd thought it was, how elegant. Dorothy had a set of five Austrian crystal goblets each in a different gem color displayed proudly on the middle shelf. Five. One for each of the women in the *kye* group? The emerald green would be for Dorothy. The ruby red for the now deceased Jin?

Dorothy motioned for me to sit at the table. She opened a drawer in the china cabinet and from among some assorted silver and silver-plated serving utensils took out a yellow silk scrapbook with a tree and a bridge embroidered on the front.

"I will show you a picture of my *kye* group at the party we had last year." She opened the book to near the back and slid it in front of me. She tapped a photograph with one vermilion painted nail. I recognized Dorothy. Jin in what looked like an Armani suit. The rest of the women I was ashamed to admit all looked alike to me. Dorothy moved her finger around the photo, tapping each face. "Lee Joon, Chu Chu Park, and Nancy Johnson."

I looked questioningly at the last woman in the photo.

"Nancy Johnson. She married U.S. serviceman. Nice man. Pharmacist. He's dead now."

"They'll all be here tonight?" I asked.

Dorothy nodded and sighed sadly. "You come. Meet the ladies. Talk to them. Find out who they told about our *kye* party."

"Won't they wonder who I am and why I'm at the party? I'm not Korean, I don't speak Korean."

Dorothy smiled. "All of us speak English. We like to speak Korean, tell a lot of jokes. But we all know English. And at least one other language." Dorothy explained that Jin had spoken Italian and French. Nancy, German because her husband was stationed in the service there for a while. The other woman, Chu Chu, spoke Spanish. "Korean women have very high level of education. First university for women. Largest university for women in the world. Education's the most important thing for us."

"You told me Chu Chu took Japanese classes once at UCLA," added Kim.

A sour look crossed Dorothy's face. "Chu Chu's an idiot. When the Japanese were in Korea they made us stop speaking Korean, tried to make everyone speak Japanese, write Japanese. Use Japanese names. No reason for anyone to study Japanese." Dorothy waved her hand dismissively, then shifted her attention back to me. "I'll tell them you're a friend of Kim's."

"Maybe you should tell them she's a sociologist or some kind of professor researching a paper," said Lupe, who had walked over to look at the photograph. As Lupe bent over the table, Joey grabbed a fistful of my hair and gurgled happily and wetly. I'd never told Lupe that I don't like kids very much. "Which one speaks Spanish?" she asked. "I heard Koreans don't like Mexicans."

Without replying Dorothy pointed to the one she said was named Chu Chu Park.

"Maybe you should come tonight too, Lupe," I said.

Lupe shot me a poisonous look. "No. This ain't my kind of *fiesta*. I heard about this new multicultural Los Angeles. Read an article about it in the *Times*. But I thought it meant we were all going to get to eat Thai food and listen to *salsa*. I didn't know it meant you were going to end up looking for a guy who bumped some *chinita*."

Kim stepped angrily up to the table. "You're impossible. I know why Hector told me to keep Joey. You're not able to take care of him. You're a drug addict. A whore. You've been in jail."

"Watch your fucking mouth in front of my kid. I'll fucking clock you." Lupe thrust Joey into my arms and stepped toward Kim. "I'm not no drug addict."

"Hmm, that's what I thought," Kim smirked. "You *are* a whore."

Lupe drew back her arm to slap Kim. Dorothy spread her arms in a quick circular motion and then dropped into *choo-choom seogi*, horse stance. First position. Master Lee had taught me this. "You know Tae Kwon Do?" I blurted out.

The old lady bowed slightly. "Black belt. Eighty-two-year-old black belt."

I handed Joey back to Lupe. He was a heavy kid. "Tell your friends I'm writing a dissertation on local Korean economics and that I'll be contacting them individually to interview them about *kye*."

"That's a good idea. Pretend to be a scholar," said Kim. "The old ones don't like outsiders very much. And it's very important to give respect to elders. As a scholar you'll be able to approach them in a respectful way."

I asked Dorothy what she was going to tell the other women about Jin and the money.

"I'll say Jin had to go down to Buena Park to see a cousin who's in the hospital. I'll tell them a man robbed me on the street."

"Why not just tell them the truth, Godmother?" sighed Kim. "They won't blame you."

"Money can make anyone an enemy," Dorothy said. "Even someone you've known all your life."

I agreed with the old woman that I'd return at seven in the evening. I wondered to myself how she was going to get Jin's body out of there and how she was going to clean the stain off the couch. Lupe, carrying Joey, and I walked out of the apartment and down to my car. I didn't want to worry her by speculating out loud if the killer was lurking nearby and watching us. There weren't many cars parked on the street. I glanced around, but didn't see anyone.

"I can't believe it!" Lupe exploded as we stood next to my car. "You're a goddamn menace to society. Wherever you go somebody gets blown away. I thought I was going to puke on my shoes."

"Yeah, I never saw anything like it before." I shook my head. I still felt numb.

Lupe jingled her car keys, which she'd taken from Kim. "Seven hundred and fifty dollars a day is a lot of *pesos*."

Lupe stood beside her Fiat and examined it critically. The red paint had faded since I'd last seen the car. The gray primer on the passenger door was scratched.

"I can't believe Hector gave that cunt my ride," complained Lupe. "She owns a restaurant. She's got a bunch of people working for her. Doesn't she have her own fucking car?" She readjusted Joey in her arms like a sack of groceries.

I studied Joey, who continued to survey his surroundings with silent alarm. He did not, as the psychologists say, seem bonded to his mother. I wondered exactly how much time Lupe had lived with him. When I'd met her he must have been about a year old. She'd been leaving him with her mother when she was hooking then, and she'd been hooking every day. Time out for jail. I could tell from the uneasy way he was scanning the street he had practically no idea who she was. "Look, Lupe, I don't know what your plans are, where you're going to live or what you're going to do, but I think you better give Joey back to your mom until you figure it out."

A fierce look greeted my suggestion. I remembered that I had once seen a Joan Crawford movie. *Mildred Pierce*. "Oh, so now you're an expert on child rearing," snapped Lupe.

"You know I don't know fuck-all about kids." Or want to. "But let's face facts. You don't know if your mom's going to let you stay at her place after that argument you had with her this morning."

"Well, I'm not going to stay around this place, that's for sure. I can't believe it. Woman gets killed. Right in front of my little boy. By some crazy *chino*."

"Chinese?"

Lupe nodded her head. "Chinese. Japanese. Whatever. Didn't you see his throat between the stupid clown mask and his shirt? He wasn't black. He wasn't brown. What's left?"

"Yellow?" I wondered if that was a politically correct term.

Lupe shrugged. "I'm gone."

I squinted into the sun, which was behind her. "You don't know if it's safe. You might see Hector . . ."

"Oh, I'm going to see Hector, all right. Take care of a personal matter. About that whore. Jesus Christ, he talks about me, then he turns around and hooks up with a real mattress-bender." She jerked her thumb back in the direction of the apartment where we'd left Kim. "He thinks he can give my baby to some *cualquiera*!"

". . . you don't know where you're going to be working . . ." I stopped. Was it possible Lupe still thought prostitution was a viable option? Three convictions. AIDS.

"Yeah, I was wondering when we'd be getting around to this. Look, I been thinking of doing something different. Something where I can sit down."

I nodded excitedly. "Great! I'm so glad to hear that. Maybe an office. Sign up with an agency."

Lupe nodded back. "Just what I was thinking. An office."

"Can you type?"

She shook her head. The miniskirt clinging to her ass was smaller than the average desk blotter.

"Shorthand?" I asked doubtfully.

"I was thinking of working for you. Answer the phone. Take messages."

I couldn't prevent myself from laughing. The Anne Klein suit and Bally spectators she'd seen me in must have made her think I was making more money than I could carry to the bank. I'd charged them. I was two months behind with Visa. "I already have someone."

Lupe drew back angrily. Her dramatic range was limited by the weight of the boy in her arms. "You think I'm not smart enough to work for you? Habeas corpus. Writ. Prima facie. You think I just been sitting on my butt in the joint? I bet I know more fucking law than you do."

"I can't afford a full-time secretary. I use a service that charges by the hour." I bit my lip and felt silly. Lupe knew everything about charging by the hour. I didn't want to encourage her and make her think she could talk me into giving her a job.

"Part-time! Perfect. That's exactly the kind of career transition I had in mind. So I could be with my boy." She hugged the overfed kid. It seemed to rouse him from his stupor.

"Doggie! Doggie!" Joey grunted in a thick Mexican accent and pointed at an old yellow tomcat making its way slowly across the yard we stood in front of.

I wondered who Joey's father was. Some homeboy from the Flats where Lupe lived? A trick accident? Someone she'd been in love with? Probably no one who paid child support.

"You still have all those commie posters on the walls in your office?" Lupe asked. "Those tacky pink silk flowers?"

"Haven't changed a thing."

Lupe shook her head as she looked at me with the same critical eye she'd used on the Fiat. "I'll be a real asset. I could redecorate your office. Have you ever thought of German Expressionism? A glass table!"

She had a car. I could let her file papers for me, serve some subpoenas. I tried to quickly calculate what I might be able to pay her. It would mean no more Ballys. No more Walter Steigers. "Ok, a hundred bucks a week."

"One fifty."

I shook my head. "You have to learn to type. A hundred."

She could make that on the street in a couple of hours. She turned away and started to put Joey in the Fiat. "What about the money Dorothy's going to pay you?"

"I'll give you a raise in a month or so if things work out."

"Mierda," she sighed. "At least I'll be able to tell my probation officer I'm working for a lawyer."

I told Lupe I'd bring my old Sperry Remington in for her to use. I explained about subpoenas. Lupe buckled Joey in the passenger seat. I decided it was pointless to tell her it's illegal in California to drive him without an infant seat. They cost sixty or seventy bucks, which she probably didn't have.

"Don't forget to report to your p.o. You've got to do that within twenty-four hours," I said.

Lupe got into the car with a quick, careless wave in my direction. She pointed the Fiat east toward her mother's house, and I got into my old blue Datsun to search for a pay phone to call my office. I wondered what her probation officer would think of Lupe's being at the scene of a murder.

At 8th and Normandie I saw a phone in a busy supermarket parking lot. There was actually nothing super about it. No radicchio, no baby vegetables, no Sonoma goat cheese. This was a stripped-down operation full of heart attack food and a big red sign in the window that said *"Acep-*

tamos Food Stamps." Guatemalan women sold mangoes on the corner and grilled corn on the cob on barbecues. The strolling crowds of Mexican, Salvadoran, and Honduran shoppers welled in and out of adjacent cheap clothing stores from which poured latin rhythms. I had thought I was still in Koreatown. I bought an ear of corn from a woman and let her slather it with mayonnaise, lime, and chili powder.

Miraculously, I located one of the 8 percent of public phones in Los Angeles that works. I called my phone answer machine and beeped in my code. This has been a huge change in my life. I went to Circuit City and bought a machine that lets you call in for your messages. It was worth the extra money to participate in the late twentieth century. I had three calls. One from the clerk of Division 40 telling me they had a case for me to pick up if I could get there before 10:30. One from Manny Washington, my process server, asking for an advance on some paper he was supposed to lay. And one from my father, who sounded half bagged again.

"Your mother says . . . your mother says . . ." He couldn't remember why he'd called me.

I looked at my watch. It was nearly ten. That would make it nearly one back in Maryland, where he and my mother live. There are two basic kinds of phone calls from my father, Donn. I usually think of him as Donn, the irritating stranger I had to live with while I was growing up, and less often, when I'm feeling vulnerable, as the father I might someday please. Donn either wants to tell me I'm ruining my mother's life because I don't have a husband and child or a regular job with a prestigious law firm, or he wants to rant and rave about the welfare system. I hung up and looked around me at the Central American refugees swarming along the sidewalks.

I called Division 40 and told them I was on my way. I

was glad to have something to take my mind off the sickening image of the dead woman. I didn't have time to go back to my office where I keep an old suit in the closet for such last-minute court appearances, so I went into the nearest clothing store. Black iron bars were pushed back from the display window. All the apparel was made of rayon. Hot pink, purple, orange. Tropical colors. The store was run by Koreans.

The woman at the cash register watched me as I ruffled through the cheap dresses. Less than three weeks ago, and not far from here, a Korean liquor store owner had shot and killed a fifteen-year-old Salvadoran boy she believed to be high on drugs and about to steal a quart of milk. Autopsy revealed no drugs in his system and his stomach was empty. I pulled a sleeveless orange dress with a white collar from the rack. Sadly, it was not only cheap looking but matronly, but it was only eleven dollars and I was in a hurry. I told the woman I'd take it, went into the changing area, and put it on. My legs were tan enough to go without stockings and I had an old pair of black Bruno Magli heels in the car.

I sped down Seventh, past the banks and corporate headquarters representing Japanese investments, past demoralized Pershing Square, where the homeless congregate. Beneath them are eight levels of parking. Up the hill at Grand, past the civil courthouse that attempts to be modern, past the Music Center, one of America's least interesting public spaces. The denuded plaza was empty. It is not growing better with age. At Temple I turned right to the criminal courts building at Broadway. It was hot again and the air was sour.

I parked across the street, hid my gun in the trunk, and hurried up the stairs to the fifth floor. I'd never been to court without a suit; at least my arms are tight and well defined. I was benchpressing nearly my own weight now. Division 40 was crowded as usual. It's one of two large arraignment courts. Pimps, gangbangers, public drunks. The court was in recess and there was much talk talk and carrying on. I knew most of the defense attorneys and Public Defenders. George Jackson, a black guy I knew from UCLA law school, detached himself from a small group drinking coffee in the back of the room.

"Yo, Whitney, long time no see." He put his hand out to me. "How about those Bruins?"

I have an adequate sports vocabulary although it bores me, but I do like to bet and I'd be insulted to be excluded from a football pool because I'm a woman. The UCLA football team was playing Tennessee on Saturday. I shook George's hand. "Yeah, those Bruins. Kicking butt and taking names."

We traded a few more banalities before George announced, "You're going to be famous soon. They got a hot case for you. Judge Harrison himself mentioned to the clerk they should call you."

I looked warily toward the clerk, a busy no-nonsense woman I felt I'd never been able to charm. Although there's a list of attorneys signed up to take appointments and the clerk is supposed to go methodically down the list, I knew about half a dozen people were getting the majority of the business. My humble efforts, a box of candy at Christmas, happy chitchat—"Hi! Gorgeous weather, isn't it?"—had been met with disinterest. I hadn't decided yet how the judge felt about me.

Behind his back he's called Foxy Grandpa. He is a huge, obese anglo-saxon guy in his late fifties. He's lucky he was able to get a job wearing a robe. It was either that or a tent. His hair is silver and he wears it combed back. Seated on the bench he's an imposing figure, but when he opens his mouth it's a different story. He calls women "girls" and "sweetheart." He's proud to be called a good ol' boy.

I slipped George ten bucks and told him to put it on UCLA for me with a six-point spread. Then I went to find out what Foxy Grandpa had in store for me. Ignoring my greeting, the clerk handed me a complaint.

"Venus Howard. In lockup."

PC 647. I sighed. More prostitution. I had the bailiff let me into the custody area.

It was empty. The only sound I heard was the click of my heels across the concrete. Foxy Grandpa had been yelling at everyone for weeks to get the arraignments done before noon in the interests of judicial economy. I knew it was so he'd be able to get out promptly for lunch. I'd heard that one of his favorite places was the old Langer's Deli on Seventh at the edge of MacArthur Park. I could see him settling his great girth onto one of the red leather booths, surrounded by his sycophants, those fucking sharkskin lawyers who licked his enormous buttocks and made a hundred and forty grand minimum a year from the public trough for chickenshit breaking-and-entering cases. I imagined Foxy Grandpa ordering: "I'll have half a cow and the left side of the menu."

A tall, slender white woman, a redhead with hair flowing past her shoulders, napped face down on the cold gray bench in the cell adjoining Division 40. She was either asleep with her right arm pillowed under her head or she'd frozen to death in the meat-locker cold of the lockup. I shivered, wishing I'd bought a dress with a little jacket. Stretched out, the woman was at least five feet ten. A pair of cheesy gold Frederick's of Hollywood pumps stood next to the bench. Was there nothing new in the world of prostitution?

"Ms. Howard?"

The redhead didn't move. A pale, shapely calf poked out of the baggy blue county overalls.

"Ms. Howard?" I coughed to get her attention.

She still didn't move. Her skin was firm. Her hair was shiny. She couldn't be more than twenty-five. I coughed again. "Ms Howard?"

The pale arm on which her head was cushioned extended out and reached for the opposite wall. She had long nails painted red with silver stripes. I sighed again. Silver looks terrible on redheads. She turned, swung her legs over the bench, and fumbled for her shoes. Her long hair covered her face. She threw it back.

She was on the bad side of fifty. Her face was thin and heavily lined. Her lines had lines. Her face was like one of those horrible dolls made from a dried apple.

"Hail, daughter of Portia. You got a cigarette?" she asked.

I shook my head and introduced myself. "Let me go over this complaint with you, Ms. Howard—"

"Venus," she corrected me. "The Great Goddess. Queen of the Shades. Mother of the Venetian tribes of the Adriatic. Goddess of Generation. Also known as Aphrodite . . ."

I flipped quickly through the complaint. "Excuse me, ma'am, I don't see that name."

"Fuck," she muttered. "I should have known they'd give me some simpleton with no poetry in her soul. I asked for a Woman. Did they tell you that? Only a Woman can understand the mysteries I represent."

"This is the police report. It says here you've been under investigation for the last six months for prostitution, running a house of prostitution—"

"A temple."

"At 1200 N. Bronson? Hollywood?"

She nodded her head. Her red hair danced in the mucky

yellow light. "Yes, the Church of the Big Mother. I am the High Priestess."

I fiddled awkwardly with the stupid Peter Pan collar on my new dress. "I don't understand."

"Didn't they have a women's studies program at your school? Come, come, daughter, is it possible you do not know your her-story? Your matriarchal roots?" Venus Howard shoved her feet into the gold shoes as if she was going somewhere.

I read aloud from the police report. "Officers arrived at the aforenamed address, spoke with suspect who stated she would engage in sexual intercourse and oral copulation. Suspect stated 'I will absolve you of all your sins for $25.' Further—"

"Anything I must do for the Great One, I will do." Her eyes were heavily outlined with kohl and she wore green eye shadow. "Sex is the religion of the Big Mother. I am but her humble servant."

"You were going to take money to fuck these two cops?"

Venus Howard folded her garish hands over her heart. "They were guilty men with many sins to be forgiven. It is my duty and that of the Big Mother's other priestesses to absolve the sins of man."

"Wait a sec. Let me get this straight. You want me to go out in the courtroom and say that it's part of your religion to have sex with men and they give you money?"

She bowed her head before looking back up at me. "Donations. For the temple. Excuse me, fair daughter, you have heard of the First Amendment, haven't you?"

I nodded unhappily. Another fucking lunatic. Why couldn't I get a grand theft auto? "It'll be about two grand to bail you out of here. You have anyone you want me to get in contact with?"

"Adonis, my Horned God. Or either of the Vestal Virgins of the Church—Heather and Sarah. They know where I keep the donations."

She gave me directions how to get to the church, a beeper number for Adonis, and told me to stand up straight and be proud of my breasts.

I could barely wait to get out of the courthouse. I sauntered, as grandly as I could, out of Division 40 with the laughter of the DA and all the other defense lawyers ringing in my ears. All I wanted was to go back to the office and talk with Harvey.

West up Sunset Boulevard through the Vietnamese outskirts of downtown, through the Mexican and Central American neighborhoods with *carnicerías*, Pentecostal churches, and brightly colored auto repair shops all painted with images of the Virgin of Guadalupe and the names of dead gang members. I went past the gay bars, the funky laundromats and old movie theaters to the fork in the road that turns into Hollywood Boulevard. My office is at Wilton on a seedy-looking block with Thai restaurants and several of the new backbone of the Los Angeles economy: the ninety-nine-cent store. Everything in the store costs ninety-nine cents and is made in some other country.

Harvey Kaplan, my landlord, was in his office reclining on his couch rereading one of the tedious and incomprehensible books detailing the life of his guru. Harvey wore an old white T-shirt with what looked like a spaghetti sauce stain on the left pec. His long gray hair was pulled into a ponytail held back by a blue Dodgers baseball cap. He had on a pair of jeans that were faded to nearly white and a pair of those terrible religious-fanatic Birkenstocks from which his big naked toes protruded. This is the man I prefer to think of as my real father. Harvey used to be a great criminal lawyer. I used to read about him in the paper when he was doing death penalty cases.

I closed Harvey's open door behind me. "Hey, man, you busy?" I sat down on the arm of the couch without waiting for his reply.

Harvey dropped the book on the floor. His eyes were glassy behind the thick Coca-Cola bottles he wears for reading, and I saw he was stoned again.

"You know anything about Koreatown?" I wouldn't tell him why I was asking. To tell Harvey I'd seen a woman murdered and had agreed for the sum of $750 per day to search for her killer would be to invite criticism. He'd tell me to stick to possession and prostitution cases. Harvey believes in karma and hard cash.

"The DMZ that divides the North and South is the most militarized area in the world. The U.S. military and nuclear presence in the South is the greatest obstacle to peace in the region," Harvey mumbled as he scratched his beard lazily. The beard is new. It's nearly all gray and looks like pubic hair. "A people divided against themselves."

"So what's that have to do with Koreatown?"

"Same people who live in Korea live in Koreatown. Except now most of the people who live in Koreatown are Central American."

I got up, nodding my head as if I understood.

"You don't by any chance have any cookies or anything to eat in your office, do you?" Harvey asked.

On my way out I left his door open as I had found it. I checked my mail quickly and tossed the overdue notice from the *Daily Journal* into the trash. I had to go home to figure out what to wear to the *kye* party at Dorothy's house that evening.

I decided on a navy pantsuit with a white silk blouse and

a pair of black Ferragamo flats. I looked preppy. Harmless. As if I'd gone to Sweet Briar or one of the other not very difficult women's colleges in the South. To complete my soft look I pinned a navy silk flower to my lapel. Before putting it in my purse, I cleaned and loaded my .38.

The sun was in its last slow amber arc in the west as I crested over Mulholland Drive and zoomed through the leafy green of Laurel Canyon. I turned up the volume on the Bob Marley cassette in my tape player, pushed my old Datsun into a turn, and felt the back wheels swing out into the gravel. This was a hell of a lot more fun than being a lawyer.

I cruised down Fairfax still bopping to the reggae. Orthodox Jews shopped and visited with each other on the street. I wondered why they had to wear wool with long sleeves all year round. It was still over ninety. September and the beginning of October are the hottest months in Los Angeles. The seasons have been stretched beyond definition and you need air-conditioning.

The lights were just coming on in Koreatown when I turned off Olympic Boulevard onto Dorothy's street. I parked. It wasn't until I had walked across the yellow lawn and past the border of birds of paradise in front of her building and started up the stairs that I felt scared. What had I gotten myself into? I glanced at my watch. It was less than eleven hours since I'd first been there and seen Jin murdered.

I knocked on the door of Dorothy's apartment.

It swung open. Kim smiled and bowed. From inside I heard a scratchy old record of Andy Williams singing "Moon River."

Kim stood back, and I saw Lee Joon and Chu Chu Park with Nancy Johnson sitting on the immaculate white couch.

Dorothy appeared from the kitchen carrying six drinks in short frosty glasses on a silver tray. Kim closed the door behind me. I couldn't help but remember the killer running down the hallway and out onto the stairs. Shooting at him. Him shooting at me. My stomach turned over again. I made myself take a deep breath and stand up taller. The women on the couch stopped talking and stared at me. I felt my face flush the same unnatural color as the cherry floating on top of the drink Dorothy handed me.

"How wonderful! A Manhattan!" I gushed. It's hard to get one's daily requirement of Red Dye No. 40.

The women's attention shifted momentarily from me to the drinks as Dorothy distributed them. Kim took her drink from her godmother and walked over to stand near the cabinet from which the man earlier in the day had removed the carved box containing the *kye* money. I glanced down at the white carpeting, expecting to see a smudged red trail where Jin would have been dragged from the living room. A colorful throw rug had been tossed down to cover the spot. I wondered what they'd done with her body.

"Yes, I make the best Manhattan in town. We always have Manhattan at our parties, isn't that right, girls?" Dorothy prodded the ancient crones.

I made a quick survey while I waited for someone to reply. They wore bright clothes and—unlike Dorothy, who wore her white hair long and straight—they had curled their hair into stiff dated 'dos. Clearly Dorothy was the oldest of the group. She was in her eighties. Two of the others were in their mid to late seventies, I judged, but the portly one squeezed in the middle of the couch was a spring chicken, not a day over sixty-five. No one moved. No one spoke. Perhaps their vocal cords had atrophied with age. Perhaps they couldn't speak English as well as Dorothy had indicated. Did they wonder what a white girl was doing at their party? What had Dorothy told them about me?

"Come on, girls, drink up," insisted Dorothy. "Skoal. Let's have a nice toast to welcome Whitney Logan. She's the lawyer I was telling you about who could help us form a limited partnership."

We'd agreed earlier that I was going to tell them I was a scholar. I'd dressed as a grad student. Why was Dorothy changing the story?

"Can we avoid taxes? In case one of us kicks the bucket?" asked the tall woman seated at the end of the couch closest to the kitchen.

Had Dorothy told them before I arrived that Jin was dead? What did they know? They watched me and waited for my answer. My mind raced back to my second year in law school. It had been compulsory to take corporate law. It was on the bar exam. It didn't interest me. I was busy taking "Law and Social Responsibility" and working in the prisoners rights project at the federal pen on Terminal Island.

I glanced over at the flamboyant woman who'd asked the question. I'd thought Lupe's clothes were weird. I made a quick mental note to lay off criticizing Lupe's wardrobe. To accessorize an aqua-and-pink Pucci dress, the Korean woman wore silver Mexican necklaces mixed with strands of gray and white seed pearls, a large not-inexpensive-looking ring with a green stone, and dangling gold Middle Eastern earrings that jingled when she moved. She looked as if she'd dressed in a boutique on a cruise ship.

I didn't remember anything about limited partnerships or taxation.

The youngest of the three old women said something in Korean as I contemplated an answer. She sounded angry.

"Lee, we're all going to speak English here tonight. I told Whitney we all speak English," said Dorothy.

"Why don't we get Korean lawyer? Korean lawyer is best." The woman frowned.

Dorothy placed her serving tray on the mahogany coffee table in front of the couch. "I haven't even introduced everyone yet, Lee, and you're already making snap judgments."

Kim stepped into the circle of women. She was wearing the same dark brown Armani pantsuit Jin Oh wore in the photo Dorothy had shown me of last year's *kye* party. Death is death, but Armani is forever. I wondered if Kim helped cart Jin's body out. Maybe it was in the bedroom. Maybe it was propped up in the shower stall. Maybe they'd driven it somewhere. I felt a bit sick juggling the possibilities. "Auntie Lee, she's a good lawyer. She went to UCLA law school."

I sipped the Manhattan so as not to let surprise register on my face. Kim must have been to the library and looked me up in a Martindale-Hubbell directory to be sure her godmother wasn't throwing money away on bunko services.

"Besides, she's not going to charge very much money," Kim added, smiling in my direction.

"Miss Logan, come here," said Dorothy. "These are my friends. Lee Joon Song . . ."

The argumentative woman nodded but didn't say anything. She had a thin mouth and deepset eyes in a broad face. Although Lee Joon was the youngest, I doubted she'd ever been a beauty. She was dressed in the same kind of full-length traditional dress Dorothy and Jin had worn earlier in the day. Hers was lime green and topped by a short orange jacket tied on one side by a wide strip of black cloth in a single bowknot. With it she wore a good-looking pair of black Bally pumps.

". . . Nancy Johnson . . ."

I put my hand out to the woman sitting where the bloodstain had been. She tentatively gave me her hand. I shook it. It was scrawny but warm. Later I would learn it was considered bad manners to touch an older person or offer to shake hands.

"I was married to U.S. serviceman. Dr. Bill Johnson. Pharmacist. From Connecticut. He called me Nancy."

I nodded, uncertain where to go with this information. She wore rose-tinted glasses. Her face was heavily lined, more so than Dorothy's and Dorothy was older. Perhaps she'd spent a lot of time in the sun. I'd seen that same aged-football look creeping up on my mother, who spent a lot of time outdoors playing tennis. I wouldn't be caught dead al fresco without SPF 30.

". . . and Chu Chu Park."

Chu Chu Park, the dotty-looking one, nodded slightly so her earrings tinkled a tune. She had on a pair of gold Turkish mules, the toes of which curved up into little crescents. "My husband was an obstetrician," she said, looking at me but apparently addressing herself more to Nancy Johnson in an offhand boast. "He's dead now. All of our husbands are dead. We're the 'Black Widows.' "

Kim giggled politely with her hand in front of her mouth.

"All widows. That's why it's so important that we take good care of our money," said Nancy Johnson, giggling in the same formal way with hand over mouth.

Dorothy took this opportunity to sit down in the red easy chair next to the couch. She pulled at the knees of her black silk trousers to adjust them, then leaned forward toward the other women. "Something very bad has happened."

The icy glass in my hand felt heavy, but I didn't want to put it down. Was she going to tell them Jin had been murdered in this room? I'd asked her not to. She'd said she was only going to tell them about the money, but she'd been changing everything else we'd discussed earlier.

The trio looked back expectantly.

Dorothy looked from Lee Joon to Chu Chu Park and then to Nancy Johnson. "A man stole our *kye*."

"What? What? What?" they exploded nearly in unison.

They'd each put in $15,000. Dorothy had explained to me that the money was awarded by lottery at the party. Each woman wrote her name on a piece of paper and the winning name was drawn by one of them from a bowl. Seventy-five thousand dollars plus interest would mean a lot to anyone.

"This morning . . ." Dorothy tried to explain.

Lee Joon began beating her breast and wailing in a primordial ritual. As if on cue, all the other women set down their drinks and began wailing along with her. They rocked back and forth moaning and weeping.

I looked uncomfortably away and examined a lithograph of craggy mauve mountains on the far wall. I come from a family where little is said about feelings. I'd never cry in front of anyone. I couldn't remember ever having seen my mother cry. The wailing grew louder. I'd seen my father cry once when he was really drunk. It was the summer after my first year in law school and I'd gone back to Maryland to visit them. Donn asked me to go with him to the country club they belong to. Although my mother's an excellent tennis player, she doesn't like to hang around the club the way my father does. Donn and I drank martinis and tried to find things to talk about. Somewhere between martini five and six Donn started to babble about Tina, one of the younger women my mother plays tennis with. He began to cry, and I realized he'd had an affair with her.

The wailing of the Korean women increased to an agitated pitch, then just as suddenly died away. The women dabbed at their faces with cocktail napkins and snuffled their runny noses. They picked up their drinks again.

Lee Joon grunted apprehensively. "Why couldn't you keep the money in the freezer like everyone else does? It was one of those Mexicans, wasn't it? One of the ones who burned Koreatown down last April."

The Pico-Union bordering Koreatown is primarily Mexican and Central American. Even Koreatown seemed to be largely latino now. Someday all of Southern California would return to its rightful owner, Mexico. It was not an invasion but a reabsorption.

"Where's Jin?" Nancy Johnson interrupted, looking worried. "Did something happen to Jin? Is that why she's not here?"

Dorothy shook her head. "No, Jin's fine. She had to go to Buena Park because one of our cousins is in the hospital."

I looked at Dorothy as I bent over my drink again. She was a cool liar.

"Our cousin Charles," added Kim, but no one seemed interested in the story about the hospital.

"What happened to our money?" Chu Chu Park demanded.

Kim held her hand up to stop the old women from talking. "Dorothy was walking home from the bank—"

"Not good to keep *kye* in bank," said Lee Joon.

"Walking?" wailed Nancy Johnson. "Why didn't you call a cab? Why didn't Kim come get you?"

Dorothy leaned forward slightly. "Kim was at work. You know I always walk everywhere. Two miles a day. Every day."

"Yes, yes, we know. Walk everywhere. That's why you are Grandmother Tiger. All the special health foods, the herbs. The tonics," Lee Joon said. She looked as if the herbs and tonics pissed her off, that she'd heard this routine one too many times. "So what happened to the money?"

"I'm trying to tell you. You act like a group of old ladies. Just hold onto your pants." Dorothy paused to make sure she had the floor. "I was walking from the bank, I was on San Marino, near the corner of Western—"

"That's where those Mexicans hang out," Nancy Johnson wailed again. Folding her arms across her orange jacket, Lee Joon nodded knowingly.

I was glad Lupe hadn't come with me. I wouldn't want her to have to hear the racist ramblings of the angry old women.

"I don't know if he was Mexican," Dorothy said. "He had on a mask—"

"A mask! In broad daylight!" exclaimed Chu Chu Park. "I tell you the riots made those people bolder than ever. It's not safe to walk in your own neighborhood! It's unbelievable. Why, you can walk anywhere in London, in Paris, in Madrid, in—"

Kim put her hand on Chu Chu Park's garishly swathed arm. "I know, Auntie, I try to tell her it isn't safe anymore."

"A Chusok festival mask," Dorothy said.

I started to ask what that meant, but Dorothy quickly explained to me that we were only a few days away from

Chusok, the festival celebrating the harvest and the autumn moon.

Lupe had called the killer a *chino*. Now Dorothy was saying he was Korean.

Dorothy sat up a bit straighter and looked directly at the women. "I was about to cross the street. It was eleven-thirty in the morning . . ."

Jin had been killed much earlier. She was stiff as a plank by that time. Why was Dorothy creating this story? Why these details?

". . . I had our *kye* money in crisp new thousand dollar bills in the bottom of my bag. The man ran up to me . . ."

How had the man gotten into Dorothy's apartment? There'd been no sign of forced entry.

". . . he must have been hiding behind one of the buildings . . ."

Had she let him in? Was it someone she knew? Someone whose voice she recognized? Was that why he was wearing the mask?

". . . he pushed me off balance and grabbed my purse. It all happened so quickly that's all I remember."

The three women looked stunned. Kim hugged her godmother. Lee Joon recovered most quickly. "Who besides us knew you'd be going for the money today?"

"Just us," Dorothy replied. A somber silence hung heavily in the air.

"One of us must have told someone," said Lee Joon.

"Of course we did," Chu Chu Park retorted. "Everyone we know knows we belong to *kye* group and that we have our lottery party same time every year."

Nancy Johnson sipped at her drink. "That's right. For Chusok."

"It was your idea to put the *kye* in a bank," Chu Chu Park added grumpily.

Every year the party was at a different person's house. The hostess went to the bank, wrapped the money up in red tissue paper, and prepared a supper, Kim explained to me.

"Did you report it to the police?" asked Nancy Johnson.

Dorothy shook her head.

The syrupy drink in Nancy Johnson's hand nearly spilled as she gestured with it. "Didn't report it! You could have walked right over to the Koreatown Police Community Center on 8th and Normandie, since you like to walk so much," she sputtered.

Lee Joon laughed, but not pleasantly. "Nancy, you think because the police come around now to Koreatown Civic Association and give us pep talks that they're gonna take care of us? They didn't during the riots. Our men did."

I'd seen the live television coverage of armed Korean merchants guarding their businesses during the Uprising. Uzis. Semiautomatics.

Chu Chu Park smacked her empty glass down on the coffee table. "This isn't time to discuss politics. And we don't want to hear about your volunteer job at the civic association again. We're sick of you bragging about it. What happened to our *kye*? Someone here knows what happened to our money."

The old ladies looked at each other as though for the first time. The gold-and-black enamel clock on the cabinet near where Kim stood ticked loudly in the silence.

"Dorothy, when did you tell her about our money?" asked Lee Joon in a shrill voice, pointing a bony accusing finger at me.

Could these old bats possibly think that I was involved in the theft of their money?

"Just yesterday," Dorothy replied calmly. Then she explained that she'd been thinking about what to do with the money if she was the winner of the *kye* lottery. She said she'd been thinking for a while of changing her will, but the lawyer who had originally done it for her had died, so she called the Los Angeles County Bar Association and asked for referrals. They gave her my name. She decided my name had a propitious number of letters in it so she called me, explained the situation, and I'd told her I could come over for an appointment with her and meet the group to explain the benefits of a limited partnership for future *kye*.

A propitious number? I quickly counted the letters in my name. Seven for Whitney. Five for Logan. Twelve! What was the meaning of twelve? Did Dorothy believe in onomancy, the divination of destinies deciphered from names? She was more than a little wack, I decided. And where was she coming up with these stories? This multicultural business was tough work. It occurred to me that, in law, a document in the handwriting of one person with the signature in the hand of another is called onomastic. They teach you so little in law school that you can actually use. I studied each of the old women again. I hadn't seen any money except for the $750 Dorothy had given me earlier in the day. All I'd seen was the wooden box.

"That's ridiculous, to think this young woman could have anything to do with it," snapped Dorothy. "You sit around your house too much. You've been watching too much television."

"How about another drink, everyone?" Kim collected the glasses and took the serving tray into the kitchen without waiting for a reply. I heard the reassuring sound of ice clinking in glasses and the burbly burble of booze being poured.

Chu Chu Park shook her jewelry dismissively at her friends. "How could a white woman possibly steal our money in the middle of Koreatown now?"

There, the cat was out of the bag. They all knew I was white.

"It's too ridiculous," repeated Chu Chu, stretching her arms out in front of her. She had a squeaky voice that was probably quite ugly if she got excited. "You know everyone keeps an eye on the *hiyun.*"

"White man," Dorothy whispered so I'd understand.

It had not previously occurred to me that I was a foreigner. My forefathers had been among the very earliest groups of criminals sent to this country by England.

The other women examined me as though I was an exotic but not particularly appealing or clean animal.

"Why do we need her here now if the money's gone?" asked Lee Joon, glaring angrily from me to Dorothy.

Because your friend Jim was murdered in this room. Because Dorothy wants to find out who killed her sister. Because I think Dorothy doesn't really trust you.

Dorothy didn't say anything. I was about to pick up my purse to beat a dignified retreat when Kim reentered the room and handed me another drink.

"I say Miss Logan stays," said Dorothy.

The women looked anxiously back and forth from one to another like kids choosing up competing kickball teams.

"Call me Whitney." I tried to look appealing and clean. I had bills to pay. Lupe's salary.

Dorothy smiled at me. I smiled back. Maybe if they kicked me out she'd let me keep the $750 anyway, for having made the trip over the hill. "Whitney is going to figure out if we can deduct the loss of our money on our income taxes."

I felt my knees buckle. Now I was a tax expert.

There was an excited murmur of assent from all the seated women except Lee Joon.

Kim finished handing out the round of drinks. She placed a plate of shrimp crackers and another of silvery dried fish on the coffee table. As she bent over, her pants' legs crept up her ankles. I noticed she had a small blue-and-red circle tattooed on her left ankle.

I bowed slightly to the group. "I'm sorry I'm meeting you on an occasion of such loss. . . ."

Dorothy sighed, but none of the others seemed to notice. She must have been thinking of her sister.

". . . You must be in shock about the theft of your money."

Nancy Johnson shoved a handful of the tiny dried fish into her mouth and tried to insist the others have something to eat also.

"Nancy." Chu Chu Park waved aside the proffered snacks. "Did you tell your nephew Henry about the money?"

Nancy Johnson chewed deliberately and swallowed. She wiped her fingers carefully with the cocktail napkin. She set it aside with great precision. "Why do you ask that?"

"He was arrested once, wasn't he?"

Kim shook her head. "That was for driving with a suspended license, Auntie. That doesn't count."

"Arrested is arrested. They took him to the police station, didn't they? Nobody in my family's ever been arrested."

"It wasn't Henry," argued Nancy Johnson. "He doesn't need our money. He's in Seoul on business. Our little seventy-five thousand dollars is peanuts to him." Nancy Johnson puffed up and looked very proud of her nephew.

"I always wondered where he got the money to start his business," muttered Chu Chu Park.

"What did you say, Chu Chu?" demanded Nancy Johnson. "How do you go on all those trips? Europe. Mexico. Hong Kong. Didn't you get that ring in Hong Kong?"

"You told us it's an emerald," added Lee Joon.

Chu Chu instinctively twisted the ring on her right hand

to display the stone more prominently. "It *is* an emerald. You're both jealous because I'm the only one who wears nice clothes and looks good all the time."

I couldn't help bending forward slightly to get a better look at the ring. It was a good green rock about half the size of Ireland.

"I save my money," Chu Chu said. "I still have a lot of money my husband left me. He left me a lot of money. I didn't put it in those crazy aerospace industry and movie studio stocks like Lee's brother-in-law talked her into."

Lee Joon clicked her teeth and waved her hand angrily. "My stocks are good stocks. Not government bonds like you have. I'm smart enough to know how to play the market. And commodities. I invest in Korea. Strong Korea. I don't waste my money in bonds. Maybe you stole the money because—"

"Sisters, sisters!" Dorothy clapped her hands, trying to bring order to the room. "It's not going to do any good to fight among ourselves. The money is gone. We can't prove who took it. We don't want to report to the police until we calm down a little so we don't say hasty things that are going to cause us harm. We've known each other a long time. We must give each other respect. We are family."

Did the bickering women consider Dorothy their leader or were they simply being polite because they were in her house? Each of them seemed to have some reason to want the money. How long had they known each other? I thought of Lupe. Would I know her for a long time? I thought again of the $750 a day Dorothy had said she'd pay me to find out who'd killed her sister. I needed it. And I wasn't afraid of old ladies.

"I may have to take some statements from you. I'll need to come and speak with each of you individually."

"Depositions," Nancy Johnson announced importantly but inaccurately. "I've seen that on 'Perry Mason.' " The other women murmured an affirmation of this.

I took a grateful drink from the glass. I was on solid ground. None of them knew anything about the law except what they'd learned from television. I would have to remember to use legal terminology with them more often.

The next day I went to my office early in the morning to wait for Lupe to begin her job as my secretary. I cleaned off the top of my desk and set up the antiquated electric typewriter I'd brought from home. It surged on when I plugged it in and the carriage jumped slightly. Ready to go! I sharpened all the pencils and replaced them in their pink-and-orange Mexican papier-mâché jug shaped like a mermaid that I'd bought on Olvera Street. I put all the books I wasn't using back on the bookshelf. Since Lupe had last been in my office I'd acquired used sets of *Bender's Criminal Defense* and *Witkin on Evidence*. Then I sat down to wait. I read some back issues of the *Daily Journal* and noted in the classifieds that real legal secretaries were making a minimum of $22,500 a year. After an hour of waiting, I went out for a cup of coffee at the Viet restaurant down the block.

The caffeine made me nervous as a bird dog. I raced back up the stairs to my office. From the second floor wafted the moving sounds of the Delfonics. "LaLaLa Means I Love You."

I opened the door.

Lupe stood beside the desk. She had on a gray pinstripe flannel suit with a midcalf-length skirt and a jacket belted at the waist. A plastic cameo was pinned to the lapel. Her shiny black hair was twisted up into a bun. Soft curls framed her face. She wore blood red lipstick and a pair of black pumps with a thick heel from the forties. A steno pad was in one hand, a pencil in the other. "Professional, no?" she said. "Rosalind Russell in *His Girl Friday*."

"It's perfect. Unfortunately, not a lot of clients come in here. It's ok for you to wear jeans. That'd probably be best since you'll be delivering papers."

"You said I was going to be an executive secretary." Lupe frowned and waved the steno pad at the desk. "Look, I've been typing already."

I walked over to look at the paper in the typewriter. It said LUPE RAMOS LUPE RAMOD LUPE RAMOS.

She leaned past me and peered at the paper. I heard her grunt with displeasure at it.

"No preocupese," I mispronounced. "It's only your first day. You'll get better. You're on your own for right now 'cause I gotta go back to Koreatown. To talk with one of the old ladies I met last night at Kim's godmother's." I intentionally did not mention the dead woman, Jin.

"Did Dorothy pay you yet?"

I shook my head. I quickly explained there were barely constrained tensions among the old women and I needed to learn what those tensions were if I expected to find out who was responsible for the theft of the *kye* and the murder. I was hoping to skirt around the edges so Lupe wouldn't freak out on me again.

"Man, that's so *chingón*. Someone you actually know

stealing your *pan*." Lupe tsk'ed in disapproval. "What are you going to ask this *vieja*?"

"I'm gonna find out if she believes Dorothy's story about the robbery for starters. I can't imagine anyone saying anything incriminating to me if she thinks a murder's involved. Snitching off a thief's a different matter. Also, I been wondering why the guy only shot Jin. With determinate sentencing you might as well kill as many people as you want; you get the same punishment. It's like two for the price of one."

"He didn't have to shoot Dorothy. Got her too scared to go to the cops. She's lucky," said Lupe. "I'm glad. She seemed nice to me. Took good care of Joey."

"I guess since she was the older sister she always looked after Jin." I wondered why Dorothy hadn't tried to kick the guy if she knew Tae Kwon Do. Why did she leave that to Jin? I supposed that she was afraid. It's one thing to practice the forms and another thing to spar. One thing to shoot at a paper target. Another thing to shoot at someone. "She must feel awful that she couldn't have done anything to protect her." I waited to see if Lupe would add anything. If she would understand the way I was hinting at our tangled relationship from Dogtown to the present.

"Get her to talk about Jin," suggested Lupe, without indicating she'd understood my allusion. "Find out who was Jin's best friend."

I didn't have a best friend. Always been a loner. It's easier that way. Don't have to explain my father's drinking or any of the wack things he does. Never have to have my mother look down her nose at anyone I might've brought home. I studied Lupe. Did she have a best friend? This might be an appropriate time for a direct personal question. To connect with her. To show her I cared about her life. "What'd your mom say when you got home yesterday with Joey?"

"Nothing." Lupe smoothed her skirt and edged closer to the desk as though there was something she didn't want me to see.

I waited for her to tell me more, but she busied herself shifting a file from one side of the desk to the other. "Are you going to be staying there? I need to know how to get in touch with you. About work."

"Yeah, we'll be staying there till I make enough to get our own place. Things are cool."

Would she laugh at me if I told her I was worried about her? "What about Hector? Where's he?"

"You don't understand English, or what? I don't feel like talking about it. Hector and me, it's not finished, but it don't have nothing to do with you." She paused. "Doesn't got nothing to do with you," she corrected herself, apparently mindful of her new employment position. She adjusted a gold picture frame with a 5×7 of Joey so I could see it. "Don't get me wrong, I appreciate what you're doing for me and all, but it's none of your business."

"I may run into Hector while—"

She snapped open the steno pad to a fresh, attentive page. "What do you want me to do here today?"

I told her to review all the files, be sure they were alphabetized, and check that all upcoming court cases were recorded both on the calendar I carry and on the desk calendar. This double calendaring is one of the requirements of being insured for malpractice. The insurers don't want to pay out big bucks because some careless lawyer let a statute of limitations or an appeal period run. For a while I didn't carry insurance, but I'd had too many sleepless nights worrying about what would happen if I fucked up someone's case. Most lawyers are conscientious about their work not because they have the deep abiding desire to do good but because they want to avoid judgments being taken against them. The sheriff coming in and ripping your Charles Jourdan shoes out of the closet along with everything else you own. I am ashamed that I, a member of the National Lawyers Guild, think about such things too, but there you have it.

I showed Lupe the message pad I wanted her to use to record phone messages in duplicate. I told her that all the supplies she'd need were in the file cabinet.

"Don't worry about a thing," Lupe assured me. She turned busily away to check the contents of the cabinet. She wore black stockings with seams up the back. Her skirt was slit all the way up to her butt.

I drove west on Hollywood Boulevard so I could go down Vermont and check out how much of the damage from the riots had been repaired. I shoved a Peter Tosh cassette into my tape player. Koreatown was busy with shoppers, both Korean and Central American, that Wednesday morning. In the aftermath of the riots there had been a call for a rainbow coalition. Whites from the Westside had poured into South Central, the Pico-Union, and Koreatown armed with brooms and dustpans to begin cleaning up the city. I still felt guilty I hadn't helped. Sweeping up burned things had seemed an unsatisfactory response to the disaster. I'd picked up a lot of cases in the arraignment courts in the days following the violence. Looting, possession of narcotics, drunk in public, curfew violations. I told myself that this was my contribution to society. Serve the people.

The gutted furniture and clothing stores had been leveled, but the memory of smoke and burning plastics hung in the air. The sky was blue, but greasy with smog. Big dumpsters covered and then re-covered with competing gang graffiti stood on the sidewalks in front of empty businesses. On the eastern edge of Koreatown the *placas* of Salvatrucha began appearing spray-painted on walls. In Salvadoran slang it means something like bad dudes. It's the largest gang in the area.

I found Irolo Street, where I intended to look for Lee Joon. Since she was the most openly hostile to me the night before, I'd decided to start my questioning with her. I had to talk to two telephone operators and then a supervisor before they could find any phone listing or address for a Koreatown Civic Association. I was guessing this was the same place Chu Chu Park was talking about when she'd been ragging on Lee Joon.

The Koreatown Civic Association was a light-brown stone building on the corner of 8th surrounded by the usual crummy dress shops, Salvadoran restaurants, and a video rental store covered with thick black bars. I went around the block and ended up parking on Ardmore in front of an early-twenties bungalow court with an Islamic facade. A sloped and painted driveway led from the street into a narrow entrance. Pairs of small towers adorned each of the two wings of the court. I thought of Chu Chu Park's crazy Middle Eastern slippers. I locked my pull-out radio in the trunk next to my gun.

Some Salvadoran boys leaning on an old dented gold El Dorado yelled and whistled at me as I walked to the Korean civic association. I was wearing the same navy pantsuit and blouse I'd worn the night before. I hoped it would make me look familiar to Lee Joon. I wondered if many whites went to the association.

I opened the door and stepped from the bright sunlight into a small cool room painted ivory. A large Korean flag hung on the wall behind a wooden desk. A fat old man with many liver spots on his face dozed at the desk with his arm resting next to a red leather guest book and a white ballpoint pen. A pile of fliers announced an exhibition of contemporary art. He started awake and mumbled something as I closed the door.

"I'm sorry. I don't speak Korean. Do you speak English?"

"Of course. I'm Korean-American. Eighty-five percent of Koreans are here less than twenty years, but we all speak English. Koreans are good students. Education most important to us," he said with a heavy accent I could barely understand.

I nodded and looked down the hall to my right, where I could see doors to other rooms. Was Lee Joon there?

"Your first time here? You come to see exhibit of paintings?"

I nodded, glad to be able to agree.

He pointed to the flag behind him. In the center of a white background was a circle divided in two parts, the upper part red and the lower blue. In the four corners were black lines, three rows each. "The circle is universe in perfect balance and harmony. These symbols represent heaven, earth, fire, and water." He handed me a flier and gestured to where the gallery was. "Have a nice day."

I looked in the first room. A small group of women sat making green clay bowls and figurines at a long table covered with white butcher paper. They didn't bother to look up. Traditional music of plucked instruments came from a tape player in a corner. Lee Joon wasn't among the women. I moved on to the next room, where five tables of men and women played cards. I stepped into the doorway to get a better look at them. No Lee Joon. The cigarette smoke was heavy, and there was laughter and joking. They all stopped talking when they noticed me.

"Art gallery there," barked a guy who pointed a nicotine-stained finger farther down the hall.

I stepped back into the hall, and the laughter and talking

resumed. As I walked away I heard an argument coming from a room at the far end of the hall and on the opposite side of the corridor. A teenage girl's voice was raised in anger. Then a woman's voice snapped in response. I walked past the entrance to the gallery, which was empty, toward the voices.

The door to the room was partially closed. I stood so I could see into it. It was a large kitchen with restaurant-size and -quality appliances. In the center of the room the teenage girl glanced up at me in fierce confusion. She wore a Depeche Mode t-shirt with a pair of skimpy denim cutoffs over a pair of black tights and unlaced Doc Martens. The girl threw a knife coated with peanut butter down on the tile counter next to the sink, grabbed a sandwich from the counter, and rushed past me.

"Old cunt," she snarled at the slight figure who stood between us.

Lee Joon turned and barked something Korean in response at the girl's retreating back. The old woman looked startled to see me standing in the doorway. Had she understood what the girl had said to her? Her timeworn features rearranged themselves, but were unable to completely erase her ire or her surprise.

"She stole food," Lee Joon said. "We only eat at certain times. Everyone pays or has special voucher."

"Perhaps I should have called to make an appointment to see you." I tried to look apologetic but professional.

"Junk food. That's all the young people want nowadays is junk food. Here we fix good food. Real food." She wiped the already clean counter furiously with a damp sponge.

A large pot simmered on the stove. I walked over and looked in at steaming chunks of fish floating plump and white on the bubbling surface. I had never tasted Korean food. A ladle lay nearby. I picked it up. "May I?"

Lee Joon frowned with annoyance but handed me a small styrofoam cup from a cabinet. She took the ladle from me and gave me a minute amount of the boiling broth.

It burned my lips. It was spicy, hot, and complex. I murmured my appreciation.

"*Maeuntang,*" she named it.

"Did you make this? It's wonderful."

She took the paper cup from me without saying anything and threw it in the trash.

"You're a great cook," I offered enthusiastically.

"Yes, I am very good cook." She folded her arms across her chest. "Why do you come here? I got nothing to say to you."

"I'm just trying to help. You must be upset about the *kye* It'll make you feel better to talk about what happened."

She waved her hand dismissively as if she didn't have any use for touchy-feely bullshit. "Maybe somebody did steal our money. I didn't see money."

I hadn't seen any either. Only the box. Had it really contained the money? The guy who stole it had seemed happy about whatever was in it. I hoped this old lady would tell me more if I treated her right. Being gracious didn't seem to work. That was too bad: I like being gracious. "You've known Dorothy a long time, haven't you?"

"Long enough." With some encouragement Lee Joon said she'd known both sisters since her husband opened a store on Olympic. She said the name of the store as if it was Neiman-Marcus.

"I haven't met Jin yet," I said. "Is she a good friend of yours?"

Lee Joon nodded without answering.

"It must be wonderful to have a friend like Dorothy too," I gushed like a sorority girl at a rush party. "She's beautiful.

I can see everyone adores her and looks up to her because she's so wise. She's a natural-born leader."

"Dorothy always try to run the show, all right," exploded Lee Joon. "Tell everyone what to do."

I gazed down at the floor awkwardly as if her anger discomforted me. I held it for a second as if she'd surprised me and embarrassed both of us with her unseemly outburst. It's like fishing. One of the few valuable things I ever learned from my father. You let the fish have the line and you wait and then you play it. When a decent length of time had passed, I looked up. She was slightly flushed. I had embarrassed her. Time to throw some nice. I told her I hadn't understood the name of her husband's store. I apologized and asked her to repeat it for me.

Inspecting me with disdain, she repeated it. "Hangul is most sensible language in the world. Simplest." She shook her head as though I should learn it but I was probably too dumb.

"Is your store still in existence?" The uprising was like an economic holocaust for the Korean business community. Nearly 90 percent of the destroyed businesses hadn't been able to rebuild.

"Best grocery store in town. You bet. My son runs it now."

"Was it damaged in the riots?"

Lee Joon turned away and stirred the soup briskly before turning off the fire beneath it.

"I'm sorry. I don't mean to pry. I'm just trying to think of all the possible tax implications. The news said storeowners lost everything, their entire life savings."

"We have insurance," she insisted.

I wondered if it was true. I'd read that many merchants had not been carrying insurance because of prohibitive costs due to redlining. Even if they did have coverage, it was unlikely that the companies were making prompt payment. Seventy-five thousand could come in very handy to a damaged business. I watched Lee Joon. She'd probably told her son about the *kye* money. She'd want to help him out. Wouldn't she choose her son above all others?

"Are you still involved in the store? I imagine you worked with your husband when it got started."

"Of course I helped my husband," she retorted, adding that they'd worked fifteen-hour days and the store was very successful. "When my husband died two years ago, I wanted to keep working, keep track of the books and accounts. But my son said, 'Mom, you take vacation.' "

I nodded. "So now you volunteer your time here."

"I always volunteer here. Many years," she corrected me.

"That's wonderful. If you change your mind and want to talk to me about the tax situation, give me a call." I handed her one of my business cards. "Would you show me around before I leave?"

Lee Joon walked past me without responding, turned out the kitchen light, and started down the hall. I hurried after her. Her lips were set grimly, but then, not without some pride, she barked, "There's art gallery, card room, room for sculpture and painting."

I let her show me the rooms I'd already seen and asked what was in the rest of the building. We shuffled silently toward the other hall, past the old man at the reception desk. He was asleep again, snoring this time, with an unlit but still stinky cigar perched in a red enamel ashtray.

"Library." Lee Joon opened the door and pointed inside a small empty room whose walls were covered with shelves laden with both musty books and shiny magazines. "Meeting room." She opened the door and showed me a larger room with about fifty metal folding chairs stacked in the rear corners. At the end of the hall she stopped and opened the last door. "Exercise room." I peered in. The angry teenage girl I'd seen with the sandwich danced alone while smoking a cigarette. She wore a Sony Walkman, which was turned up full blast. She glanced at us, did an aggressive Roger Rabbit, then continued her solitary hip-hop routine.

"Do many young people come here?" I wondered aloud as Lee Joon started to lead me back out the door. Shouldn't the girl be in school? They were always talking about how important education was.

"We have very nice dances. Boys and girls dress up nice." She sniffed disapprovingly at the lonely dancer. "The Koreatown Civic Association is very popular with the girls and boys. Very popular."

The girl ripped off her headphones before running out of the room. "Are you kidding me! This is the most boring fucking place on earth! I can't wait till the new sports center's finished so there'll be something to do, somewhere to go where you don't have to look like a mummy."

Lee Joon stamped her little foot in its sensible collegiate Bass Weejun. I wondered where she had bought them. I hadn't seen any for years.

"I'm sorry she was rude to you," I said. "You've had an awful day. Her, me, both of us bothering you." I put my hand out toward her to steady her or comfort her.

The old woman ignored my hand. "Sports center! I'm sick of hearing about sports center. Just another place for gangsters and hooligans."

I stopped in my tracks. I was charmed. Hooligans. "What's the sports center?"

"On Normandie. Near Olympic. New center for Mexicans. Salvadorans. Going to have boxing." She shook her head as though she couldn't imagine anyone of any value liking boxing.

"Mexicans? Salvadorans?"

Lee Joon smiled slightly, pleased with my apparent stupidity. She'd be able to tell Dorothy I was an idiot. "When Koreatown was burned down, it wasn't the blacks. Mexicans and Salvadorans burn down Koreatown. Here everybody from Mexico and Central America. Now just a few from Korea."

I gestured in the air as if I didn't understand what she was getting at.

"Korean businessman, Mr. Ko Won Bae, gives money to the community to build this sports center." She looked proud of this civic effort but doubtful of its success. "Get Mexicans and others off the street. They say no more trouble."

I nodded my head. "Great idea! Give kids somewhere to go. Let people from all countries be together, play together."

Lee Joon snorted with disdain. "Place for all criminals to be together. Make more trouble. Look, don'tgetmewrong . . ."

Had Lee Joon learned English from old gangster movies? George Raft? This would thrill Lupe, all these old biddies talking like B movies. Why do they always talk so fast in those old movies?

". . . Ko Won Bae, plenty smart businessman. Makes a lot of money. Gives a lot of money to people of Koreatown. To our association. I support Ko Won, respect Ko Won, but I don't want more Mexicans in Koreatown with their loud music and noisy children. They're the kind of people who throw trash on the streets. Koreatown for Koreans."

Did many of the Koreans feel like Lee Joon? I wondered again where Hector "Manos" Ramos had met Kim and why the Ivory Princess was sleeping with a bullethead like Hector. Lee Joon showed me to the front door. I wondered if I should bow. She opened the door. Blaring *salsa* music and the roar of traffic rushed in. Then the sound of flutes and small drums wafted down the hall of the Koreatown Civic Association. A woman's voice soared in a high-pitched but sweet traditional song. I closed my eyes for a second. I smelled rose incense and oranges. I opened my eyes and once again examined the old woman in front of me. I felt suffused with the lovely mysteries of the Orient and a deep aching to be part of the new multicultural Los Angeles. I bowed.

Lee Joon slammed the door between us.

I got in my car, shoved the Peter Tosh Equal Rights tape in again, adjusted it to full blast, and drove out to North Hollywood. It was hotter than hell in the Valley and everything was pale, sundrenched, bleached of sharp edges. I drove past Universal City, the old lot of Universal Studios that has been turned into an amusement park with a public transportation system more sophisticated than that of the city surrounding it. Above the freeway the three black glass towers of the City loom menacingly on a hill, their smooth surfaces marred by huge horizontal brown travertine marble slabs like the eruptions of some terrifying tropical disease. I drove down the wide boulevard through what were once the immeasurable wheat fields of Isaac Lankershim. The film industry found the Valley photogenic and western. Less hazy at one time than the LA basin.

I drove up Burbank Boulevard past a mile or so of burger stands and Xerox places, then turned left near a Methodist church built in the Spanish Colonial revival style now reserved for taco take-out franchises. I parked in front of a run-down but clean white stucco store next to a vet's. It was the temple of my master.

It was cool and quiet inside the *do jang*. The stucco walls covered with white rice paper, the concrete floor with thick white matting. The room was empty. I took off my high heels and placed them on a wooden rack next to the door.

I glanced at my watch. The next class wasn't until four. It was just a little past one. I saw the flicker of candlelight from the end of the hall where Master Kyung Sun Lee, Golden Tiger, maintains his red and gold altar.

As though expecting me, Sun Lee, dressed in his immaculate white *do bak* covered with colorful silk patches of tournaments he has won, stepped from the hallway into the space. With his receding nebbish brown hair clipped short and his Wonder Bread skin, he looks like a computer nerd. He's as anglo as you can get. I suspect his real name is Bob.

I bowed. He bowed in return.

"I hope I'm not disturbing you. There's something I wanted to ask you . . ." I stopped. I still have trouble calling him Master Tiger. A year ago I had found an ad for his Tae Kwon Do school in my local throwaway paper. Tae Kwon Do, original Korean karate, ancient, sophisticated. I've never really told him why I wanted to learn martial arts. Never told him about my gun, the shooting range. It's well enough if he thinks I want to protect myself from rapists and muggers. Bob is training warriors, yes, but not killers.

"I got a job over in Koreatown. I don't understand the people. They won't talk with me. There are things I need to find out."

Sun Lee turned toward his kitchen to make us some tea. "Every stranger is a stranger. And the mountain is tall."

I shook my head as I followed him silently to the kitchen. Great. Someday fish will fly. Why did I have to come from such a dysfunctional family?

Geologically the Korean peninsula is mostly paleozoic and mesozoic like southern Manchuria, but the southeastern part of the country, like Japan, is more recent. The people of this mountainous island bounded by the Yellow Sea and the Sea of Japan are related to the Mongolian race and can probably be traced back to the fossil men of Tzuyang and Liuchang. The Golden Tiger had spoken in a stilted formal way, as if he was narrating a travelogue.

I didn't pay much attention to the scenery in Laurel Canyon on my way back over the hill to Hollywood. I was trying to digest everything he'd told me because I needed a basis for understanding the old women. One of them had to have been involved in the theft of the *kye*. And the death of a friend. But which one?

As part of our warm-up exercises at the *do jang* I'd learned to count to 100 in Korean while we did sit-ups and push-ups, but I realized I didn't know the slightest thing about Korea or Koreans. Despite my professed desire to sing the

Internationale on top of all the barricades across the world wherever human rights were endangered, hadn't I been as guilty as anyone of buying into the stereotype of Koreans in LA as just greedy liquor store owners? Before I met Kim and Dorothy, the only Korean I'd ever spoken to was a guy who ran a minimart with take-out pizza near my apartment.

The Golden Tiger had described ancient competing states to me. Like Big Hazard and *Tres Puntos* in East LA, like South Central and Koreatown, I thought. The founding mythologies of these Korean states were more or less the same: the immigrant leader of a more advanced culture was invariably called the Heavenly Son. He marries a girl of the native people with a less developed culture and founds a royal family. The social system is then a dual organization, an upper class of immigrants and a lower class of native peoples. You can't get away from it, I admonished myself, it's always the story of class struggle. These ancient people made clay figurines. They built huts in a round dugout form. They fished with nets and hunted with spears. They knew how to sew with bone needles, how to select seeds, and how to destroy weeds to protect their crops. They cast bronze trinkets, axes, and arrowheads. They believed all things in nature had powerful spirits, and shamans were their intermediaries with the spirits.

I hugged the curve and downshifted, slowing up behind a ragged old baby blue Cadillac with a bumper sticker that proclaimed: PROSPERITY IS MY CHOICE.

"They worshiped their ancestors," Sun Lee had said. I'd seen that Kim was devoted to Dorothy. Was I a good daughter? Probably not. I moved to Los Angeles to put as much distance as possible between myself and my parents.

I started to feel the old anxiety and guilt in my stomach about my family, so I tried to remember what else the Golden Tiger had told me. That Korean history was the story of these competing local tribes and their efforts to remain free of the Chinese and Japanese, who both wanted to dominate the strategic landbridge. It was the history of a people who wanted to remain isolated. They invented woodblock printing and the first encyclopedia, they printed with metal type two hundred years before Gutenberg. He explained that during much of this century and the last the Japanese had occupied Korea with a military government that tried to eliminate Korean culture. Natural resources were exported, civil rights almost completely wiped out. During World War II, Japan used Korea as a factory and arsenal. Korean citizens were drafted into the Japanese army.

"They had a history before they came here," he reminded me.

He also said that Korean people are typically inclined to possess a self-motivated, self-effacing, extroversive, and sociable character. So why wouldn't they talk with me? I was trying to help them.

I decided I should drive over to central Hollywood to Bronson before I returned to Koreatown. At the south end of Bronson is the Paramount Studio lot with its black iron Spanish Renaissance gate. At the north end, according to my Thomas map guide, is the location of the Church of the Big Mother. I thought I should find out if anyone was going to bail Venus Howard out of jail.

I cruised slowly up the street toward Franklin, looking for the address I had written in her file. A crack dealer stood on a quiet corner blanched by the ferocious September sun. Number 1200 was a white stone Hansel and Gretel cottage probably built in the mid-twenties. It looked like medieval rural England except for two enormous royal palms behind it dancing and swaying in the filthy breeze.

The yard was immaculate emerald grass, and I followed

a curving red brick path across it to a heavy dark wood door hinged on the right with two large black triangles of metal. I was unable to hear anything inside. On either side of the door were windows with heavy leaded glass tinted red. I knocked on the door.

When no one answered, I tried the doorknob. Was the church truly a place of worship open to all? The door creaked and swung slowly inward. I stepped inside.

I was in a small white anteroom bathed with red sunlight from the windows. On either side of me stood copper vases nearly as high as my waist. They were filled with water, and on the surface of each floated a gardenia. In front of me was a narrow arch shaped like a vagina. This entrance was cloaked with many strands of clear crystal beads that hung like a spooky psychedelic hymen, the sunlight breaking and shattering against the beads into red, blue, purple, and yellow all over the innocent walls.

I waited for permission to go farther, but no one appeared. From the next room I heard Pachelbel's unmistakable Canon in D. I paused warily, feeling something was wrong. Disco, yes. Rod Stewart, yes. This I would expect. Perhaps the kinkiest libido might demand Mötley Crue or Guns n' Roses. But Pachelbel? I pushed through the beads.

The air was heavy with jasmine and musk incense. At my feet was a red, black, and orange Persian rug, the kind sold outdoors on Highland Avenue down near Sunset for $29.99 by guys who drive old Toyota Celicas. I was flanked by two white marble columns—these sold on La Brea south of Wilshire by black men going "checkitout, checkitout." On each column smoked a bronze incense burner. The walls were white, the ceiling a pale pale blue over which someone had clumsily daubed white paint to indicate clouds.

In front of me stood the goddess Aphrodite.

Made from a mannequin. She wore a sheer red nylon

nightie. Her feet were stuffed into a cracked pair of black patent stilettos to which had been added black ribbon winding around her calves like ancient sandals. The flame red wig on her head was crowned with a wreath of bay leaves. Her arms stretched out stiffly to me.

"Step forward. The Mother will receive you," rasped a live voice.

I looked around the room. Off to my right I saw a small dirty kitchen. I stepped toward it and peered in. It was empty except for the usual grimy broken appliances left by people who have moved out in a hurry.

"The Mother is waiting," the voice croaked.

In the flickering shadows, moving deeper into the main room I passed the statue of Aphrodite and nearly tripped on a wooden kneeler stationed in front of a throne covered with black fur and mottled with old come stains. The throne was empty, but flanked by mirrors so that my own image was thrown back at me. Platinum hair blown straight that morning after I washed it and held back from my face now by a narrow black grosgrain ribbon. The careful makeup I had been taught to apply by a nice man at the Chanel counter of I. Magnin. Translucent powder, slight highlights of copper on my cheeks and eyes, black mascara. Tempting Red lipstick. Of course I have good skin and a regular routine. And I always dab a discreet touch of Chanel No. 22 on my wrists.

"Behold the Mother." The voice interrupted my careful appraisal of myself.

A pale slender teenage girl rose silently from where she had been coiled on the red satin sheets of a king-size bed. Directly behind her stood a gold altar with two flickering white candles. Above the altar was a black-and-white poster of Marilyn Monroe with her skirt blown up toward her waist.

The girl walked to the edge of the bed and posed above me with her arms stretched out, her long black hair past her waist but not completely covering her nakedness. I stared at her navel in confusion. A small black spider was tattooed on her left pelvic bone.

"I'm here about Venus," I stammered, withdrawing my attention from her shaved private part. I wondered how this was done. Every time I try to shave my bikini area I end up with a rash of small red bumps.

"You want Venus? For the mother-daughter number? A hundred and seventy-five dollars gets you Mom in an apron and a Catholic schoolgirl uniform for yourself. Mom goes down on you or you can go down on Mom. It's two hundred and fifty dollars for 69."

I'd never even seen my mother naked! Who'd want to see their mother naked? I don't want any kind of family activity. Even the conventional visit-the-family-for-Thanksgiving kind of thing. No, thank you. Families, they fuck you up. It had taken me years to get away from mine. Was this neurotic on my part? Other people wanted to be close to their families. Lupe wanted to be with her mother and her son. Kim and Dorothy were a family. I've always been a loner. "No, Venus—"

"Oh, you want the secrets of Venus." She cupped her breast like Botticelli's Venus rising from the sea. "The secrets of love. The secrets of erotic enchantment . . ." A strong blast of mouthwash emanated from her ruby lips.

"Venus sent me—"

"After you give your offering, I will teach you the ancient wisdom." She dropped to her knees on the bed, knocked a *TV Guide* to the floor, and placed a basket of fruit between us. She grabbed a banana. "Watch this. We'll start with blowjobs. Is that gonna be cash or credit card?"

"I'm Venus's lawyer." I explained I'd been told to come here so someone could get the cash to spring the High Priestess from jail. I asked if she was Heather or Sarah.

The girl tossed her hair nonchalantly aside, peeled the banana, and chomped into it. "Sarah," she said with a mouthful of food. "Larry, I mean Adonis, is the only one who can get the money. He's gone. You'll have to come back later." She pushed the rest of the banana into her mouth. "Sure you don't need to know any of the ancient secrets? It's supposed to be forty-five dollars, but if you give me cash, I can show you for thirty. Your husband'll never look at another woman."

"I'm not married."

"Ok, your boyfriend then."

"I don't have a boyfriend. Not for several years."

"Man." She shook her head thoughtfully. Her hair parted, letting one of her small breasts peek out. "Then you're gonna need the whole series. How to meet men. How to dress." She pointed disapprovingly at my navy linen pants. "You can pay it in installments."

I told her I'd get back to her on that and that I had another appointment I had to go to.

Back at my car I hung my navy jacket carefully on the passenger seat so it wouldn't get any more wrinkled. What did I know about men? The last time I had a real boyfriend was four years ago while I was still in law school. Bill Hughes was my age but was behind me in school because he had worked as an engineer for two years after graduating from Stanford. I noticed him the very first day. He was nearly six feet tall and had light brown hair that fell past his shoulder blades. I hung out in the morning on the patio where he drank coffee with other guys from his class, but he never noticed me. After several weeks I followed him down the hall to his torts class and introduced myself. We were together for nearly a year after that.

I started the car. There was no point in going through the whole stupid thing about Bill again. Where I'd gone wrong, the skinny brunette I found out he was fucking every time he wasn't with me. I turned the radio on, punched the stations a few times, then found a Howlin' Wolf tape. I didn't want to think about those things. It was ancient history. The day was growing hotter by the minute, and I had business in Koreatown.

On Vermont I stopped to use a pay phone. I called Dorothy, but no one was there. I called Cafe James Dean and asked for Kim. There was some haggling in Korean in the background before Kim answered. I told her I planned to go talk with Nancy Johnson that afternoon and I wanted to know how to get hold of her. I said it would be best if I could drop in on Nancy Johnson without her knowing I was coming.

"That's a good idea," Kim agreed. "You and I didn't get to talk much last night. I want to be able to fill you in on anything you need to know. Nancy wasn't Jin's best friend, but they did spend some time together." She told me that nearly every Wednesday afternoon Nancy went to the United Korean Methodist Church on New Hampshire to attend a service and then drink tea with the other wizened Methodists.

"You will find out who did this, won't you?" Kim implored. "My godmother Dorothy's frantic. She's so old, I don't know how much more stress she can take. She hasn't stopped crying over Jin. She's ashamed the money was stolen. For us it's very important not to lose face. We need someone who will help us now, someone good."

I've always had the feeling that no matter what I do it will never be good enough. UCLA law school, cum laude. I will end up a bag lady on the streets of Los Angeles. I promised Kim I'd find out who'd been responsible for the tragedy. I would find out. I would prove myself to them. To Lupe. To Kim. To my father. And all the jerks who ever laughed at me. To Bill Hughes. To Bill's fucking skinny brunette slut. To all the creeps who tried to put me down.

The United Korean Methodist Church was west of the intersection of New Hampshire and 9th and adjacent to the burned-out shell of a former market. I pulled into a lot behind the church and parked next to a Hyundai. Shouldn't Koreans be Buddhists? I made a note to ask the Golden Tiger the next time I went to the *do jang*. I put my suit jacket on and more lipstick. The back door of the church was unlocked and the unilluminated hallway cool. I heard talking and laughing, voices calling out in greeting to one another.

Services had just ended. I hurried toward the departing parishioners. Nancy Johnson straggled out at the end of the group. She was dressed like Pat Nixon in a blue-and-black floral print dress with matching short-sleeve jacket. Her hair was stiff and shiny, as though she had just had it done that morning and then had it frozen. Like cryogenics.

I stepped up to her and said hello. She looked quickly from me to the women she was talking with. A frown flashed across her face as she recognized me, and she spoke hastily in Korean to the other women. They nodded and made their way toward the exit.

"What did you say about me?" I wondered.

"I told them you are life insurance agent," she said, pointing at my crumpled suit. "Come, we'll go sit in the library and drink some tea. You can explain how I'll get tax deduction for theft of the *kye* money."

I followed her into the library. She gestured for me to make myself a cup of tea. I had expected some kind of ceremony with a ceramic teapot and dainty cups without handles, but instead I was handed a chipped mug and a Lipton's tea bag.

"You should have made an appointment so I could have my tax returns with me."

I felt queasy. Tax was the hardest class I ever took. Zero comprehension. I'm good at memorizing things, though, so I learned it like a foreign language for the exams and then forgot it. I took a deep breath and dove in. "It won't be necessary to see the returns at this time since we won't be averaging the loss. We'll be extrapolating from capital gain and then reassessing in the next quarter with a division between—"

"Ok, ok. I never understand all that stuff. My husband always took care of it."

I nodded sympathetically. "Yes, you said he was a U.S. soldier. Did you meet him during the Korean War?" I paused awkwardly. Maybe her family had been killed or their house destroyed. Maybe they had been bombed.

She said she'd met him at the end of the war, and he brought her to the United States. "I'm a citizen."

"Did you know Dorothy in Korea?"

She looked at me incredulously. Like I was some Midwesterner asking a person from Hollywood if he knew Charlton Heston. "No. I met Dorothy when she opened her restaurant . . ."

"In Koreatown?"

She nodded. "Same street where Kim has her restaurant. At that time not so many Koreans here as now. Not so many restaurants. Dorothy made it just like the Shining Pearl, her restaurant in Seoul."

Nancy Johnson was a real chatterbox. Too helpful. It made me wonder if she was telling me the truth. Her story would need double-checking. I'd have to play all the old women against each other to find the essential elements. I asked if she'd gone often to the restaurant in Koreatown.

"Oh, yes. All the time for lunch. My husband want to eat hamburger every day, but I get tired of Bob's Big Boy. I want *saengson chigye*, fish and vegetable stew. Too much trouble to make for just one person."

I wanted to know how tight she was with Dorothy, so I asked her if she had lived in Koreatown since she arrived as a war bride.

"My husband bought us a house in San Fernando Valley, Studio City. In those days you buy good house, with big yard, lemon and orange trees. I am only Korean person, only person not white. They treat me like I'm a little doll, not a real person. I feel bad. All alone. Don't have any children because my husband doesn't want any. He sees I am lonely, don't have any friends, so he teaches me to play poker. We go to other people's houses, they come to ours, but still I don't get close with anyone. Finally he understands how lonely I am. I get him to give me car so I can go over to Koreatown in daytime, talk my language, eat food I like. So I meet Jin."

"I haven't met Jin yet," I said. "Didn't she just come here recently from Korea?"

"No, she came same time as Dorothy in beginning of sixties." Nancy Johnson said the Shining Pearl restaurant made good money for the two sisters in Korea. Seoul, which suffered more destruction during World War II than Berlin, was a very busy place after the war. "They have money, but also have old parents, and parents don't want to leave Seoul so Jin and Dorothy don't move here until their mother and father die. We take care of family."

More of the arcane and tedious familial obligations. I shuddered. "You became a good friend of Jin's?"

"She's like big sister to me. I go to the restaurant every

day, see Jin. We talk. I teach Jin to play poker. We laugh. Sometimes drink a little *jinro*."

"Is she as beautiful as Dorothy?"

Nancy Johnson laughed. She told me that although Dorothy and Jin were perfect sisters, Jin was certainly the more beautiful. She said she'd learned in the long afternoons over cards that Jin had been an excellent student but was only able to attend school until she was fifteen because the economic situation under the Japanese occupation of their country was so terrible she needed to get a job to help her family. Jin had wanted to be a teacher and teach at a university but instead had to work in a factory.

"When Jin was just seventeen she marry one of her teachers. He was a lot older than her. They had a son, but he was killed in Korean War. Jin's husband died too, long time ago. She never get married again."

I looked down at the empty mug in my hand. I'd been lost in Nancy Johnson's story and didn't remember drinking the tea. "Last night someone said they thought your nephew Henry stole the *kye* money."

"That's Chu Chu Park. Big talk. Henry owns clothing business. Very rich. Went to Seoul last week to make deal to buy another business. Even though he's gone much of the time, he still remember to send me a little check every month. He's good nephew. Somebody want to find out what happened to our money, they find out about Chu Chu."

"What about Chu Chu?"

Nancy Johnson slumped back in her chair. "This is church. I don't talk bad about another person in church. You ask someone else who Chu Chu owes money to."

I quickly reviewed with myself what I knew. That Nancy Johnson's husband had been a pharmacist. He left her the house when he died, probably insurance and a pension fund. There would be some Social Security. How much would that be? I asked her if she still lived in Studio City. "In case I need to see you again. I want to get back to you as soon as possible with your tax information."

She shook her head. "When my husband died I sold the house and buy other house in Koreatown, near Crenshaw. But now almost all nigger black people there. Like a jungle."

I'd felt bad about her losing her *kye* money until she said that. I stood up. I got Nancy Johnson to tell me the name of her nephew's business, and I wrote down her address and phone number as well. There will be a day when the color of a man's skin is of no more significance than the color of his eyes. The day will come. I believe that. I drove through Koreatown toward my office and thought about the excitement I'd felt watching the televised riots and the disappointment when it was over.

Lupe sat at the desk reading one of my files and drinking a diet Coke. She glanced up when I came in. "Man, you got some sick dudes. No wonder you don't have much interest in finding a boyfriend. This guy, he had his *pito* out in public. Right in front of a school. How can you defend these sleazebags?"

"It's one of the fundamental rights of the Constitution, equal protection, due process . . ."

"You only got paid two hundred and fifty dollars for this?" She pointed accusingly at my financial declaration in the file. "You did this for two hundred and fifty dollars? Let this guy go back out on the street so he can shake his wienie at little kids?" She closed the file abruptly and pushed it aside. "I don't know about you. Oh, that reminds me, you got a couple messages from some cretin calls himself Adonis."

I took the slips of paper she handed me. "I been in Koreatown all day. Found out a lot." I told her I talked with Lee Joon, the old woman who'd given me the most attitude.

Lee Joon was resentful that her son had stopped her from working. I didn't think she liked Dorothy very much and suspected she envied her independence. She could have taken the *kye* so she'd have something of her own or something to give her son. Nancy Johnson disliked her black neighbors. Maybe she was unable to sell her place in the depressed housing market and took the money to be able to move. There was all throughout Los Angeles a gathering sense of unease and a premonition that *el futuro* would be parched and empty.

"*Oye,* I been thinking about this," Lupe interrupted. "I read your files. You're hardly making any money. Nobody's going to tell you anything about what happened to that *kye,* let alone who killed the old lady. You don't even know if Dorothy's really going to pay you. You should cut your losses now."

Didn't Lupe realize the killer might come back? I intentionally hadn't mentioned it because I didn't want to spook her, but I also couldn't believe she hadn't been thinking of it herself. And no matter what happens or what I have to go through, I will not give up my vision of creating a life for myself here. Under no circumstances. No matter how crazy or dangerous LA, this is the last stop, the last desperate brink before we all drop off the edge of the page.

I picked up the phone and punched in Adonis's number so I could take care of business with him, but it was busy. Probably arranging out-calls for miscreant penitents and other would-be saints.

"So I been thinking about how you could make more money so you could pay me more," Lupe said. "I was reading in the paper about these guys who fake car accidents—"

"Lupe!"

"Well, it was just an idea. I'm only trying to help you.

Ok, then, if you're going to go ahead with this, here's what you're going to have to do. It's just like Paul Muni in *The Good Earth*. He had to experiment with makeup until he was able to look Chinese. You know they made all those old movies with white people made up to look Asian." She rummaged excitedly through her purse and triumphantly pulled out a black eyeliner pencil. She pushed me into one of the matching vinyl chairs in front of the desk. "Yeah, this is going to be great. But we're going to have to do something with your hair."

Lupe and I started the night at Yee Mee Loo's on Spring and Ord in Chinatown. It was dark and everything was painted gold and red. Racks of booze formed a pagoda behind the bar. I couldn't believe I'd let her talk me into this. I didn't want to stay because I was afraid we'd run into someone I knew. Who could miss my blond hair? The place was full of downtown artists, off-duty cops, and haggard Public Defenders. They might ask about Lupe or my bizarre black eye makeup.

"Great place to pick up sheriffs near retirement age," Lupe observed. She ordered Mai Tais with extra cherries and orange slices, then began instructing me on how to act Oriental.

"Keep your eyes down when you speak. Giggle at the end of every sentence. Didn't you see *Flower Drum Song*?"

"That was about Chinese, not Koreans," I argued. "What are we doing in Chinatown?"

Lupe shrugged. "It's all basically the same. Watch the women for any pointers you can pick up." She ordered egg rolls and a couple of dishes of little barbecue ribs. The kind that look like they come from dwarf pigs.

Later we went over to a karaoke bar on Beverly Boulevard and had more Mai Tais at a place with a waterfall. Rollicking patrons sang along to Frank Sinatra as the lyrics to "My Blue Heaven" flashed on video monitors bracketed overhead. Lupe pointed out a table with a group of salesmen from Taiwan and pushed me toward them so I could practice my "Orientalness."

"A hundred thousand miracles are happening every day. A hundred thousand miracles," Lupe crooned off-key.

"Knock it off, would you?" I moaned in embarrassment, hoping no one could hear her. I turned away from her barstool. The group she had pointed out stared back at us. Lupe was a little drunk and her voice was getting loud.

One of the men stood up, then came over to the bar. He asked us to sit with them. He told us he'd graduated from the University of Ohio business school. With a greedy look in her eye, Lupe pulled me to the table with her. She smiled and bowed at everyone until she finally chose a chair next to the oldest of the men and drew it up close beside him. The businessmen, who were plenty drunk, ordered another round of drinks for us and kept speaking to each other in Taiwanese and the occasional English phrase.

"Macintosh," shouted one of the men on the opposite side of the table.

"Apple," shouted another in response.

The man next to me leaned close and put his hand on my knee. "I love your eye makeup. It's so European. So French."

I hoped Lupe noticed the heavy cruise the guy was giving me. I'd told her I could get as many men as I wanted. Didn't this prove it? His hand rubbed up toward the inside of my thigh. I picked the hand off my leg and kicked Lupe under the table while the businessmen screamed about computers. The Esperanto of the fin de siècle. We turned back and forth between the arguing men like spectators at a tennis match. I was bored out of my skull, but trying to be polite.

"What kind of watch is that? Does it have different time zones on it?" Lupe asked the old guy next to her. "I always get so confused when I travel. How many hours' difference is there between LA and Hong Kong?"

He told her how many hours' difference there was. His English wasn't as good as the other men's. I tried to catch Lupe's eye to tell her I wanted to leave.

"You must do a lot of traveling in your business. How many time zones does it keep track of?" She touched his hand, which he extended toward her so she could get a better look at the Rolex.

"It's very heavy," Lupe murmured. "Heavy," she repeated in slow breathy English.

He took the watch off and handed it to her. She strapped it on her wrist with a satisfied look. The conversation around us went on in more and more technical terms. It was endless, and I could no longer tell what language they were speaking.

"IBM," shouted one of the partisans.

"Epson!"

Lupe giggled uncontrollably at something the old guy said. Her arms flailed wildly above her head, knocking the tray of drinks out of the hand of the passing cocktail waitress. Ice flew everywhere. Lupe and her gentleman friend were drenched with Mai Tais and grasshoppers. The old guy jumped up, wiping furiously at his green-stained lap, and stalked off to the men's loo. (I made a mental note to find out if this was a Chinese word.)

Lupe got up, apologizing and bowing as she'd instructed me to do earlier. She bowed her way out the front door. I caught up with her by the car. I told her to go back inside and give back the Rolex.

"He said I could have it."

"Lupe, if you want to keep your job at my office, take it right back in there and—"

"He did say I could have it, because I'm so pretty." She shifted slightly so the streetlight caught the right side of her face and cast the left into a shadow.

She was staggeringly beautiful. I've always been intimidated by girls who are prettier than me. "My place is totally legit and if you work there, so are you," I insisted.

"He did give it to me . . ." I heard her muttering as she went back inside the bar. She was back in a minute and we got into the car.

"Did you give it back?"

"Of course," she pouted.

"Scout's honor?"

She tossed her hair impatiently and buckled her seat belt. "Yes."

We moved on to a Japanese place on Beverly. With geishas. They wore kimonos with vibrant pink and purple silk sashes. A couple of the more contemporary geishas wore Chanel suits. At the door a guy charged us twenty-five dollars admission. It seemed like a lot of money, but Lupe insisted we go in. When we got inside and ordered a drink, the waitress told us it was another twenty-five dollars for the table. Hang on, Visa, it's going to be a bumpy night. We were the only women in the place besides the geishas. Then Lupe insisted we switch to scotch. "More sophisticated," she assured me. They were nearly eight bucks a shot.

"Check this out," Lupe instructed, nodding toward the geishas, her voice filled with admiration. "These are some real pros."

I watched the attentive way the geishas leaned toward the

men, the graceful arching of necks, the delicate flutter of white hands.

"They make some real money in one of these clubs. Ten grand a month. And tips," Lupe said. "Man, I hear they get diamond rings, apartments, sometimes a Porsche Targa."

I took a closer look at the geishas. The exquisite ivory skin. The magnificent long red nails. The room was permeated with the gentle smell of costly perfume. The geisha closest to me was wearing a new pair of Manolo Blahnik purple stilettos. Kicky. Fun. Deadly expensive. I'd seen the same pair in *Vogue* magazine. As I admired the shoes, I noticed she had a small black circle tattooed on her ankle. I tried to decide if it ruined the shoes or showed a strong sense of style. Actually, it was cheap looking.

It reminded me of Kim's tattoo.

"Supposedly, these places are run by gangs. Organized crime," Lupe said, nudging me out of my contemplation of the tattoo. "I don't know. Whenever someone who's not white makes a lot of money, somebody says it's organized crime. Looks like a good job to me."

I remember getting my Visa card out of my wallet and in exchange receiving a bill for fifty-seven dollars accompanied by two cellophane-wrapped peppermint candies. Lupe grabbed the receipt and handed it to me. "Expenses."

I dropped Lupe off in front of the office and told her it would be ok if she came in a little late for work. It was already Thursday morning and she'd need to check on Joey and get some sleep. Then I stopped at an all-night coffee shop on Sunset and had a cup of mud. I'd had only one drink at each place, I calculated. Maybe two at Yee Mee Loo's. Or was it more? Two at the geisha bar?

I coasted over the hill. The San Fernando Valley, a million red and white twitching lights, spread before me. Eucalyptus perfumed the balmy night. The car twisted into a curve, but I held it steady. The Beach Boys sang "good, good vibrations." I didn't want to think about Kim's tattoo anymore.

I was legally drunk.

It is not true that alcoholism is genetic. I had only one drink an hour. It occurred to me that Lupe hadn't finished either of her drinks at the last two bars.

I rolled carefully down Coldwater Canyon and turned left onto my street, Dickens. My apartment's the basic two-story stucco box with a flat gravel roof. It shared a common driveway with an identical building that faced it. Both were owned and minimally maintained by an Armenian named Mr. Zarifian. It was the same dump I lived in while I was going to law school.

I was the only person still awake on my block. I turned off my radio and cut the engine as I turned into my driveway. I coasted to the back of the apartment building and into my assigned parking space. It was dark. Fuck. Neither Mr. Zarifian nor his surly, obese wife had fixed the lights above the parking stalls. A passing cloud covered the moon. I got out of the car holding the keys in my right hand.

I began to walk across the asphalt toward my apartment. The click of my high heels resounded in the empty night. I was steady on my feet, but I tightened the grip on my car keys. I'm always aware. Be aware of your surroundings, that's what the Golden Tiger says. I felt good. They could have tested me right there. My blood alcohol might be more than .10, but I could pass the field sobriety test. Walk a straight line. Stand on one foot with my eyes closed. Fuck the police. I whistled the beginning of the goofy song Lupe had sung in the bar.

Something singed the air near my ears.

I heard the dull whoosh of a flying object.

Then I felt something tighten around my shoulders. A rough rope cut into my chest.

My hands flew up to loosen the grip. I stumbled in my black heels. I was wrenched backward toward the shadowy area where the dumpster was pushed against a concrete wall. At that same instant I heard the muffled footsteps of someone in sneakers closing the distance between us.

I worked my left hand desperately between the thick, scratchy rope and my chest. I smelled the musky pine of aftershave. I was jerked off balance as my assailant wrestled for control. I fell back against him.

He began to grope at the front of my silk blouse, ripping off the mother-of-pearl buttons. He shoved his hand into my bra. He grabbed my breast roughly and I heard him breathing hard. I glanced down. His right hand was pretty beat up looking. As if he'd been in more than a few fights. Everything turned black and swam in front of my eyes. My knees buckled. I felt myself start to sink to the ground. I was about to become a rape statistic. Was he going to kill me when he was finished?

"Horse stance. Balance." I heard the Golden Tiger's voice in the back of my mind. I slid my left foot to the side, bent my knees until I resembled a mounted rider; I felt my elbow smash backward into the unprotected stomach of my attacker.

He let out a gasp as I reached between his legs, pounding with my right fist and the car keys dead into his crotch. "Aim for the zipper," the Golden Tiger taught us. The man dropped the rope. He groaned as he stumbled backward.

"Always follow through. Now what do you do?" I'd heard the Golden Tiger urging many times in the *do jang*. I pivoted quickly on my left foot and with my right kicked the black sweatsuited form in the nuts.

He screamed as he fell into Mrs. Zarifian's camellia bushes. I didn't get a good look at him because he had the hood of the sweatsuit over his head.

Pulling the rope off, I ran toward the stairs to my apartment as I'd never run in my life. I hit the stairs like a pro track star and made it to my front door on the second floor. With shaking hands I fumbled the key into the lock. Listening for him following me, I unlocked the door. I was panting out of control. It had all happened in less than twenty seconds.

I locked the door behind me and fell against it. I couldn't catch my breath. The loud ragged sound of my wheezing filled the room. I dropped the rope I still carried onto the floor. I made my way to the window overlooking the parking area.

The man was just climbing to his feet. He kept his head down, but the hood of the sweatshirt had dropped off. It looked as if he had black hair tied back in a ponytail, but it was dark and I couldn't be certain. I couldn't see his face. He limped as he ran down the driveway to the street. He looked crazy, like some B movie werewolf loping into the darkness. He disappeared and shortly thereafter I heard a car start up. With screeching tires it pulled away fast and sped down Dickens Avenue until everything was quiet again.

I saw something lying in the driveway. From the kitchen I took the large, sharp Reed & Barton silver meat carver my mother gave me for Christmas, then I opened the front door and stepped out onto the landing. None of the neighbors had woken up during the fight. I tiptoed down the stairs. The moonlight sparkled on the oil-stained driveway.

I knelt beside the trampled pink mask.

Black eyes. Garish red mouth. It was the same kind of mask the man who killed Jin Oh not two days ago had worn.

I picked it up and got weakly to my feet. How had he

found me? I knew he hadn't been following me all night. I would have noticed. Wouldn't I?

I climbed numbly back up the stairs to the safety of my apartment. I turned on the light and sank down onto the couch. I put the meat carver on the floor next to me. I examined the mask more closely. Who knew me? Only Dorothy. Who could find out where I lived? Lee Joon? Nancy Johnson? Chu Chu Park? I wasn't listed in the phone book. I hadn't even been out to talk with Chu Chu Park yet. How could any of them know where I lived? For Christ's sake. They were little old ladies. Did they have enough money left to hire the thug who jumped me?

Would the guy who attacked me try to hurt Lupe? I tossed the mask on the coffee table and tore open my wallet looking for the piece of paper with her home phone number. I glanced at my Timex. It was nearly 4:00 A.M. With shaking hands I dialed her mother's place in East LA.

The phone rang and rang. I imagined the door of their old stucco busted down, the walls riddled with bullet holes, Lupe and her old lady in a pool of blood. Joey, dumb with shock, wandering vacantly between the bodies . . .

"*¿Qué?*" the old woman answered groggily.

"*¿Está Lupe? Necesito—*"

"I don't understand. What do you want?"

"I'm looking for Lupe—"

"She's not here. I don't know where she is." Lupe's mother slammed down the receiver.

I turned off the light and sat in the dark. It didn't do much good to have a gun if you left it locked in the car. But man, my Tae Kwon Do moves! It worked! I saw my rapid-fire punches and kicks like a superspectacular cinerama all action flying fists movie.

Why hadn't he punched me back? In class the Golden Tiger had shown us how to block a kick. We learned defensive moves. If my attacker was Korean, wouldn't he know Tae Kwon Do? Better than I did? Maybe it was just a stereotype for me to think he knew Tae Kwon Do. Not all American men play baseball. Or had he intentionally taken it easy on me? The mask grinned nastily back at me. Eventually I slept.

It was nearly ten when I woke up. I had a headache. While staring at the cottage-cheese ceiling, reviewing all that had happened, I decided to go to Koreatown to see Kim. I took a long hot shower, then put on a sleeveless white silk dress and my brown-and-white Bally spectator pumps. It seemed too difficult to get all of the Chanel makeup on, so I had to settle for lipstick and mascara. There was a faint red mark across my chest where the rope had chafed my skin.

It was nearly ten-thirty. I called the office to leave a message for Lupe.

The phone was answered on the first ring. "Law offices. *A sus ordenes.*" Lupe sounded bright and cheerful.

"How'd you get there so early this morning?" I asked.

"I didn't get home that late."

"Your mom said you weren't there."

"Why are you checking up on me? I already got a probation officer. Who, incidentally, is coming here this afternoon. I wish you'd let me hang some different pictures in here. Monet. Some of those cute water lilies—"

"Lupe, a guy tried to rape me last night."

"No me jodas."

"I'm not joking. When I got home he was hiding in one of the parking spaces and he grabbed me."

"Did he . . . ?"

"No. He just tore my blouse and felt my tit." I felt sick thinking about it again. His hot, clammy hand fondling me. "I'm ok." I felt dirty. I wanted to take another shower.

Quickly I explained that the man wore a mask identical to the one worn by Jin Oh's killer.

"It's the same guy!"

"I'm not sure. The mask fell off while I was trying to get away, but I didn't see his face." I wondered if there was more than one of these guys. It had been a strange killing. Professional, but squirrelly.

"That creep could come after me too! Jesus, I feel just like Ava Gardner in *The Killers*."

"Do you have a gun?"

"Of course not! I'm on probation, *¿recuerdas?*"

"Want me to get one for you?"

Lupe didn't say anything for a long time. "I don't need a gun. What are you gonna do? Take the money for it out of my slave wages, then sell it to me?"

I hung up. Damn. Why did I ever think I wanted to be her friend? She was a cold bitch. Or was she afraid of guns because of what had happened in Dogtown? She hadn't even said she was sorry I got molested.

I took the freeway to Koreatown. I felt a kind of dismal Monday morning of the soul. I didn't notice much when I got off on Vermont. It was all the same. Incomprehensible. Foreign and closed to outsiders. A liquor store. A furniture store. A video store. I passed an aqua and purple building with a yellow FOR LEASE sign. Mexicans and Central American men from El Salvador, Guatemala, Honduras stood on Olympic outside a large building supply store waiting to help rebuild the city in a multicultural kind of a way. I supposed I did have an ugly attitude. I parked in front of Cafe James Dean.

It was lunchtime. Inside I stood for a second by the door next to a Lotto machine, checking the place out. Only two of the tables were occupied. At court I'd heard people say there were extortion rackets in all the businesses in the Southeast Asian immigrant communities. Kim herself carried a couple of meals to one of the waiting tables. She wore a yellow silk suit. Her long, thick black hair was pulled back with a black chiffon scarf, and she smiled when she looked up and saw me. She put the food down quickly and hurried over to me. I wondered if she had to pay out to keep her place running. If this was a typical noon crowd, it looked as if she'd have a hard time coming up with the necessary extra cash.

"Did you find out something?" she asked without formality.

"I'd like to have lunch. Something not too fancy."

She apologized for not guessing that I was hungry and put me at a table near the kitchen. She went into the kitchen. There was a small stiff cardboard announcement printed in Korean and English propped up on the table. All the tables had one, I noticed. It asked people to contribute to the new Koreatown Sports Center that would be opening soon. I pushed it aside when Kim reappeared and sat down with me. "I told them to grill you some fish."

"A guy jumped me last night. Wearing a Chusok mask."

Kim gasped. She leaned across the table to grasp my forearm. The color drained out of her face and she looked very white under her face powder.

A Mexican busboy came to the table and placed six small white ceramic dishes with different foods in front of me. Kim waved him away with her free hand. "What happened?"

I told her. "Who do you think he is?"

She shook her head. "I wish I knew. Did he hurt you? Did he . . . ?"

"No, he was just rubbing my breasts and . . ." I broke down, near tears, and stared at the table.

"It happened to me too," Kim said.

I looked up.

"When I was in college at SC. The year before I graduated."

"I'm sorry, Kim . . ." Why had I been so hung up on the tattoo on her ankle? Lots of college girls have tattoos nowadays.

She let go of my forearm and looked away before continuing. "I was walking to my car after a class. It was about ten at night. This big black guy jumped out of the bushes. I was too scared to scream. After he left I just lay there in the dirt. I couldn't believe he didn't kill me."

"Oh, Kim . . ."

She said they wrote about it in the *Trojan*, and later she helped organize student watch groups to walk girls to their cars at night. Kim sighed heavily, then, shrugging off the memory, snapped her fingers. The busboy came running over. "Beer?" she asked me.

I shook my head again. "I'm so sorry, Kim. I was lucky. This scumbag wasn't much taller than me. I kicked him in the nuts. I don't think he's going be using his dick for a while."

"Good for you!" She patted my arm again. "Have something to eat. That's kimchi." She pointed at the dishes, explaining that there were spinach, mung bean sprouts, and pickled taro. She told me kimchi is made in the fall. In the average family they use fifty heads of cabbage per family member. The cabbage is seasoned with salt, ground up with hot red peppers, then mixed with pickled turnips, radishes, cucumbers, or other vegetables. It is left to ferment for several weeks in huge earthenware jars buried up to their necks in the ground.

I watched Kim as she explained this. It was apparent she'd said all she was going to say about the attack upon her, but I knew I'd touched something within her. Maybe she felt the same way, because she seemed less guarded and angry than the first time I'd met her. Granted the first time there had been the issue of Joey and the murky offscreen presence of Lupe's potatohead brother, Hector "Manos" Ramos.

I told Kim I'd talked with Nancy Johnson and Lee Joon.

"Not Chu Chu Park?" asked Kim.

I shook my head. "Is that a real Korean name? Seems pretty unusual."

"That's just my point!" Kim exclaimed. "It's not a real name. It's invented. It would be like someone calling herself La Fifi or The Mimi. I don't know why Jin put up with her. Dorothy can't stand her."

"Dorothy means a lot to you, doesn't she?"

"She's been my godmother since I was born. She raised me."

The busboy brought a large white plate containing a thick fillet of salmon to the table. Kim inspected it quickly. It was perfectly grilled with the requisite crosshatches indicating it had been charbroiled. A delicate fragrant sauce in a small white bowl accompanied the fish. I glanced around the dining room, wondering why it wasn't full. Cafe James Dean was a good restaurant.

Kim also glanced around the room and seemed a bit dissatisfied with what she saw. "Dorothy was a friend of my grandmother. Both my mother and my grandmother are dead. I have no family. Dorothy took me in."

"Dorothy helped you get started with the restaurant? With *kye* money, right?"

Kim nodded. "Yeah, after I graduated from SC. There wasn't much I could do with an anthropology degree. Dorothy's always been generous. She's always given me everything I've ever asked for. Jin was like that too."

The fish was delicious. I realized how hungry I was.

"Look, there's something Dorothy didn't tell you about the box that was stolen," Kim said. "I told her she must tell you everything if she expects you to find out who killed Jin. We had sort of an argument about it, and she said I could go ahead and tell you. I think it's part of the reason why she didn't want to call the police. The old people, and the new ones just off the boat, are reluctant to report crimes to the police. A lot of them are self-conscious about their English and they're unsure of the system. A lot of them come from countries where the cops are crooks."

I'd seen that downtown. I often got appointed to represent Mexicans and Central Americans who were afraid of the system. A few months ago I'd been appointed to represent a woman from El Salvador who'd been battered almost to a pulp by her husband, and she'd been more afraid of the police than of her husband.

"It's kind of nutty"—Kim's voice trailed off apologetically—"but she insists the box is valuable. She didn't want people knowing she had it because she thought they'd criticize her for keeping it instead of giving it to a museum or maybe that someone would try to steal it from her. She says it belonged to Queen Min."

I put down the chopsticks. "Who?"

"Queen Min. The last Korean queen before the Japanese occupation of Korea. When they took over they killed the royal family. Dragged Queen Min out of the palace and set her on fire."

Was the box what the guy in the Chusok mask had been asking Dorothy and Jin about before he killed Jin? "How'd Dorothy get the box?"

Kim shrugged. "I never paid any attention to Korean history. Jin was the one who loved history, knew all that stuff. I wish I'd listened more to her stories. . . ." Kim looked as if she was going to cry. "Korean people have what's called *han*. That means bitter feelings because of injustices committed by government, the Japanese occupation, even by your family members or friends. The box must be valuable to old people like Jin and Dorothy for *han*—"

Kim's story was interrupted by a dark shadow falling over the table. Hector "Manos" Ramos bent down and kissed Kim on the mouth.

"Hey, ain't you the dyke my sister Lupe hangs out with?" he growled at me.

I saw that my chances for a pleasant lunch were over.

Hector was heavier than the last time I'd seen him, a year ago. Although I searched the sports page for his name, I never saw it. The fight scene in LA is minimal compared with what they say it was like in the forties and fifties, when there were weekly matches at the Hollywood Legion Hall. All the stars attended. The great gyms were down on Main Street. The action moved to the Olympic Auditorium for a couple of decades. Then the old auditorium was taken over by wrestling mania and punk thrash bands who tore the place apart. Now the fights are limited to the Forum on Monday nights, where beers cost five bucks, or to the smoky confines of a nearly bust night spot like the Diamond Girl Bar in Reseda. No, there'd been no mention of Hector in the papers, and he was ominously over the weight requirements for a light welterweight.

Hector pulled out a chair and plopped down next to Kim. He threw his arm territorially around her shoulder and began squeezing it. Kim flinched slightly, as if it was irritating her. "What's she doing here?" he barked, jerking his chin in my direction.

Kim glanced uncertainly at me. I wondered if Hector had known Jin or Dorothy. Had Kim told him she'd dumped Joey off on them? "She wanted to talk about Joey," Kim lied. Her eyes beseeched me not to contradict her. Was she afraid of him?

"Joey!" exploded Hector, pounding his fist on the table. "Don't get me started on that! You were supposed to be taking care of him for me."

"Come on, honey," Kim cooed. "Calm down. You know I had to give him to your sister when she showed up. We can't keep him without legal papers. . . ."

"That's what I'm here about," I heard myself saying. Lord, forgive me for lying and using small children as currency. "Lupe, your sister Guadalupe Virginia, that is, sent me to enter into negotiations with you about the possible placement of her son Joey with you."

Hector frowned. He knew his sister. He knew she wouldn't give Joey to him.

"Perhaps under a temporary guardianship." Lupe would be pleased if I was able to cajole Hector into giving me the lowdown on his new life. "She's very ashamed of her recent misadventure and incarceration. She knows she has to prove herself to society and to her family." I hoped she never found out what I had to say about her to try to get him to talk.

Hector spread his fat hand on the table and stared at it with thoughtful admiration, as if he usually depended on it to make decisions for him. I was glad I'd put on my lawyer clothes that morning so Hector could take seriously what I was saying. "Just let me take care of it," I said. "I know you and your sister aren't getting along very well right now." I smiled a good white Junior League kind of smile at him, polite and beneficent.

"Ok, that's good then. She's finally coming to her senses." Hector nodded his meaty-looking head at me. "Lupe don't take care of him. In and outta jail. My mother's getting too old for this shit." He gave Kim's shoulder another mauling. "There you go, babydoll, just like I told you. Everything'll work out. We'll be able to get married. Like I promised you."

I shot a quick look at Kim. She looked radiant. Transfixed. It didn't figure. She was attractive. He was not. She was smart. He was dumb. Is it really all about sex? Is the whole meaning of life just the old in/out in/out? Nietzsche, Sartre, Aristotle? Maybe it is all just splayed beaver and pounding dick.

"There are still some very important things we'd have to discuss," I insisted in my best Pasadena matron tone. "I need some information about your residence, your day-care plan. Your income." I wondered how he'd met Kim. What was he doing in Koreatown?

Hector glared at me suspiciously.

"There's a form we have to fill out and file with the court about your income," I continued right in my jurist stride. "To show you're financially capable of assuming the responsibility for your nephew."

He removed his arm from Kim's shoulder and leaned toward me, placing both hands on the table.

I stared at his hands again. They were square and mahogany brown. He was much darker than Lupe. The right hand was larger than the left, the knuckles puffy, as if he'd busted his hand a few times.

"Money won't be a problem," Hector bragged. "I'm the director of the new sports center that's opening here in Koreatown."

I congratulated him and told him I'd heard of it. I pointed at the cardboard announcement on the table touting the sports center. Why had a chicano been hired as director rather than a Korean? I wondered if Hector had experienced any of the racism some of the old Korean ladies expressed to me. I asked him to tell me more about the new job.

Hector sat back in his chair looking expansive. "It's a five-million-dollar dream come true. State of the art. Gym. Weights. Boxing ring. Sauna. Jacuzzi. It's even got an indoor court for basketball or volleyball. I was specially hired to run it, to start a boxing program . . ."

Wouldn't it be Tae Kwon Do in Koreatown?

". . . help get kids off the street. You know, after the riots and all of that."

I nodded encouragement. "Because you're the best-known boxer in LA." Why Hector? In the last eight years two young guys from East LA had fought in the Olympics. Both had won medals in their weight categories. Their names were in the papers. If the sports center was really a big deal, wouldn't they have tried to get one of them?

"It's not just a job. It's an opportunity to serve the community," Hector recited. "Bring Koreans and latinos together."

I tilted my head in dumb but appreciative bemusement. "I thought most latinos living in Koreatown were Central American, not chicano like you. . . ."

"Community in the big sense." Hector was on a roll. "It was very visionary of Mr. Ko Won—"

"Who?" I interrupted, although Lee Joon had mentioned him.

"Ko Won Bae," chimed Kim in a singsongy voice.

"Ko Won," Hector said. "He's a big businessman here in Koreatown, isn't that right, Kim, honey? He owns, I don't know, maybe three, four, or five businesses. A big electronics store. One of the only ones in this area that wasn't looted and destroyed by the riots. He put his guys with Uzis right up on the roof. It was, like, you know, 'Fuck this shit!' "

What would a big man in Koreatown want with a has-been like Hector, I wondered, but I nodded and looked impressed. "I saw that on television!"

Hector looked well pleased by his connection to greatness. "Yeah, he's on television all the time. Plus, that's how I met Kim."

Kim nodded. "Mr. Won's a big fight fan."

"That's right," said Hector. "I was fighting an exhibition about three months ago out in Monterey Park, and Ko came to it and brought Kim with him. With his group. A big group. It wasn't like Kim was his girlfriend or nothing. That's the kinda guy he is. Brought ten people, paid for everyone. Guy's got class. Total class.

"Anyhow, I won my match. Stupid duffer *mayate* outta Nickerson Gardens. Ko comes back to the dressing room to tell me how great I was. Kim was with him. He invited me out to dinner with his friends. And that was it! Love at first sight, ain't that right, baby?" He threw his arm back around Kim and gave her another ferocious squeeze.

Kim put her hand on his thigh high up near his groin. "That's right, baby."

"Man, whatta night!" Hector sighed, placing his hand over his heart. As his sleeve pulled up slightly I noticed the blue hem of a tattoo of the Blessed Virgin Mary on his forearm. "Ko took us to Pacific Dining Car. You heard about that? Old place near downtown. Right in the middle of *Varrio* 13. Man, if those homeboys only knew. Steaks cost like thirty bucks each. We were drinking French wine and champagne like there was no tomorrow. He sure knows how to party."

"Fantastic!" I agreed. I imagined Hector puking Château

Lafite and hastily gobbled filet mignon in the men's room of the Pacific Dining Car, returning to the table to paw Kim some more. "Is that when he offered you the job as director of the sports center?"

"Do you need all this for your papers?" Hector asked with annoyance. "What do you really want? You don't care about my life, so don't try to jerk me off."

"Yes, I have to file all this information with the court, and I'm doing this for Lupe—"

"You want to stick your face in her box."

"Don't talk to me like that. You don't know me either, so don't be shooting your mouth off about stuff you don't know anything about. I give you respect, so you give me some. I'm willing to help Lupe, give her a job. You want her out on the streets again? Fine, I'll fire her and tell her to go turn tricks right in front of your sports center. I'll tell her to wear a big sign that says she's your sister. We'll see how long you get to be the big *queso* in Koreatown."

Hector thought about this. Kim nodded at him to assist him with understanding the logic of my proposal. "Ok," he said grumpily. "What else do you need to know? Ko Won hired me 'cause I gave him some real good ideas on programs on how to get the latino kids involved. That's the idea, you know. Get the latino kids and the Korean kids involved with each other. Sports instead of bangin' on the streets. All they're gonna think about is gangin', bangin', and slangin' unless the community gets involved to provide them with an alternative."

Hector sounded as if he was reading a press release, but with real unstudied sincerity. Kim motioned for the busboy to clear my dishes away. Hector gave the boy a *vato* handshake: a quick shake, then hand curled into a fist and knocked against the other's knuckles. The busboy flushed with pleasure at this recognition. It was possible that I had been wrong about everything. Maybe Hector was famous all over town. Perhaps he was not the monster Lupe had made him out to be.

"You wouldn't mind if I spoke with Mr. Won, would you?" I asked Hector. "Just to verify the required information for the guardianship forms?"

"Whenever you like. My main man. He'll be glad to do anything for me." Kim nodded in agreement, took Hector's hand in hers, and gave it a squeeze. Hector told me he'd call the next day to get me an appointment. I stood up. I got his assurance he wouldn't talk to Lupe about the guardianship.

"Hey," he chortled across the restaurant as I was leaving. "Remember to keep your hands off Lupe. Or I'll have to kill you."

I drove up Vermont toward the office. I was in a bad mood. I wanted to hurt someone. I tried psychotherapy once. I went to a woman in Westwood with an office decorated in soothing blues and beiges. A waiting room with old issues of *Time*. Like someone who's about to kill himself wants to read about last year's news. Leaving out the parts I considered most damaging, I told her my story. She suggested that my family was dysfunctional. That I was out of contact with my inner child. That I felt victimized. She told me to sit on the floor. She gave me a piece of chalk and asked me to draw a circle around myself. To make a boundary that expressed the amount of intimacy I was comfortable with. It cost me a hundred dollars.

I never went back.

Instead I went to the gym. I built my deltoids and my biceps. Sculpted my abdomen. Made my thighs into steel.

I do not believe in the inner child. The idea of a little Whitney Logan inside of me crying out for a teddy bear—I don't buy it. We are filled with dragons and demons and primordial ooze. At least I am. And so I guessed were Hector and Lupe and the guy who tried to rape me last night. I shoved a Bob Marley tape into the tape player. "Positive vibrations, positive vibrations," sang the great Rasta. Positive vibrations, oh yeah.

Lupe was in the office, wearing the same pinstripe suit she'd had on yesterday.

"Didn't go home last night?" I asked, gesturing at her getup.

She didn't answer. Instead she showed me a stack of newly created index cards she had filled out to make a filing system for my disordered cases. She had small, neat block printing. The product of a Catholic school education, I guessed. I imagined Lupe's mother slaving to pay for school and tried to picture Lupe as a girl in a plaid uniform and one of those boxy blue wool blazers with a sacred bleeding heart of Jesus embroidered on the pocket.

"I just saw Hector," I told her.

"So?" Lupe shrugged without looking up from the cards. She nervously shuffled them into a pile.

"I told him you wanted me to do the papers so he can get guardianship of Joey."

Lupe sprang angrily to her feet. "What the fuck are you talking about? I told you to stay out of my business!"

"Relax. I only told him that so I could get him to cooperate with me." I informed Lupe I'd discovered how her brother knew Kim and that there seemed to be something fishy indeed about it.

"Hector's not much for *sesos,*" Lupe agreed after I told her all I'd learned. "I'd love to find out more about this gig he has going in Koreatown. I'm sick of hearing my mother talk about how great Hector is. Hector's important new job. You'd think I never brought home a paycheck," she muttered.

I dropped my purse on the desk. "Your mom sounded pissed when I called last night. Why didn't you go home? What about Joey? You're always talking about him, for Christ's sake. Talk, talk, talk. You don't spend any time with him." I shook my head in disgust.

"My mom won't let me stay there no more. Ok? Got it? You need me to draw a picture? My old lady threw me out and I slept on your stupid fucking *pinchi* floor. You'll probably want to deduct that from my crummy salary too. How can you even call this a job? Look, look what I found here." Lupe stepped behind the desk and jerked the top drawer open. "A number 2 pencil, a couple of ballpoint pens, one of which is out of ink"—Lupe threw the pen angrily into the trash—"a two-for-one coupon for Taco Bell, and this." Lupe pulled open the bottom drawer and pointed at a nearly empty bottle of Southern Comfort. "You are seriously undercapitalized. Even worse than I thought. How can you call yourself a professional? I can't believe I let you talk me into working in this shithole."

I walked across the room and pointed out the window at Hollywood Boulevard. A skinny black hooker in a leopard-skin mini and a silver halter top lurked in the shade of the video store across the street. I recognized her. She was about thirty. Last year she'd had a friend, a black woman who wore a blond wig, who'd often worked the same corner. I'd seen them many times talking and sharing a smoke. I heard the blonde died. "Come here. Take a look out there."

Lupe sauntered across the room to the window and glanced out. "Yeah, it's the Boulevard. Same old same old. I've done it before, I can do it again. It's not so bad."

"You don't like it here? Want to go back out there? You want to get AIDS? Go on. The door's open. You don't have to be a secretary." I leaned against the windowsill and wouldn't look at her.

"There's a lot to be said for the street. Meet new people. Be my own boss. Keep all the money. Not have to put up with a lot of bullshit from some white chick thinks she knows everything." I heard the click of Lupe's high heels moving away from me across the old wooden floor. "See ya around, *gringa.*" The door slammed closed.

I looked at the Boulevard again. For the second time that day I was near tears. I turned to go after her.

Lupe stood beside the door grinning. "Want me to stay? Cut me in on half of what that old lady Dorothy's gonna pay you."

"You should stay out of this Koreatown stuff. You got Joey to think about, your probation . . ." I wrapped my arms around myself without thinking, but when I realized how silly that looked I felt foolish and let go. "I'm sorry you got involved. Sorry you saw Jin killed. I told you what happened to me last night. Almost happened," I corrected myself.

"I'll take my chances. Plus I'm gonna use this opportunity to find out about Hector, and I'm gonna finish him off once and for all so he stays out of my business and leaves me and Joey the fuck alone."

I straightened a book in the bookshelf before looking over at her. She was serious. "Ok, if you help me, I'll give you a third. That's it. No deals, no bargains."

"Fucking lawyers," Lupe mumbled as she walked back across the room to take her seat at the desk. She rearranged the papers on top of the desk to her satisfaction. "I had to order some business cards. I charged them to you." She unfolded a yellow paper and showed me a receipt.

MS. VIRGINIA G. RAMOS

PARALEGAL

"You're not a paralegal! You have to go to school for that. It takes about a year—"

"The printer's only gonna take about three hours, so could you let me have the money now? Tell you what, if I like working here, I'll go to school and make it legit. I was good in school. I ever tell you that? Had a 3.8 at East LA City College. Biology major. Got a B in English or I would've had all A's. I was a cheerleader too. Vice president of the coin collectors club. . . ."

I told Lupe to call Dorothy and find out if she knew Ko Won or the names and locations of his businesses in Koreatown. Lupe and I would go that afternoon to talk with him. As I left to get some tacos I heard Lupe on the speaker phone.

"Dorothy? Ms. Ramos here. Ms. Logan's investigative partner. . . ."

Dorothy knew who Ko Won was. She seemed impressed by his name. "Very important man in the community," I heard her say, but her voice was soft and distant as though she didn't really approve of him.

We were given an address on Olympic in Koreatown, and we drove over in my car. Ko Won's place was an electronics emporium in a large minimall about half a mile east of Cafe James Dean. The parking lot was crowded, and while we waited for a space Lupe gave her makeup a quick touch-up—another swoop of crimson across her full lips, then black liner under her lower lashes.

She surveyed herself with pleasure in the mirror of a shiny black compact. "Hmm, I wish I had time to get into the whole beading the eyelashes thing. Like Garbo. By the way, Dorothy doesn't know Kim's already friends with this guy."

I rolled up the window and locked the doors. "How do you know that?"

"What do you think, I'm psychic? I asked her if she and Kim knew him. She said they didn't. Not personally, anyhow. I'll tell you something." She tossed her lipstick into her purse. "I don't like this Ko Won guy already. He's a pimp." She got out of the car tugging her skintight skirt into place.

"We can't go in there with attitude or we won't find anything out," I argued. "As far as we know he's an outstanding citizen." I wondered why Kim hadn't told her godmother she knew Ko Won.

"Then why'd he fix my *pinchi* brother up with that whore Kim?"

"We don't know if she is or not. She's a wannabe rich girl. Went to USC. Besides, she seems to like Hector. Maybe she should marry him and get him off your back."

"I know a working girl when I see one." Lupe frowned.

"Leave it alone," I warned. Had I made a mistake in telling her she could be my partner? Lupe always had to act as if she knew everything. I didn't want her to blow this.

A couple blocked the door of the store readjusting and securing a color tv in a box on a dolly. Lupe tapped her foot impatiently, waiting for them to get out of our way, then pushed past them into the store. The unavoidable slit in her skirt gaped open as she walked, revealing her shapely brown legs.

Don't be sticking your butt in Mr. Won's face. Please, I begged silently.

The store was crammed from floor to ceiling with every kind of tv, vcr, video camera, cellular phone, and laser disc player made in the Far East. There were many shoppers. We stood in the tv sales area as I looked about for a salesperson who could direct us to Ko Won. Lupe stepped in front of one of the cameras that was hooked up to a monitor. Immediately she appeared on the screen of a big fifty-inch

Mitsubishi. She threw back her hair and gave the camera some good profile.

"Give me a whiskey, baby. And don't be stingy," she said in a low, gravelly, not-quite-accurate Swedish accent.

"Would you get over here?" I hissed.

"Lighting's not very good," she muttered, leaning into the camera to examine her eye makeup.

A short, fat, bespectacled, friendly-looking salesman in a black suit bore down on us. I raised my hand, motioning him over.

"You want to see some televisions?" he asked, bowing at both of us. "Best prices in town. That Mitsubishi you were just looking at—and I must say, Miss, haven't I seen you on tv before?"

Lupe shot me a smug glance. "Yes. I'm—"

"We're not here to buy anything," I interrupted. "We're here to see Ko Won Bae. Is he here?"

The man bowed again. "Do you have an appointment?"

"No. I'm from *Esquire* magazine," I lied. I hoped he'd heard of it. Koreans seemed to like big names. While driving through Koreatown I'd noticed a Cafe Van Gogh, a Club Annie Hall, and a noodle shop called the Al Pacino. "We're doing an article, 'Where Now, LA? Six Months After the Rebellion'—I mean riots—and we want to meet some prominent members of this community to schedule interviews with. That's why we want to speak with Mr. Ko Won Bae."

The man nodded. "Follow me." He led us down the aisle on the east side of the store to a small office. He opened the door without knocking. An ebony wood desk was nearly buried beneath papers and receipts. Two black lacquer chairs with red silk seats flanked the desk, and he motioned us into them. I sat down. It felt as if the legs of the chair had been sawed down. My knees were nearly in my chest, and I had to look up at the desk. The salesman moved behind the desk and drew the chair out. I glanced down. He was wearing $900 English oxfords of deep buttery rich cordovan leather. Handmade. Right out of the pages of *Town & Country* magazine, which my mother had made me read.

"You're Ko Won Bae!" I exclaimed.

He nodded.

"These chairs are real comfortable," said Lupe. "A lot of times my legs just dangle and I can't touch the floor." She smiled graciously and crossed one leg over the other, hiking her skirt up in the process.

"My photographer, Miss Lopez," I hastened. "The reason I was so interested in meeting you is the sports center. I understand you're the driving force behind it."

He bowed again. All this bowing stuff was getting repetitious. He looked like an accountant. "I couldn't have done it without the support of a lot of people. It's for all the people of the community. Koreans, Pan-Asians . . ."

"Pan-latinos?" Lupe asked. I couldn't tell if she was putting him on or not.

"How did the sports center idea come into being? It's so wonderful, so necessary, bringing people together . . ." I faltered. What would the sports center mean to Koreatown? Would it be used by all the people of the area? Could people of all colors come together in utopian games or would it become just a graffiti-covered outpost where people were afraid to use the bathroom? Not everyone had forgotten the Uzis on the roofs yet.

"The community responded to the call, and there's been a tremendous outpouring of public support. It's one hundred percent community funded." Ko Won smiled.

Beware those who brag about their charitable work. When I was a little kid I believed in Santa Claus and the Easter Bunny too. The Easter I was seven, I climbed on top of the kitchen cabinets and found the green plastic grass that would fill my Easter basket and a carton of waxy chocolate eggs. I no longer believed all the stories I was told. "I've heard that some people think you just started the ball rolling so you'll get a huge tax deduction."

"No!" He smacked his hand on the desk. "I don't contribute money, I contribute my heart. I get people together so they can support it, so it can belong to them. Koreatown's given me a lot and I'm proud to be able to give something back to all the people who live here. What you say's the kind of talk that keeps our town divided. Everybody suspicious of everyone who's different from them. Now's the time for everybody to come together. Work together. Play together."

"I hear you hired Hector Ramos to run the program," interrupted Lupe, obviously bored with my line of questioning.

"Yes," Ko Won agreed. "The great welterweight 'Manos' Ramos. And he's a real nice guy. You might want to do a photo of him for your article."

"He's washed up. He hasn't had a big fight since late in eighty-eight." Lupe stopped abruptly, but Ko Won didn't seem to notice.

Ko Won nodded. "You must be a fight fan."

"A real fan. He fought Manny Estrada at the Forum. Got his butt kicked. Six rounds. TKO. I had a hundred and fifty dollars on Estrada and I cleaned up."

I pushed myself out of the tiny chair and to my feet. I wanted to get Lupe out of there. I didn't want Ko Won to guess she was Hector's sister. "We won't keep you. You must be awfully busy. Several businesses. The sports center." I shook my head in admiration. "May I call on you again for an in-depth interview?"

"And the photos," he added agreeably, pointing us to the office door. "I'd love to see one of your articles. Send me a copy of something you've published recently. I'll bet you must be a young lady who knows her way around this town. Would that be a good bet for me to take, Miss Lopez?"

Lupe didn't have much to say on the way back to my office. I saw her chewing her lower lip thoughtfully. She stared out the window at the streets of faltering businesses and dying palms.

"What do you think Ko Won meant when we were leaving?" I finally asked Lupe, interrupting her inspection of the Mexicans, *salvadorenos, guatemaltecos,* and Colombians waiting for buses and milling about the corner of Vermont and Santa Monica Boulevard. This was the northern boundary of Koreatown, and the city seemed to reassert its tropical heat. A car pulled up next to us playing a loud *cumbia.* Lupe nodded her head in time to the music.

"Did you hear me? What did he mean?" I repeated.

Lupe glanced over at me. "He meant he thought you were a smartass. I think he knows Hector's my brother. This Koreatown shit looks like it's going to be a harder roll than I thought." She turned back away from me and listened to her music.

I wondered if she was thinking about Dogtown, where we'd seen a man die. I dropped her in front of the office and headed for downtown.

I parked behind a chain link fence next to a warehouse in the light industrial area south of Little Tokyo. I got my gun out of the trunk of the car and went into the warehouse. It's an indoor shooting range. Guns are illegal in Japan, so this is a favorite destination of Japanese tourists. Ten bucks to rent anything you want: .357 Magnum, Smith & Wesson, Lambretta. Bullets are expensive if you have to buy them at the range. I was glad I'd brought my own. I wanted to stay awhile. I felt edgy.

The northern edge of Exposition Park, a racetrack in the last century, is a lonely though busy intersection. I left my car at a meter and trekked onto the campus of USC. I imagined Kim walking the same path. I was going to find out as much as I could about her. The tattoo on her ankle looked like the one I'd seen on the geisha. Her restaurant looked dramatically unsuccessful. The lofty campanile of the Colonel Seeley Wintersmith Mudd Memorial Hall of Philosophy was overshadowed by dull high rises in which were being educated greedy assholes who drove BMWs, carried cellular phones, and ate at the Hard Rock Cafe. I made my way through crowds of students dressed predictably in $200 athletic shoes and ripped prefaded Levi 501s. Yuppie fucks. They probably asked Mommy and Daddy for money whenever they wanted it.

I wondered if Kim had had the money to keep up with them. She liked nice things. The real Chanel purse. The disdainful way she'd looked at my old car. When did she get the tattoo? As I continued past Northern Italian Romanesque castles to the administration building, I wondered if she'd felt like an outsider here.

There was no record of Kim's graduating. She'd dropped out after the first semester. The demographics say Asian-Americans are more likely than any other racial group to finish high school and go to college. Why had she made such a big deal of her attendance? Was this simply part of the Asian stereotype that they all went to school and got the best grades? Or should it tell me something about Kim's propensity for telling the truth? I'd watch her, but I wouldn't tell her I'd found out she'd lied to me. I didn't like the story she'd told about having been raped here either.

On the way back to my car I stopped at the school of architecture to use a pay phone to call Chu Chu Park, the only member of the *kye* group I hadn't questioned yet. The other women were suspicious that she traveled so much and bought so many clothes and expensive jewelry. Nancy Johnson said Chu Chu was in debt up to her eyeballs. Were creditors after her? Threatening her? Lawsuits? Did she need $75,000 enough to kill for it? I was living on a little over two grand a month and barely staying alive; $75,000 seemed like enough money to solve a few problems with. Yeah, pay off Visa and the department stores, book a trip to the Bahamas. You could squeeze a few pleasurable moments out of $75,000. Might be worth murdering a friend for. I dropped my last quarter in the phone and dialed. The architecture school had a depressing funereal atmosphere. It looked like a savings and loan.

Chu Chu Park answered the phone after three rings. I reminded her who I was, but she cut me off and said hurriedly in her heavy accent, "I was just on my way out. I have couple errands, then I go to the bass. You come there at eight-thirty." She quickly gave me an address on Oxford

Street near Western and hung up. I wondered what the bass was.

It was nearly six-thirty by the time I ate some Kentucky Fried Chicken and vinegary potato salad in my car on the south end of Figueroa, where an uneasy commercial DMZ separates USC from the black ghetto south of Martin Luther King Boulevard. It was all check-cashing places and fast food. McDonald's and Taco Bell with drive-through service so people wouldn't have to risk getting out of their cars. The sky turned a poisonous amber as the sun set miles away in Pacific Palisades or Malibu, where lawns were green and homeowners secure.

The Thursday evening traffic seemed purposeful, as though everyone but me was fleeing for home before night fell. I drove up to 1st Street and then west over the bridge through Newton Division. "Rootin' tootin' shootin' Newton," a cop on a GTA had told me. Since the Uprising the streets are uneasily quiet, as if people are concentrated on furtive plans like survivalists stocking their spare bedrooms with Spam. But still nothing could stop a warm *pachanga* breeze that blew through the Salvadoran night. A man and a woman stopped in front of a *panaderia* and kissed. They walked on, oblivious to the deepening shadows.

I drove into the lot on Oxford Chu Chu Park had told me about. It was on a side street in a busy commercial part of Koreatown, and many of the nearby stores were still open. I was early, but I wanted to case the joint. I was trying to get into talking like that to myself. I'd said I was a detective. I should try to talk like one, even if it was corny. I never made $750 a day practicing law. My office open over two years, and I had yet to rise above doing lame-ass possession cases. The lot was full of Mercedeses. New Jaguars. I left my shabby old blue Datsun with a parking attendant. I was embarrassed my car was so messy. The interior of my car's like a giant purse. Old lipsticks, Evian bottles, newspapers I'm never going to read.

The sign above the entrance to the building said Baths.

The lobby was fine-veined ivory marble with red velvet easy chairs. A two-story-high rough granite wall stood before me. Water cascaded over the granite and formed a pool separated from the entranceway by a polished brass railing. A mahogany grand piano crowned by a large gold vase filled with orange and crimson cymbidium orchids and sprays of eucalyptus stood to the side of the entrance.

Was Chu Chu Park expecting to meet me in the lobby or was I to go inside? Why, if she thought I was a tax attorney, would she ask me to meet her here? I glanced around. If I went in would I have to take off my clothes? I watched two well-dressed Korean businessmen pay the admission and be directed across the lobby to an elevator. I'd be taking off my clothes with men I'd never met before! The woman at the reception desk watched me with an impatient frown as if I should make up my mind or get out. It was getting close to time to meet Chu Chu Park.

I stepped forward and paid my money. I started for the elevator.

"No! Not for you. You go there." The woman gave me a withering glance and pointed me toward a door on the opposite side of the lobby.

At this entrance a middle-aged woman in a white smock handed me two white towels and a blue-and-white seersucker robe, then pointed toward another door down a corridor. Did Chu Chu Park know Jin was dead? What did she know about me? In a large, empty, mirrored dressing area I was shown by another attendant where to store my clothing. I started to put everything into a locker, but the attendant stopped me and with some disdain showed me a special wooden compartment for my shoes. I stared at myself in the mirror covering the far wall. I was in better shape than I'd ever been in. My arms were carved. My stomach flat.

I put on the robe and went into the baths. It was hot and muggy. The woman at the desk had said it was the only natural hot spring in Los Angeles County. Only a few dim circles of light illuminated the cloudy room. Did Chu Chu Park think that by bringing me into her territory and treating this as a social rather than a business meeting she could throw me off? Naked Korean women lounged by the side of the steaming pool. Women with long wet black hair sprawled carelessly, their legs open. They leaned close to each other whispering. A woman lolled in the water, her pear-shaped breasts half submerged and her eyes closed. Another woman crouched upon a smooth low stone with her arms resting on her knees as still another woman washed her back with jasmine-scented soap.

Dropping the robe I slipped into the water. It was exquisitely hot, and I ached all over from the tension and pain of the last two days. I touched my shoulders and chest where the guy who'd tried to rape me had caught me with the rope. Lassoed me like a damn cow. It made me furious all over again, but I let myself sink into the incredible heat of the healing water. I closed my eyes. I might have fallen asleep, but I couldn't get out of my mind the image of the grinning Chusok mask dropped by my attacker. Who was he? The only thing I'd really seen of him was his hands, but it had been dark. Who told him where to find me? He couldn't have followed me home. Even though I'd been drinking I'd kept an eye on the rearview mirror for cops. He'd been waiting for me. Was he really the same man who killed Jin? Could old ladies be malevolent enough to hire a killer?

I opened my eyes and peered around the room for Chu Chu Park. No one in the bath was as old as Chu Chu. No sagging skin. No extended abdomens, no shrivelly dehydrated bosoms. One of the women caught me staring at her and shot me an angry look. I pulled myself out of the water to explore a room whose entrance I could make out on the far side of the pool.

I walked slowly toward the room through the heavy mist past more silent reclining forms. I heard murmuring I couldn't understand and the splatter of heavy drops of water. A woman shuffled by. For an instant I thought it was Lee Joon, but it was too hard to see. I stumbled over an outstretched arm.

"Be careful!" someone snapped.

I apologized and continued into the room ahead of me. There on a massage table was Chu Chu being scrubbed and massaged with cucumbers and milk by two women wearing red bikini bottoms. Chu Chu's soft skin barely sagged. She was nearly porcelain. The two attendants turned their backs to me and attacked Chu Chu more vigorously. They rinsed off the cucumbers and milk and began to massage her with golden honey.

Chu Chu must have heard my voice because she opened her eyes and looked at me. "Go wait," she murmured.

I glanced around the room for a chair, but there weren't any.

"In steam room." She sounded annoyed. "You know steam room?"

Yeah, I knew steam room. Did she think I was a barbarian? I'd been in jacuzzis before too. Naked. With my old boyfriend, Bill Hughes, in the middle of the night at his apartment building in Westwood. We did the wild thing underwater.

I found a plastic bowl, which I filled with icy water from the cold pool. I peered through the hazy light. Now the room was nearly empty, and the remaining women were rinsing their luminescent topaz skin and finishing their ablutions. I carried the bowl of cold water with me into the sauna. It was deserted. I arranged my towels on the lowest of the wooden platforms. I wondered if I should wrap myself in one of the towels to conduct the interview. No. I would meet her bush to bush.

After a few minutes the door opened, cutting into my futher ruminations about why Kim had lied to me. Chu Chu Park stepped inside. "Why you want to see me? I don't need your help."

"All of your friends, the other women—I've talked with all of them already . . ." I paused for effect as if I felt uncomfortable with what I had to say. I was going to tell her they'd been badmouthing her and then see whom she put the finger on. "They think you're the one responsible for the theft of the *kye* money."

"Who said that?" she snapped, throwing the towel she carried up onto the wooden platform above me.

I shrugged. "Nancy Johnson . . ."

"Of course." Chu Chu Park flicked her hand as if she was batting away an ugly bug. "She's always been jealous of me. She even tells people I'm older than she is. She—"

"Lee Joon."

"You're lying!"

I shook my head as I prepared another lie. "Lee Joon said you told her you wanted to take the money out of the bank early this year. Not wait for Chusok."

"That stinking sow! That slack-breasted dried-up ancient mongrel! I never said that. What about Kim?"

I nodded my head. "Her too. Even Dorothy said you'd steal anything that wasn't nailed down."

"Not Kim! She didn't say that. It's Dorothy!" Her face twisted in fury as she leaned toward me. It was a startling, rubbery grimace made even more horrible by the dim lighting. "Don't tell me anything about Dorothy. Bah, Dorothy. I've known Dorothy to tell many lies."

"Like what?"

She looked at me suspiciously, but her anger pushed her forward. "Everything. If it wasn't because of Jin I wouldn't have anything to do with Dorothy and also I act nice because she's Kim's grandmother."

"Grandmother? You're wrong. She's Kim's godmother." I pronounced it slowly so she could hear the difference between the two words. Her English wasn't as good as I'd thought.

Chu Chu Park climbed nimbly onto her towel, then leaned down to put her face in mine again. "That's the tale Dorothy tells, but it's not the true one," she hissed. "I'll tell you the true story so that you see the real Dorothy." Chu Chu Park leaned back resplendent with fury to tell her account.

Dorothy was said to have been a plain-looking young girl with long legs and a willful temperament. She displayed artistic and creative ability at a very early age. She wanted to go to a classical dance academy.

"That was when the Japanese occupied our country," spat Chu Chu.

"Dorothy said you studied Japanese."

"Never! That bitch Dorothy! You see the kind of poison she spreads? Our classical dance was forbidden. A person could be sent to jail for dancing, so the training was secret."

Since Dorothy was unable to be a dancer she went to work in a bar.

"She called it a restaurant, but it was a bar," Chu Chu gloated.

Dorothy was nearly eighteen. It was 1928.

"She never married," continued Chu Chu. "But she had

a daughter. A daughter she named Chungmi. Isn't that a beautiful name? It means 'The Shining Pearl.' "

I nodded, puzzled, but wanting her to continue.

"There was a father."

I nodded again.

"This father, he was also a husband."

I nodded, less certain. I wondered where she was going with this. It was as complicated as the bizarre cosmologies my Tae Kwon Do instructor had tried to teach me yesterday afternoon in the *do jang*. "This father, he was also a husband," I repeated, to show my efforts to keep up with the story.

"He was Jin's husband."

Dorothy had a child by her sister's husband!

She never told Jin or their family who the father of her child was. She said only that it was a man who frequented the restaurant where she worked. She said he begged many times to marry her, but that she refused him because he was too old.

"He was old when he married Jin, who had been his student," sniffed Chu Chu Park.

"Wait a sec. You mean Jin knew her husband and her sister had an affair? And a baby?" I asked.

Chu Chu laughed, but her laugh became a mean racking cough. "He, like so many men, was a fool. On his deathbed he confessed to Jin what he'd done."

I wiped at the sweat running down my breasts. "Everyone says Dorothy and Jin were perfect sisters. . . ."

Chu Chu Park nodded her head and looked smug. "Jin never told Dorothy that she knew."

I hugged my knees to me as I considered the enormity of this lie between the two sisters. Chu Chu Park continued the story.

Eventually Dorothy was able to afford to buy a tiny restaurant of her own in Seoul near the East Gate. She named it the Shining Pearl.

"Dorothy's always been able to make money. She's got plenty of it. Now she's probably got seventy-five thousand dollars more," said Chu Chu bitterly. "After the war she bought a bigger restaurant. Then she built onto it, making it even bigger. She never changed the name. Always the Shining Pearl."

"She must have loved her daughter very much." I wondered if my mother would have named anything after me. Although I was an only child, I had not seemed to have figured very prominently in her life. It was always tennis, the country club, bridge. Mostly tennis. I guess I'm lucky she didn't name me Schlazenger after her favorite racket. "Where's Dorothy's daughter?"

Chu Chu Park fell silent and examined her body with satisfaction. "You ask Dorothy about that."

"Is her daughter dead?"

"I don't know. Ask Dorothy." Chu Chu Park gathered her towel around herself as though she was going to get up to leave.

I didn't want her to leave. There was so much more I had to find out. "Let me make sure I understand this. You said Kim was Dorothy's granddaughter. . . ."

"Yes."

"And Jin knew Kim was the daughter of Chungmi?"

Chu Chu Park nodded and tossed her towel down impatiently. "Why do you keep talking about Jin like she was in the past? That's the second time now you do that."

I hadn't realized it. I tried to think quickly whether I should tell Chu Chu Park what I knew. Should I tell her her friend was dead? My intuition said no. I might need this later on.

"I have a bad feeling about Jin," insisted Chu Chu Park. "I feel in my heart she is very far away from me."

"Yeah, Buena Park. Visiting a relative." I repeated Dorothy's original story.

Chu Chu shook her head and looked deep into my face. "Jin is old. I am old. I feel a cold wind in my heart when I say her name. It makes me feel she's already dead. You can do no good in here. Whatever it is that Dorothy's talked you into doing, maybe covering up that she lost our money in bad investments, turn your back on it. Walk away."

I glanced down at my hands. I am only twenty-seven years old. I can't believe my hands will ever be wrinkled and spotted like Chu Chu Park's.

"You think we Korean women all spend our time gambling." Chu Chu grunted. "Or haggling in open air markets. You think because we're old we don't know what's going on. Because we don't speak your language we are stupid. Jin was born the same year Albert Einstein formulated the theory of relativity. We old women are not outside of history. We are history."

Chu Chu paused to catch her breath before telling me more about Jin. Jin was introspective and could be stubborn. She was quiet, but when she spoke she chose her words well. She loved beauty. She was a clotheshorse who knew just the right way to drape an Hermès scarf across an old coat and make it look new. She was a subscriber to the Los Angeles Philharmonic and never missed a Saturday matinee performance. She loved Scriabin's strange, mysterious music.

Yes, Jin sounded like a wonderful old woman, but my attention was starting to wander. None of this explained why she was killed.

". . . composed his music while in a trance."

"Excuse me?" I glanced up at Chu Chu Park, wondering if I'd missed something.

"Scriabin composed his music while in a trance. I like Bach myself, but Jin believed in that kind of stuff. That's how Dorothy held the reins over her."

"What are you trying to tell me?"

"Dorothy's a witch."

I plunged my hands into the plastic bowl of icy water and rinsed my face off. Were all of these little old ladies as mad as hatters? Is this what I had to look forward to? I couldn't imagine being thirty, let alone a million years old with my brain abraded to a smidgen like a worn-down gummy pink eraser on a number 2 pencil.

"You don't believe me?" Chu Chu Park pressed. "I've seen her turn herself into a bird, even a wild dog."

I put my head down on my knees. It was really hot in the sauna. I was starting to feel a bit dizzy.

"She dances in the moonlight wearing nothing but a red cape."

I lifted my head to look at Chu Chu Park.

She smiled knowingly at me. "You don't believe me, do you? You think I'm a crazy old woman."

"No, ma'am. I didn't say that. I was just wondering if this is Korean. Like if there's a shamanic tradition, thousands of years old. An emphasis on nature. Anthropomorphism. Animals that talk, that sort of thing."

Chu Chu Park glared angrily back at me. "Oh, you once took an anthropology class. Splendid. You understand all of our quaint customs, then."

I nodded. "I understand you. So far I figured out you don't like Dorothy much."

Chu Chu Park leaned forward with her hands on her knees. Her breasts dangled toward me. I tried not to stare at her tiny nipples. "She ruins everyone's life. Kim doesn't know Dorothy's her grandmother. And don't you tell her. Kim doesn't remember anything about her mother. Dorothy won't tell her. She doesn't remember anything about Korea, where she was born. That's what Dorothy has done! Stolen Kim's life! Imagine not knowing your own mother or your own country."

The volcanic rocks hissed as Chu Chu Park flung my water on them. They flared, then glowed a brighter red. She stood and looked satisfied as she wrapped the large white towel around herself. She opened the door and went out toward the mineral pool. Almost immediately I lost track of her outline as she moved into the heavy mist.

I lay down on the pine bench with my knees up. They looked far away. I felt my bones turning to liquid. I closed my eyes. Would it be so bad not to know your parents? I thought of my father raging through the house drunk at night, the sound of breaking glass, a door slamming. I tried to push myself farther back into the past. Tried to recall a special blue-and-green dress my mother bought me for Easter one year when I was small. Tried to imagine playing in the snow with my father at my side. My father placing the snowman's head on top of its icy body. My mother sticking a carrot in the snowman's face to make a nose. We all laugh with delight. I'm pushing it. I don't remember any of this.

I doubt that it ever happened.

I hear my father at the door of my mother's bedroom. I am fifteen. It's about three in the morning.

". . . you never want to," my father whines at the locked door.

I pull the pillow over my head so I won't have to listen anymore. What if he comes to my room? I'll pretend I'm asleep. The way he looks at me sometimes gives me the willies. I push the pillow aside. I force myself to listen for what will happen next. He stands outside my mother's room for a while. I hear him turn toward my door. I clutch my pillow. I am barely breathing. Finally he shuffles back toward his bedroom. Then the water runs in the bathroom sink and I know he is taking more Miltown.

I opened my eyes in the steam room. I pushed myself up to a sitting position and blotted my face. It had to be at least 120 degrees. I'd lost track of time. My watch was locked safely in the other room. I had to go talk to Dorothy. I had to find out more about her. But what was I going to do? Ask her if she was a witch?

I stood up. I felt wobbly. My head was starting to pound. No wonder they usually have signs that say not to stay in steam rooms more than ten minutes. I wished Chu Chu Park hadn't thrown the cold water out. That was pretty damn inconsiderate. I draped the towel around my waist and walked to the door. I could barely draw a breath in the heavy hot dampness. I put my hand on the door handle and pushed it.

It wouldn't move.

I rattled the handle as hard as I could. It still wouldn't budge. It was getting harder and harder to breathe.

"Hey," I yelled. I thought the baths were closing for the night and the attendants had forgotten me.

A shrill hiss of steam spit out at me. Wiping at the fog on the glass in the door I cleared a circle so I could look out. I didn't see anyone. I saw only a thick, blunt board jammed through the handle, making it impossible to open the door from the inside.

"Hey!" I screamed again more loudly and banged on the door.

A smoldering blast of heat filled the small room. It scorched my back. A new wave of steam took over the room. I gasped for air, but the heavy boiling cloud wouldn't let me breathe.

"Help!" I screamed at the top of my lungs.

In response another cloud of burning steam flooded the small space. I dropped to my knees and pulling the towel off, wrapped it around my face. I crawled back to the fake volcanic rocks. I could barely see. I inched my fingers cautiously around the smoldering fixture, looking for the control switch. The hot metal burned me. I nearly bit through my lip in pain. There was no switch. The heat was controlled from outside.

Whoever had intentionally locked me in the sauna while I'd had my eyes closed intended to boil me alive. Chu Chu Park? Had that been Lee Joon I thought I'd seen earlier?

I crawled back toward the door. I slipped once and skidded along the floor into one of the wooden benches, hitting my shoulder hard. I pushed myself back onto my knees. My head hung like a dog's.

Another blast of steam filled the room. I got to the door and knelt before it.

"Holy Mary Mother of God pray for . . ." I'd never told Lupe my folks sent me for a year to Catholic school. Was Lupe raised as a Catholic or was I stereotyping her?

My eyes began to close again, and I started to pass out. I saw the Golden Tiger in the *do jang* as though he was veiled in mist. He crouched. His white-robed arms spread like a mighty heron and whipped through the air as he demonstrated how to break a board. Then a brick.

I wrapped the towel around my right fist. I hit the glass as hard as I could. The glass shattered. Cool air rushed in. I smashed the glass again and again. I wrenched the wooden bar from the door handle, staggered out of the steam room, and collapsed on the moist granite floor.

"Lupe?" I whispered into the phone. I thought that she might be afraid to go home to face her mother and that she might still be at the office.

"Where are you?" her sleepy voice answered. *"¿Que horas son?"*

"Midnight."

" 'Bout time you called in. You gotta go right over to the Church of the Big Mother. Venus Howard's pimp's been calling every ten minutes. Just a sec . . ."

I heard Lupe fumbling with the things on top of the desk. Something crashed to the floor.

"Ok, got it. I wrote down exactly what he told me. 'Significant constitutional issues you chose to ignore. Make immediate application for writ to Appellate Court. Or we sue you. For everything you own.' Says for you to come by no matter how late it is. He's driving me *loca*. It's hard enough to get any shut-eye here. The traffic. Your landlord. I mean, how many times in a row can you listen to 'Like a Rolling Stone'? And now he's got a *chingada* harmonica."

I sat up in bed. "Lupe, I don't have time right now for Venus Howard. Someone—"

"I'm ready to go over to that freaky church myself and show them something about tort action," she exploded.

I looked down at my hands. They were still shaking. "Someone tried to kill me in Koreatown tonight."

"*¿Qué?*" She sounded as if she didn't believe me.

Leaving out the relatively unimportant part about the manager going bonkers over the broken door and threatening to call the cops to have me arrested for vandalism, I quickly filled Lupe in on what had happened to me at the baths after I met Chu Chu Park.

"Chu Chu Park! The first time I saw her I could see she was living grand. She racked that *plata*, for sure."

I looked over at my clothes, which I'd thrown in a pile on the floor when I dragged in about an hour earlier. My mother would be so disappointed. She always told me, "No skirt of mine has ever been on a chair unless I was in it." I examined the empty bottle of Southern Comfort on the night table and drained the last drops. "I'm totally exhausted, Lupe, but I can't sleep. I got to go to Dorothy's. Find out more of what she knows about Chu Chu and the other women." Did Lupe care what happened to me? I felt embarrassed I was so transparent. Sickened with myself. Begging for her attention. "I was just calling to tell you I don't know when I'll come by the office. Finish organizing the files tomorrow."

I hung up and ran my fingers through my hair, which was still slightly damp. I had to go back to Koreatown. Weren't murderers supposed to return to the scene of the crime? I'd be there waiting, ready. Better that than waiting for him to come for me. He knew where I lived. Had he been at the baths or was it Chu Chu Park? Lee Joon? I pushed myself out of bed. At least I didn't need a shower. I was as clean as a boiled chicken. I pulled on an old pair of jeans, a white t-shirt, and my high-tops.

I pulled up in front of Dorothy's place in Koreatown around two and cut the engine. In the dark it looked like a peaceful neighborhood. There were porches with swings; a statue of Buddha stood in a front yard. A diseased-looking dwarf pine tree attested to the desperate desire to establish roots. I got out of the car and walked up the stairs to Dorothy's apartment.

Outside her door I looked around to see if anyone was watching. I put my ear against the door. Soft chanting came from the living room. It was only one voice. Dorothy's. I pressed against the door, trying to hear more of what was happening. The drone repeated over and over. I turned away. The dead deserved their honor. Dorothy was praying.

Back in the car, I turned my radio down real low. It was the blues station from Long Beach. The groove was good. Esther Phillips. I started to relax for the first time since I escaped from the steam bath.

". . . got the black-eyed blues . . . ," sang Esther, dead too and buried somewhere in Inglewood.

An hour or more passed while the ebony night smothered the city. I wondered what they'd done with Jin's body. I wondered whether Buddhists believe in heaven. Or would Jin immediately reincarnate? Dorothy had told me Jin's name meant "Star." I looked upward. Off in the distance, where the stars should be, lights on top of a Wilshire high rise blinked.

A car split the silent night, screeching around the corner and roaring fast in my direction. It groaned into an anguished third, popped into a flat-out fourth.

I was right. He was coming back!

The headlights swerved as the car wove across the imaginary center line and raced toward me. In one movement I reached under the seat for my gun then flattened myself across the passenger seat to avoid being spotted.

An old Fiat roared to a stop parallel to my car.

Lupe turned off the motor, which continued to kick and sputter. She stepped out as though unaware of the clatter of her heap. She strolled over to my car and leaned in. Then she pulled a brand-new half pint of Southern Comfort from her purse, unscrewed the top, took a drink. "Here. I thought you might want this. Tastes like fucking cough syrup to me." She handed me the bottle.

"I put a spell on you . . . ," moaned Screamin' Jay Hawkins. How many places in the world can you listen to Screamin' Jay Hawkins in the middle of the night?

I took a drink. It was good.

"Thought I'd drop by and go undercover with you," Lupe said.

"Thanks." I pushed the gun farther back under my seat so she wouldn't see it.

"De nada." Lupe got into the car. "Plus this way I can keep an eye on my money. You're getting seven fifty a day, right? Let's see, a third is two fifty. Plus my expenses. Let's say three hundred, OK?"

"You'd risk your life for that? What about right and wrong? The underlying truth? Unraveling the complexities of the human mind?"

"Complexities! Ayyy, you give me a headache." She shook her head with disgust. "There's plenty of guys who just wanna go boom boom boom and take everything you've ever worked for. I don't have any trouble at all believing some *vato* blew Jin away for seventy-five grand. Where I come from there are guys who'd do a hit for a hundred bucks. Or just to prove they're *macho*."

"So you think it's a jungle out there?"

She nodded. "Absolutely. It's just you. And your family. Fuck everybody else."

I took another drink. What Lupe said made me bluer than the blues. What about community? Friendship? "When I gave you a job, it was supposed to be your chance to go straight, so you could get Joey back. I wanted to help you. You're my only friend."

"Ohhh, get out the violins. What about law school? You must have friends from there. Late-night studying, talking about the lectures as you walk the ivy-covered arcades. The great professors. Like Robert Donat in *Goodbye Mr. Chips*. Everyone wearing tweed . . ."

"I don't know anyone from school. I didn't really hang out with anyone. . . ."

"*Jesus!* That's it. That's what's wrong with you. You don't know how to hang out. Yeah, I read once in *People* magazine about this famous guy who went up into a bell tower and killed, like, seven nurses. And they were interviewing everyone who knew him and this one guy said, 'Oh, yeah, he was weird, like he didn't even know how to hang out, he didn't hang out anywhere, he didn't even know how to roller-skate.' " Lupe stopped breathlessly to study me.

I stared out the window. I don't know how to roller-skate. I hate adults on roller skates. We both slumped back in our seats listening to the blues. What did I have to do to make her acknowledge the screwed-up situation we were in?

"You think families are so important? So sacred? Well, explain this then. Last night I found out Dorothy's Kim's grandmother. Not her godmother. And you were right that Kim's probably a pro." I laid out the rest of the facts as I'd been pondering them in the dark. An armed robbery turns into murder. An old lady I don't know, whose language I can't speak, hires me to find the killer of her beloved sister.

She lies to me about her family because she had an illegitimate daughter fathered by her sister's husband. She won't go to the police because she's got a righteous grudge against them and she's been threatened by her sister's killer.

Lupe put her hand up to stop me. "Don't make this so difficult. All you have to do is figure out who's responsible, not put 'em in jail. We're not playing 'Gunsmoke.' This is a real gig. With real money."

I slapped the dash in frustration. "Why don't you think that whoever killed Jin couldn't come back to kill us? They've already tried twice to hurt me. It's not just about the money anymore."

"Not just about the money! What do you think I was doing out here with all those guys for twenty-five dollars? Having a Coke and a chat? Getting stock tips? Nah, I've sucked enough dicks for one lifetime. Shit, that's ten blowjobs per day to make what I can get from Dorothy, so don't be telling me what's dangerous and what I ought or ought not be doing—"

I snapped my fingers in front of her face. "Hey, girlfriend! Haven't you heard what I was telling you?"

"So she lied because she had an illegitimate kid. That's not the worst thing in the world. How do you think I felt when I found out I was pregnant with Joey?"

I held my breath and let it out slowly. I didn't want to start yelling at her. "Maybe Dorothy doesn't have any money."

"Then what are we sitting here for?" She reached angrily for the car door handle. "Let's go up there right now and find out. I'm not gonna waste my time and put my tail on the line if there's no money."

From behind Dorothy's building, a car started up, gunned its engine, and then came down the driveway. We both ducked. I glanced at my watch. Nearly five-thirty. Dorothy drove past in a gold Acura. I let her get to the end of the block. She hung a fast right and skidded around the corner. I started my engine and followed her north.

"Would it be racist if I said Orientals are really bad drivers?" Lupe asked as the Acura wove in and out of traffic.

The sun was coming up. It was autumn in Los Angeles. Although the air was balmy it would be staggeringly hot by 11:00 A.M. A bank of clouds moved sluggishly over the mottled green Hollywood Hills. Dorothy swung over to Hoover and up through the Central American streets of orange blossoms, mango stands, and rubber trees towards Wilshire.

"Over there," said Lupe, pointing out my window. "About a block over's the apartment where Kid McCoy killed his girlfriend in the twenties. He was once the welterweight and the middleweight champion of the world. You think I haven't been wondering about my bonehead brother and that Kim? I wouldn't be surprised to find out Hector's up to his neck in this whole thing. He could have gotten one of his homies he was in the pen with to be the shooter."

I glanced over at Lupe. "Hector was in state prison?"

"Sure. I can't believe I never told you that. I must have told you."

I shook my head. "What for?"

"Assault with a deadly weapon. Busted down from manslaughter. Maybe that's part of the reason Hector has trouble getting fights."

I was starting to feel unwell.

"It was at some *ruca*'s place in East LA. He was drinking with this broad and screwing around while her husband was at work. The *esposo* came home and caught them. There was a fight. Hector broke the bottle of whiskey and cut the guy bad. That's how he is. He thought this woman belonged to him even though she was married to someone else."

We passed a more benign collection of houses and apartments in the stately Queen Anne style. A pair of apartments modified with classical American colonial revival detailing. Then a jungle of palms appeared before us at the intersection of Wilshire. It was Lafayette Park.

I slowed up to fall behind as Dorothy circled the park looking for a good place to leave her car. Finally she decided on a spot at the far end near Wilshire Boulevard and the old Sheraton–Town House hotel. "Hector did that?"

She nodded. "He's the real McCoy."

We watched as Dorothy, dressed in a pair of baggy black sweats and an oversize black sweatshirt, got out of her car. She headed away from the hotel.

"What's she doing? Is she nuts? This is a dangerous park," muttered Lupe. "I thought she was going to breakfast at the Sheraton." Lupe quickly explained the building was constructed in 1929 as luxury apartments and converted to a hotel by Conrad Hilton in 1942. Howard Hughes rented a suite there for a time. In the fifties the hotel's Zebra Room was one of the city's ritziest nightclubs. "Mae West's last film was shot there."

Dorothy crossed the street and went down a slope into the park. There were several white-haired old ladies and men dressed the same as Dorothy waiting for her. They bowed in greeting to her.

I pulled the car onto the side street and as close as possible to see what was happening.

"What the hell are they doing here?" Lupe wondered.

Dorothy stood before the assembled group. She bowed to them in return. She crouched low to the ground with her hands out before her. The others imitated her to the best of their ability. She was leading them in *kicho il bo,* the first *poomsae* of the stances, blocks, and punches of Tae Kwon Do.

We sat silently in the car watching the old people practicing the defensive techniques.

"You know anything about self-defense?" I asked Lupe.

"No."

"What about when you were out on the streets?"

Lupe sat up proudly. "I never been hurt on the streets by any man. They treated me good."

I wondered who gave her the bruise I'd noticed on her face the day I saw her arraigned in court. "They could try anything once they're alone with you. There are a lot of sickies out here. You said so yourself. I'll teach you some martial arts." I nodded toward Dorothy and her group. "If those dinosaurs can do it, you can do it."

"Nothing's gonna happen to me." Lupe shook her head. "When I walk that walk, I'm the dream come true. They'd die to feel the touch of my hand." She opened her purse and took out her makeup bag. She put on foundation, mascara, a brown blusher, two different purple eyeshadows, and magenta lipstick, then touched her eyebrows with black pencil. She examined her face in the mirror before dropping the makeup bag back in her purse. "Enough of being nice. Let's go find out about our money." She gestured toward the martial arts group concluding its exercise.

We waited until Dorothy and the other old people finished chatting and Dorothy was on her way back to her car alone. The promising pink light of a new day pushed forth as Lupe and I hurried into the park, which was starting to get busy with drug deals. Lupe looked with a combination of pity and disdain at a young strawberry in yellow stretch pants and a filthy floral blouse giving a frantic handjob behind a eucalyptus tree to a ragged Salvadoran too stoned to come.

I looked at Lupe. She'd never told me how she started prostituting. I knew she once worked in a dance hall, dancing for thirty cents a minute with lonely Mexicans and Central Americans on Pico near downtown. What was the turning point, the day, the hour, the slant of the sun, the direction of the moon; what were the forces at play at the moment Lupe became a whore?

"Yo, Mrs. Oh!" Lupe called after Dorothy's retreating figure.

Dorothy turned. If she was surprised to see us there among the flotsam and jetsam of the park, she didn't show it. She stopped and waited until we caught up with her. I stood beside her. She wasn't even winded from her exercise. She was tiny. Smaller than I remembered. Maybe only five feet. She bowed slightly when she saw me. She was less pleased to see Lupe.

"What's this about Kim being your granddaughter?" Lupe asked.

So much for cunning and subtlety. I had wanted to invite her to the Sheraton, sit down for a cup of tea, have some lead-in.

Dorothy looked questioningly at me. I reported what Chu Chu Park had told me.

"My oldest friend!" Dorothy responded with disdain. "Chu Chu Park's a very bitter woman. Don't listen to her." Dorothy started to walk again across the park toward her car, with us tagging along beside her. "Her own children never even spend any time with her."

"Why'd you lie?" I asked. "Why'd you say Kim's not your flesh and blood?"

Dorothy stopped and put her hands on her hips. At that instant she looked ancient. Older than the earth upon which we stood. "I don't know if she is or not."

Dorothy spun away from us and began to walk more quickly. Lupe ran around in front of her, forcing her to a halt. "Why don't you ask your daughter? Where is she?"

With an impatient look Dorothy stepped around Lupe. "I don't know. The last time I saw my daughter she was twelve years old."

I touched Lupe on the arm to get her out of Dorothy's way, but she wouldn't budge. She was going to screw everything up. She pushed her face up close to Dorothy's. "Tell us where she is. We don't got all day."

"Don't talk to me like that," snapped Dorothy. "Whitney's the one helping me."

I nodded soothingly. "That's right. I want to help you, but I need for you to tell me about your daughter. Help me to help you."

"The Japanese took her," Dorothy said.

"What do you mean, took her?" Lupe demanded.

Dorothy stepped back slightly. "During the war. They took her to a comfort camp. To comfort the soldiers." Dorothy saw our lack of comprehension. "For prostitution. At least eighty thousand women. The little girls too."

"*¡Jesús y María!*" Lupe exploded. "A brothel!"

Dorothy stumbled past Lupe. "After the war she wouldn't come home. She was too ashamed. She was seventeen. She wrote and said she had another life. For me to forget her."

A junkie in stinking jeans and no shirt approached with his hand out. There were open sores on his chest. I pulled a dollar out of my pocket and thrust it at him. He turned to Dorothy, who waved her hands at him to brush him away. She broke away from us and started toward her car, as he lumbered behind us mumbling inarticulately.

"Get the fuck out of here," Lupe screamed at him, pushing him aside. She grabbed Dorothy by the arm, jerking her to a standstill. "What kind of mother are you? Why didn't you go get her? Why didn't you stop her?"

Dorothy shook her head. "She wouldn't even send me

her address. All I knew was that she was in Kaesong. Not so far from Seoul, but after our civil war, after our country was divided, it wasn't possible."

Lupe let go of Dorothy's arm. She stared away from us and toward the growing traffic on Wilshire. Beneath her careful makeup I saw under her left eye the tiny black tear tattoo she'd gotten in jail. The first time I'd seen it I assumed she'd drawn it on with eyeliner pencil. Now I realized it was real and a permanent part of her.

"You never saw your daughter again?" I asked Dorothy. I wondered if what I was able to find out about Chungmi would help me understand Lupe.

Dorothy shook her head, and I thought she might cry. "It was a blessing when I finally heard from a minister and his wife in 1977 . . ."

The park was rapidly filling up with Salvatrucha gangbangers, the homeless, and the mentally ill. Dorothy hurried past them as she told us about the minister and his wife who had found Kim when she was only four years old. The couple formally adopted Kim when they arrived back in the U.S.A. I could imagine the whole story in *Life* magazine. The adorable little girl with big dark eyes and black hair hanging in bangs cut neatly and precisely above her eyebrows. The little girl dressed in a sailor suit with a big red bow. The minister and his wife would have been so glad to get away from the menacing Communists on the other side of the 38th Parallel and return to the good old U.S. of A. that there would be some slightly militaristic bent in their selection of clothes for the child. When she was fourteen her adopted parents learned Kim's grandmother lived in Los Angeles and decided to do the right thing: to send Kim to Dorothy so she could know her real family and her real culture.

"How'd they find you?" I wondered.

"The orphanage had records. They spent a lot of time and money looking for me. God bless them."

It was a beautiful and inspiring story. Lupe was hushed and solemn. The sun flooded the street like a bank of klieg lights as we stepped from beneath the trees and exited the park.

I walked next to Dorothy up the hill to the street, not wanting to let on yet how much I knew about Kim. "Tell me again what the man said before he shot Jin. He was speaking Korean, wasn't he?"

Dorothy stopped beside her gold Acura. She pulled up her sweatshirt and fished her car keys out of a neon green fannypack she wore around her waist. "Sort of."

I asked her what she meant.

"He's not a real Korean. Not from Korea."

"Man, I hate that too," Lupe said. "*Pocho* Spanish. All those *chingón* yuppies from the Westside who gotta try to order their food in Spanish in Mexican restaurants. Who say 'boo nos day ass' to their maids—"

"Did he ask if it was the Queen Min box?" I interrupted. I wondered what Lupe thought of my Spanish.

Dorothy shook her head.

Who was this guy if Dorothy didn't think he was Korean? "What's this Queen Min box?" I asked. "I keep hearing people talking about it. How come Kim told me about it and you didn't?"

Dorothy got into her car. "It doesn't concern you. . . ."

I grabbed the door to keep her from shutting it. "What do you mean, it doesn't concern me? Look, I've been trying to be cool, but so far, since I met you, just three days ago, I've been jumped, some guy tried to rape me, and last night when I went to meet Chu Chu Park at the baths she, or someone, maybe Lee Joon, locked me in the steam room and almost burned me to death."

"And don't forget the money," Lupe added. "So far you owe Whitney twenty-two hundred and fifty dollars."

Dorothy fumbled again with the pouch fastened around her waist. She took out a wad of twenties and pushed it toward me. "Here. You want money? You say Chu Chu tried to hurt you at the baths last night. That settles it. That's all I need to know. I knew she was behind this. Thank you. You don't need to do anything more for me."

"I gotta find this guy or I could be killed. . . ."

"So could I!" Lupe snatched the money from Dorothy's hand and quickly counted it. "And so could you, Mrs. Oh. Don't overlook that. So could you." She tucked the cash into her black bra. "This'll do for starters. Now what's this about the Queen Min box?"

Dorothy put her head down on the steering wheel for a few seconds. "I feel very tired now," she whispered. I could barely hear her. I leaned toward her. "Old and tired. I need to go home and make some special vitality tea. You come to my house later. Just you, Whitney. Tonight around nine. I'll tell you about Queen Min."

We stood in the street shielding our eyes against the sun and watching the departing gold Acura as it hurried south. A flock of birds filled the sky, headed south also. They were migrating for the winter. It was nearly ninety. A breeze shivered the palm trees on the fringe of the park. It is hard to tell what's happening and read all the signs in the tropics.

12

The cook at Cafe James Dean told me where Kim was. Lupe and I hurried over to a glass-and-marble mall at the corner of Western and 9th. It was bordered by crumbling, charred apartments of Central American refugees. Inside the Korean mall water cascaded from a jade fountain into a pool the color of tourmaline. There were toy stores, boutiques of women's silk clothing, imported British tweeds for the gentlemen, and a French bakery. Gooey Muzak teased the air as we rode the escalator up through a large atrium filled with palms. Kim was getting her hair done in a black-and-white-tiled beauty salon on the second floor.

Seated in a stylist's chair at the back of the salon, Kim spotted us in the mirror as soon as we approached. The action in the salon stopped. Women stared at us, and I heard their critical, amused whispers as we walked past them. Lupe paused in front of a glass display case to examine some knockoffs of Chanel belts. "How clever," Lupe announced in a dramatic stage whisper. "Totally fake. Like Kim."

I nodded in greeting at Kim, hoping she hadn't heard Lupe.

Kim's hair was in rollers, but she was already made up. I'd never seen her sans the full Earl Scheib paint job. I wondered what she looked like without it. Probably damn good. She had real cheekbones and big sexy lips.

Kim lifted her hand to cover her mouth and giggled as though embarrassed by her pink plastic crown. "I told them to tell you where I was. I was hoping to talk to you today." She gave some curt direction in Korean to the woman doing her hair. "Why don't you wait for me in the bakery, Whitney. They make excellent cappuccino."

The salon fell quiet again as Lupe, in her tawdry gray pinstripe suit, and I turned to leave. I had no doubt they were in shock at Lupe's skirt slit high up the rear. Fuck them. What did they know? They'd probably never heard of Lana Turner or Ava Gardner. I smiled encouragingly at Lupe as we ran the silent gauntlet.

"Jesus Christ," sighed Lupe once we were outside. "I wish you'd make more of an effort to dress. Sometimes it's really embarrassing."

We went down to the bakery we'd seen near the fountain on the first floor. Lupe wanted to use a pay phone, so I waited for her a short distance away in front of a jeweler's, pretending to study the necklaces and bracelets while I strained to hear over the passing shoppers what Lupe was saying.

"Hola, hola, Joey. Soy yo, Mami . . . Joey? Joey?" She hung the phone up angrily, and I guessed her mother had taken the phone from Joey and hung up on her.

We killed about forty minutes grazing through brioches and almond croissants. I told Lupe I wanted her to be more polite to Kim. "You're acting like you're prejudiced against Koreans," I warned.

Lupe shrugged. "It's a free country. I ain't prejudiced against anybody. I just don't like this broad."

"I'm in a service industry now, so cool it if you expect Dorothy to pay me."

Kim finally showed up with her shiny, fresh-smelling hair artfully combed as though it hadn't been done at all. Although the table was littered with cups and crumbs, she insisted on ordering more of everything for us. The busboy cleared the table for the second round of coffees.

"Ever notice no matter what kind of restaurant it is, the busboys are always Mexican?" Lupe grumbled.

Kim laughed. I wondered how she felt and what she thought while she was fucking Hector Ramos.

"I'm so relieved you came, Whitney," said Kim, pointedly ignoring Lupe. "I haven't been able to stop thinking about everything that's happened. There's something else I thought of to tell you. About Lee Joon." She paused as the waiter deposited cups and carbs in front of us. She tore open a Sweet 'N Low and stirred it into her decaf caffè latte. "About a month ago Lee Joon said she was buying a timeshare in Puerto Vallarta."

"Mexico?" I asked. "I thought Chu Chu was the traveler."

"Lee loves Mexico."

Lupe set down her cup with a roar of loud, mean laughter. "*¡Qué rico!* That explains why everyone's so hot to open the new sports center. Because they love Mexicans."

"She had a little tea party to tell Jin and Dorothy and the other women. They were all planning on going there this Christmas, although the three of us were wondering how Lee was going to pay for the place—"

"You think this Lee Joon lady's the one who stole the money?" Lupe interrupted. She leaned across the table, brushing her dark black hair back from her face with one delicate brown hand as she spoke. Her hair fell in a lush curve onto her breast. "Where would she get the guy with the gun?"

Kim patted her gleaming coiffed hair into place. "Her youngest nephew. He lives in Fresno."

"Fresno?" I said. "How's he figure?"

"He's a gangbanger." Kim tore a scrap of croissant and spread it with jam. "It'd be easy to do. Drive down here, steal the money, turn around and drive back. His family sent him up there. Trying to get him away from bad influences." She paused to push croissant into her rosy painted mouth. "Nobody likes to talk about it, but there are gangs here."

"Even in Koreatown?" Lupe asked with a sneer in her voice.

I flashed her a warning look, but she just smiled. I leaned back in my chair so Kim wouldn't see I was getting irritated with Lupe. I asked Kim how she knew it was the gangbanger from Fresno.

"It's been a long time since I've seen him," she admitted. "I'm not even sure what he looks like now, but his voice was familiar. I know it was him. This had to be Lee Joon's fault. She couldn't keep her mouth shut in a swarm of flies."

"But why kill Jin?" I asked. "For the Queen Min box? Is it worth that much?" Was the box real gold? Or merely gilt? From where I'd been hiding when I saw the man take the box from Dorothy, I couldn't tell. I couldn't believe it was gold. Why wouldn't Dorothy keep it in a safe deposit box or a museum if it was real?

Kim sighed. "No. I tried to explain to you. Dorothy's built this box up in her mind because history's important to the old Koreans, probably because they'll never really fit in here. Believe me, if it was real Dorothy would have it locked up in a bank so nobody could touch it."

I told Kim we'd already seen Dorothy that morning and

she'd told us Kim was born in Korea. I wondered why Kim sounded impatient about the bank when she'd told me how generous Dorothy was.

"You weren't born here," Lupe crowed. "I was. So was my mother."

"I'm an American citizen," Kim snapped.

I grimaced at Lupe, trying to get her to shut up. "You speak English just like an American," I said to Kim in my most diplomatic tone.

"I don't even remember Korea," Kim said, angrily swiveling to face Lupe. "I don't think I'd like it. Too sexist. There, in the old days, they had to have laws to keep men off the streets in the evening so upper-class women could go visit one another. If you weren't rich, forget it. If you went outside of your house you had to wear *chan'got*—cape—covering your face."

I scooped the fuzz off my cappuccino and scraped it on the saucer. It was getting increasingly difficult to get a real cup of coffee anywhere in town. "Dorothy said you left Korea when you were a little girl with some missionaries who adopted you. . . ."

Kim broke a chocolate croissant from the basket between us into smaller pieces and smiled. "She told you about the Petersons?"

I nodded. "Yeah. She said they brought you out of North Korea. That your mom gave you to them . . ."

"My mother's dead," said Kim.

"I'm sorry," I said. "I didn't know. Dorothy said your mother'd been taken by the Japanese to . . ."

"A whorehouse," said Lupe, folding her arms across her chest and staring coldly at Kim. "You don't even know who your father was."

Kim pushed back her chair and started to stand. I leaned

forward and touched Kim on the arm. "Shut up, Lupe. Say you're sorry."

Lupe turned her mad-dog eyes to me. "First day we met she called me a whore. And her puttin' on airs like she's somebody."

"I don't think she meant it. She was upset. Nearly hysterical. It was right after Jin . . ." I fumbled. "You didn't mean it, did you, Kim?"

Kim sat down in the chair again. She shook her head and wiped at her eyes. "No. I was shook up. Please don't tell Hector. Let's be friends, ok?"

I looked back and forth between the two women, each poised on the edge of her chair as though about to spring.

Instead of answering, Lupe closed her eyes and nodded her head a couple of times as if she was thinking something out.

Can't we all just get along?

I pushed my chair back slightly in case they decided to go for it.

"Yeah, ok. I'm sorry too," Lupe said at last. "I'm sorry about your mother. That's tough not having your mother. Your real mother."

"I don't even have a photograph of her," said Kim.

We all fell silent. Adrift in Los Angeles and far from home. "Lucky for you the Petersons were able to bring you out of North Korea," I said finally.

Kim nodded. "They were the most wonderful people in the world. They're dead now. I don't remember a lot about them. Just little bits and pieces. My mom, Mrs. Peterson, bought me a bright red coat with a little white rabbit collar."

Why couldn't I have been adopted? Some nice working-class family? One with a union maid in its background. A red diaper baby. My mother singing union songs as she rocked me on some barricade, instead of swinging at tennis balls on a grass court in Maryland.

Kim went on to explain that the Petersons had been able to locate Dorothy and Jin, who were believed to have some blood relationship to Kim's mother. "Like distant cousins. That's why I call Dorothy godmother. To give her respect."

Was it possible she didn't know Dorothy was her grandmother? Was Kim lying to us? Why? I flashed a look at Lupe, begging her to keep her mouth shut while I probed some more. "Do you think you'll ever go back? To Korea? To find the rest of your family," I suggested.

Kim shrugged. "What for? This country has given me everything. A family. A good education. Everything I want's right here. My restaurant. Hector."

Lupe burst into laughter. "I can't believe you're serious about my brother. He's an idiot and meaner than a skunk on crank."

Kim put down a couple of tens to pay for our food. "You don't know him like I do. Hector's much smarter than anybody gives him credit for. He just needed the right woman. This job as director of the new multicultural sports center's only the beginning for him." She got up from the table. "And he's a very sexy guy."

I reached uneasily for my water glass. I did not like to think of Hector with a hard-on.

Kim dropped her Louis Vuitton wallet into her Gucci purse. "We're getting married next month. You'll be my maid of honor, Lupe." She turned and walked away, her pert hips moving in a tasteful way under her pale pink silk dress.

Lupe toyed with the crescent tip of an almond croissant, rolling it between her fingers for some time, before declaring, "That broad's *loca*."

I put on some lipstick. The zen way. No mirror. "Yeah.

Let's go talk to Mr. Ko Won again. I don't believe Kim. She's way too good-looking for your brother."

"What do you mean?" snarled Lupe, tossing the mangled croissant on the littered table. "It is possible that someone could be in love with my brother. He may be a shit and an asshole, but he's my brother."

I told Lupe we should meet Ko Won after work that evening and learn more about how Kim happened to accompany him to the fights the night she met Hector. We left the mall as a slobbering string arrangement of "Ain't No Mountain High Enough" tainted the air. "She ain't that good looking," Lupe kept muttering.

I glanced at my watch. I couldn't put off my meeting with Adonis at the Church of the Big Mother any longer. Not if I was serious about keeping my license to practice law. I asked Lupe to drive me there so I'd have a witness if they tried to hassle me again about the way I was handling their case. People only hear what they want to hear, and Venus Howard seemed like the type who'd try to claim I hadn't fully explained things to her. It's a shame but it's true: a lot of time is spent defending yourself from your client.

The small Tudor house looked just as it had the first time I was there, except there was a white stretch limo parked in the driveway.

"*Quelle charmante,*" said Lupe. "The seven dwarves must be here."

We went up the path. From outside the front door we heard a burst of Italian.

"What's that?" Lupe said suspiciously. "Someone in trouble?"

"No, it's opera." I knocked on the door, but no one answered. I tried the door, but it was locked. I knocked again.

It was opened by a middle-aged flabby guy in a navy Brooks Brothers suit and a pair of tortoiseshell glasses. His jacket was open, and although he wore a bow tie he was shirtless. A halter of black leather straps was bound across his chest. His sagging nipples were pierced with silver rings. From the room behind him came the murmur of a small crowd.

I stuck my hand out and introduced myself. "You Adonis?"

He tittered with pleasure as he shook his head. "Just a friend."

"How about Venus? She's here to see Venus," Lupe added, leaning against the doorframe. She sounded bored, as if she was being presented with a not very fresh or colorful sales rack of *minifaldas*. She fingered one of the black leather straps near the man's nipple. "Feels like ya bought it in TJ." She sighed, exhausted by the mediocrity of the material. "Never shop discount for restraints. You're the lowest of the low. Filthy pig," she said with scorn.

The man looked thrilled by her rejection. He stepped back to open the door for us.

I faltered in the open doorway. Lupe didn't do kink. Did she? The gilded light of the small anteroom was smudged with patchouli incense. Lupe parted the shimmering bead curtains and we stepped inside the Royal Hall.

Two clean-cut men crawled naked, except for black leather waist restraints, in a circle on the floor. The two temple maidens, Heather and Sarah, stood over them in stiletto black suede boots. Each held a riding crop. In the center of it all stood Venus Howard elevated above them on a table.

Lupe started forward. "*¡Dios mío!*" she exclaimed.

Venus wore a platinum blonde wig and a white dress. Fans on the floor were aimed up at her so that her dress blew up toward her waist. On the wall behind her, above the altar in the inner sanctuary of the Church of the Big Mother, was the famous poster of Marilyn, her white dress blown up toward her waist.

"Dios," Lupe exclaimed again as though being offered a piece of the Holy Grail. She held her trembling hand out in front of her. "Cotton piqué," she mumbled as though saying a rosary. "Just like Marilyn's dress in *The Seven Year Itch*. August 17, 1954, 2:00 A.M., the Trans-Lux Theatre, Manhattan"—Lupe paused, color returning to her face once more as she shook herself from her reverie—"but this frail here's got legs like a moose."

Venus Howard glanced toward us. She pointed with her chin for us to go into the small kitchenette. "Priestesses," she intoned in a baby voice to her foxy minions, "I am most displeased with my servants."

The handmaidens began to prod the crawling men with the riding crops as Venus Howard climbed stiffly down from the table. On her way to the kitchen she kicked one of the guys with her nasty stiletto. He looked as if he'd gone to heaven.

"What'd you want to see me about, Ms. Howard?" I asked, taking a spot in the kitchen where I could keep an eye on the other room. One of the handmaidens had one of the men bent over a chair and was spanking him. His butthole looked like an angry spider. His unattractive aryan balls dangled unevenly.

Venus Howard studied Lupe with distrust.

"My legal secretary, Ms. Ramos. She's here to take notes."

"I don't have to write it down. I have a photographic memory," Lupe said.

Venus Howard turned her attention back my way with a dramatic sweeping hand gesture. "I have a very important offer to accept: my own show on Channel 50! The word must be spread! My trial televised! Have you finished researching the constitutional issues yet?"

Television! And have the world know about the lunatics I was forced to represent? How much worse could my life get? I shook my head. "I haven't had time and I don't think it's—"

"How much are you making for this scene?" Lupe asked, indicating the other room.

"That's it! That's what I'm trying to explain. That's what we must make clear for our television audience." Venus poked me in the arm. "There's no fee. It's a donation to the church. The ancient sacred prostitutes were often known as Charities or Graces because they dealt in a unique combination of beauty and kindness called *charitas*—"

"Five hundred bucks?" guessed Lupe. "You got two girls, overhead . . . I don't think it could be done, realistically, for less than seven fifty."

Venus shook her head. "In Babylonia the custom compelled every woman of the land once in her life to sit in the temple of love and have intercourse with some stranger. It didn't matter what sum of money was offered, the woman would not refuse because the money of this act was sacred."

"A grand," Lupe insisted.

Venus turned from Lupe to me. "Get all the networks at my trial. Think of what it'll do for your career! Praise the Great Slit."

"You can't be serious, can you?" I stammered. I looked at Lupe for help.

"It's brilliant," said Lupe. "I see a series. T-shirts . . ."

I glanced back into the temple and saw the handmaiden with long hair yawn as she continued the spanking. "What's the cosmology involved here? The gods, the goddesses?"

"Ishtar, Mylitta, Attar . . ."

I walked out of the kitchenette and into the altar room. I stood towering over the prostrated man. "Hey, buddy, who's Attar?"

He looked at me blankly, a thin line of spittle oozing out of his excited mouth.

"Ishtar?" I asked.

He continued to look up at me stupidly.

"You're fucked without a cosmology. You're looking at jail time," I called to Venus Howard on my way to the front door. "You get me a pantheon of gods and goddesses before I set foot in front of a jury."

Lupe and I left the Church of the Big Mother to the uncertain chanting of "Attar, Attar, Attar."

I had Lupe drop me off at my car in Koreatown, then I sent her back to the office. I shoved another Bob Marley tape into my cassette player and drove to the Superior Court archives between Hill and Broadway.

Archives is a creepy bomb shelter beneath a not very well conceptualized or maintained minipark, one of those desperate islands of jacaranda and green that passes for public space in the Civic Center. I ordered the docket sheets for adoptions from 1965 to 1968. I wanted to see if Kim's story about being adopted by people named Peterson was true.

Koreatown was less than five miles away. I felt it pressing in on me, taunting me with its blood secrets. Jin was killed by a masked assailant who stole not only the *kye* money but the mysterious box as well. He must have known what he was looking for. Did he know Korean history? Did the other old women know the box's special meaning? Would history provide the clue I needed? Would it explain why Jin was killed? History has never been anything more than blood.

And where was Jin's killer at this moment?

The arrival of the microfiche for the documents I'd requested put an end to my conjectures. I loaded it into a machine as instructed by an obese county employee who could barely wait to get rid of me and return to watching her tiny Japanese television. I scrolled carefully through the film and found several adoptions involving people named Peterson. I ordered those files and waited again while Oprah interviewed recovering anorexics.

The files were finally delivered to me. One was for a Luke and Mary Peterson of North Hollywood who had adopted a four-year-old girl they named Kim. There were no notices to her parents. The court order had dismissed the necessity of notices or due diligences, simply stating, "Unknown in North Korea."

It was nearly five o'clock by the time I finished reading the file. The Petersons had requested the court to set aside their adoption when the girl was fourteen years old. The accompanying court order absolved them of responsibility. I copied down their address. There wouldn't be time to try to locate the Petersons before going to see Ko Won. I'd told Lupe to meet me outside his store at five-thirty. I stopped on Olympic near Normandie at a Korean place and wolfed down a quick bowl of *manduguk*, meatball soup, and a bottle of beer.

Lupe was waiting when I pulled up in front of Ko Won's electronics place. "We should follow him, try to catch him in a more relaxed setting," she said, climbing into my car. She switched the radio station to KLVE and the booming tropical sound of Juan Luis Guerra and his band 440. I pulled onto the side street so we could watch the front of the store and the parking lot behind it. There was a huge, immaculate white Mercedes in the lot, and we agreed it was probably his. About twenty minutes later the Mercedes, driven by Ko Won, pulled out of the lot, passed our street, and headed toward the magenta sunset.

He continued out of Koreatown, past the oak- and palm-lined fringe of Hancock Park, past the tire shops and soul food diners near La Brea, past San Vicente and Midway Hospital, where a guy I knew from law school had died of AIDS. He drove past Beverly Hills, past Rexford Park where men in white pants and shirts were bowling on the emerald grass, past the triangular twin towers of Century City to a southbound ramp of the 405 freeway.

"Where's he going?" Lupe wondered. I could tell she didn't know this part of town.

When he turned onto the Richard M. Nixon freeway I knew he was going to the Marina.

Marina del Rey is the largest man-made marina in the world. It was dredged out of a marsh fronting the Santa Monica Bay. An improbable Italian Renaissance hotel stands next to a place designed to look like a cannery. Condos and luxury apartments in garish architectural ménages of Vegas and the South Seas line the artificially created channels where the boats are moored. Still, it's hard to make water look bad, and I noticed Lupe was looking about eagerly. The last rays of sun struck the masts of the sailboats, gilding them gold. There are nearly a dozen steak and seafood restaurants with busy bars in the Marina. At one time there was a hot singles and pickup scene in those bars. Rumors about airline stewardesses abounded. They got off their flights, came back to the apartments they shared with fifteen other stewardesses, poured themselves into jeans and hot pants, drenched themselves with Fracas from duty free shops, and went out and fucked everyone until it was time to get back on another plane headed east. Now, with the epidemic, I wondered if anyone was still playing those games.

Ko Won drove to Via Dolce, turned onto a eucalpytus-lined street, and then disappeared into an underground garage beneath a condo called the Buccaneer. It was directly across from a restaurant. I pulled into its lot and parked at the far end. I glanced at the sign above the restaurant. The Rusty Wharf. Despite the warm breeze and the inviting dance of the palms that framed it, the restaurant didn't look very busy. There were less than half a dozen other cars in the lot, although they were all Jags and Mercedeses and BMWs.

"Are we going to get to eat?" Lupe asked. "I'm hungry."

I shook my head guiltily. We could be in for a long night. Another Mercedes pulled into the lot, and two Korean guys got out. Even from where we were I could see that both of their suits were expensive and the jackets slightly oversize to accommodate guns. They went into the restaurant. Not another five minutes went by but another luxury car pulled up in front of the Rusty Wharf. Three more Korean guys wearing the same kind of dark suits got out and went in. Two of them wore their hair in ponytails.

"Would I be off the mark if I said those guys look like gangsters?" Lupe asked.

Ko Won, in navy boat shoes, white slacks, and a navy cashmere sweater, came out of the condominium and ambled across the street toward the restaurant. I stretched my hand out toward Lupe, motioning her to remain still. Ko Won glanced in our direction. Would he be expecting to see us again? Had Kim told him about us? If Kim was tight with Ko Won, why hadn't she gotten him and his men to take care of Jin's killer? Ko Won walked quickly to the Rusty Wharf without another look in our direction and went inside.

I shook my head. "Shit. What's this nice businessman community leader doing here?"

"Let's get out of here," Lupe whispered. "We can't fuck

around with professionals. *Firme* suits and packing rods, are you kidding me? We'll get killed."

"You said you knew what you were getting into." I reached under the seat and took out the .38. I held it out to her.

Lupe looked off into the distance. The only sound was the clanking of metal fittings and ropes against the masts of the sailboats.

"Be careful with this. It's loaded." I laid the gun in her lap. I showed her the safety, but she just kept shaking her head and staring through me. "I'm going in there to talk with him."

"Right, so he'll know you followed him here. That's very smart."

"He thinks I'm a reporter."

"And I'm Little Bo Peep. Don't you think Kim's told him who you are?"

How much could I trust Kim? I knew she'd lied to me about three things. Three is an important number. I adjusted the rearview mirror toward myself and combed my hair. I looked scared. Had Lupe noticed? "Move the car to the opposite end of the street. Then I want you to get into his building, scout out his condo, see what you can learn. We'll meet back at the car in forty minutes." I glanced at my watch. I noticed Lupe wasn't wearing one. I unfastened mine and offered it to her.

Lupe shook her head. She opened her purse and took out a Rolex, which she strapped on her wrist. What were those things worth? $8,000? $15,000? A fucking felony. What else had Lupe been keeping from me, I wondered. She got out of the car and came around to the driver side. "The reporter shtick's not going to work."

I got out of the car and looked at the boats. It was so

peaceful. I heard the car start up and Lupe drive away, leaving me alone in the dark. I walked toward the Rusty Wharf. Although I'd learned to sail on the Chesapeake Bay when I was a kid, I hadn't sailed in at least fifteen years. I wondered if I still remembered how. I quit sailing because I got tired of my father yelling at me all the time. "Tack! Draw in the jib! Can't you pay attention?" It had been exhausting being the daughter who couldn't do anything right.

The entrance to the bar had a tremendous view of the south channel. The Rusty Wharf was the usual light-pine-furniture and potted-ficus kind of place popular along the beach. The kind of place everyone on earth thinks all of So Cal looks like. Pale buffed wood, big picture windows, salad bar. My favorite is the kind of dark seaside dive with little windows like portholes. When I go out I want to be waited on. I don't want to have to go to a salad bar, stand in line, then haul my own chopped greens back to the table. A hundred-foot yacht was in a slip in front of the restaurant and beyond that a cruising catamaran I guessed to be a Solaris 42.

At the bar were a couple of bleached blondes with permanent tans and guys who looked as if they smoked too much. The women wore the official LA uniform: skintight T-shirts, miniskirts, bare legs, and black cowboy boots. I spotted Ko Won sitting at a large round table near the far wall. He faced the room so he could survey everything. He was talking and laughing and the five dark suits with him looked as if they were having as much fun as possible without actually being relaxed. I hoped Lupe wasn't going to run into any trouble trying to case his condo. Would there be anyone guarding it? What would Ko Won do if he knew who I was and that I wanted to con him into telling me what he knew about Kim? I wished I'd followed Lupe's advice and changed clothes. Something a bit sexy. Exposed flesh. I wanted Ko Won to think I was just like the other bimbettes. Only with better legs.

I went over to the bar and sat down on an empty stool next to a guy in his late fifties. He was about the same age as my father. I smiled at him and ordered a glass of white wine. He was drunk. He smiled back.

I had to keep Ko Won from knowing I'd followed him to the Marina. I nodded at the drunk. I'd prostitute myself for verisimilitude. My smile felt plastered on my face. Lupe would have pulled the barstool close to him and whispered in his ear. She would have managed to bend forward when she spoke so that her exciting cleavage would be in his face. I discreetly unbuttoned the top button of my silk shirt. "I'd like for you to do something for me," I whispered.

His smile turned into a horny, stomach-churning leer. How could Lupe and Venus Howard put up with this?

"There's a guy over there, I'm trying to get a job in his company, and I don't want him to know I came here alone. I don't want him to think I'm that kind of a girl." I swiveled further in his direction to give him a peep down my blouse, but he seemed unaware of the subtlety of my movement. No wonder Lupe wore halter tops so often. I laid my hand on the forearm of the stranger and squeezed it in a way I hoped was suggestive. "Would you just wait right here for me while I go talk to him, sugar? And then you and I'll have some fun."

Ko Won didn't give any sign of recognition when I marched up to his table and stood in front of him. Was it true all of us white people looked alike? Finally he nodded and put his scotch down on the table. The men with him put their drinks on the table too. Next to Ko Won was a hot-looking guy about my age with a ponytail and a midnight black two-button Armani suit. Could he be the man who'd attacked me? He moved his hand quickly but discreetly under his jacket to his gun. Ko Won smiled at me as he shook his head almost imperceptibly at the guy. The other man with a ponytail was a few years older. Could it have been him? He had a black suit too.

"Hi," I bubbled. "I thought that was you. I was just over at the bar having a drink with a friend when I saw you."

Ko Won glanced over at the bar. I wiggled my fingers in a little wave at the drunk at the bar who looked back at me with uncertainty, then lifted his glass in my direction. I saw the other ponytailed man's eyes flicker over me, looking more at my breasts than my face. Ko Won made a slight gesture toward the table with his hand.

The younger of the ponytail guys got up and brought a chair over from another table. He held it out for me, seating me between Ko Won and himself. He was my height, just like my attacker.

The last man I'd been this close to was from one of these bars. A commodities broker I let pick me up during a tequila shooter happy hour at a Mexican restaurant on the main channel a couple of years ago.

Ko Won's man let his hand brush against me as he guided me into the chair. He sat down, drawing his chair close to mine. I glanced quickly at him as he settled into my peripheral vision. He had long black lashes and eyes the color of moss. I wondered if he had contacts. His cheekbones were carved from ice. He was the color of caramel. I felt a little wet. Yes! It was good to know all of my parts were still working. But was he the guy in the Chusok mask?

"I'm glad to see you again," I told Ko Won. I quickly inventoried his casual but expensive clothing and rings. He wore a large blue-white diamond on each hand. Was he really a gangster? I'd never met anyone in organized crime. I knew undocumented workers who got into fights in barrooms in La Puente. Black guys from Inglewood who were picked up for commercial burglaries. I knew the occasional bad-check writer. "There's something I wanted to explain to you." I wished I'd brought my drink over from the bar with me. "When I told you I worked for *Esquire* magazine, that wasn't exactly true. I'm a free-lance writer, and I'm doing an article to sell to them. I sort of exaggerated because I thought it would help me schedule an appointment with you—"

"Have you interviewed anyone else for this article?" he interrupted.

"Korean people?" I stalled. I looked around the table, hoping to catch a friendly eye. The men stared back at me with blank, hard looks. The older ponytailed man picked up his drink, with his left hand rattling the ice cubes as he brought it to his lips. I wasn't able to get a good look at his hand to see if it was the same one which had grabbed my breast.

"We're Korean-Americans," Ko Won said.

I nodded, embarrassed. "Several."

"Who?" he asked.

"Kim Oh." I had to go ahead, move. "To get a woman's perspective on the riots, their aftermath . . ."

"Kim?" He said her name without inflection or surprise.

I nodded. Had she been Ko Won's squeeze on the night they met Hector? Or was Lupe right about her? That she was just another working girl? The tattoo meant something. Was it like a brand? Did someone own her? Ko Won? "Yeah, she was great. What a role model! A woman business owner. Strong. Dynamic. Your community must be very proud of her."

"You know Kim?" he mused. Had she told him anything about me? What would she have told him? What did he know about Jin's murder? If he didn't know, why hadn't Kim told him? Maybe she didn't tell him everything. Maybe there were things she didn't want him to know. He didn't take his eyes off my face. I felt as if I was playing poker with a viper.

I nodded again. "She said you'd been instrumental in helping her." I was betting that Kim kept secrets from Ko Won and he would wonder what they were.

Ko Won looked thoughtful, and there were a few uneasy beats before he replied. "Well, why didn't you just tell me you knew Kim?" He laughed. "I wondered why your photographer didn't have a camera when you came to my store." He said something in Korean. All the men laughed.

I laughed too. "Yeah, that was crazy. I just graduated with a degree in journalism and I guess I'm still pretty green. That's why it's so important to me to get such a big story. 'The New Los Angeles!' "

Ko Won looked at his scotch as though he'd just rediscovered it. He took a big executive pull on it. They were all smoking Marlboros. There was a lot of masculine energy. I could practically smell testosterone in the air. "I'd be glad to have you interview me. To talk about redevelopment . . ."

"New businesses!" I cheered.

". . . building new relationships with blacks and Hispanics . . . ," he added.

"Brotherhood!"

". . . and the sports center," he said.

"Right on!" I wondered why he didn't offer to buy me a drink. My mouth felt dry and my heart was pounding.

"My business associates," he said, indicating the pistol-packing crew at the table. I wondered what business they were in. Drugs? "We were having an informal meeting about some new property developments in Koreatown. Let's you and I meet at Kim's restaurant the night of Chusok festival. Tomorrow," he proposed.

I didn't want Kim to find out I was using Ko Won to check up on her. "I know the article's about connectedness, interrelationship, but I don't want it to look like I'm playing favorites or just relying on a couple of sources. Maybe it would be better if we went somewhere else." That sounded pretty lame to me. I was sweating bullets.

"In Korea we say we don't really know a person until we eat a meal with them," he said.

I was worn out by the inscrutable Oriental business. I was starting to panic. Were they involved in smuggling? Hijacked electronics goodies? A protection racket? "Great. I'd love to try Korean food."

He told me that the food was good at Kim's and that it was all made from her old family recipes. He said it was just like eating in someone's home.

"Soul food," I said.

He looked puzzled.

"Means home-cooked. Family cooking."

Ko Won nodded back at me. "That's the secret of Kim's success! Family." He laughed. "Soul food." He said something in Korean to his cronies who laughed in response.

Out of the corner of my eye I saw the drunk get up from the bar and totter toward Ko Won's table. He bumped into a middle-aged couple dressed in matching nautical sweaters as he bore down upon us.

Although I'd been told several times Dorothy put up the

money, I asked Ko Won if he'd helped finance the restaurant.

He nodded and said that in '87, when Kim opened the restaurant, it was hard for women to get loans from banks. "I loaned her money and I cosigned at the bank with her to guarantee another loan."

"I know her godmother owned a restaurant in Seoul, but Kim must only have been a college student. Weren't you worried she didn't know how to run a restaurant?"

"She'd just graduated from SC."

A lie. Or had Kim lied about SC to Ko Won also? What else, how many other things, might she have lied to him about? The sun shuddered as it fell beneath the horizon.

The drunk drew closer to the table. He was wearing boat shoes and a pair of faded khakis that hung below his gut.

Ko Won looked in the direction of the approaching drunk. "Your boyfriend's getting impatient. Tomorrow night we'll have a special dinner. Soul food, right?" Everyone at the table laughed again. He turned to the guy next to me and spoke quickly in Korean. I knew that it was a language that depended on inflection for meaning. Every time he spoke he sounded angry. He turned to me and said he'd told the guy to show me to my car. "And help your friend."

I pushed back my chair and stood up from the table. The guy next to me stood up. I like ponytails on men.

I said good-bye to Ko Won.

The man took my arm. His fingers were warm and firm on my bare tanned biceps. He bowed to Ko Won and started to walk me in the direction of the entrance. "Let's go," he whispered in my ear.

I nodded dumbly. "Your English is good."

"I'm from Bellflower."

The drunk stumbled toward us.

"I don't have my car. I came with my friend." I pointed at the drunk, who'd stopped near the corner of the bar to shoot the breeze with an equally drunk sun-mottled matey in a yachting cap. "Jeez, I see I'm going to have to drive tonight." I prayed the drunk hadn't walked over to the bar from one of the neighboring condos.

I stepped away from my handsome escort, wrapped my arms around the drunk, and gave him a big kiss. He tasted like Tanqueray and tonic. He was surprised, but not too surprised to push his tongue down my throat. I wanted to barf, but I pulled away smiling. "Come on, sugar, let's go. Over to your place. Give me the car keys."

The drunk started to protest, but his pal, giving me a slimy once-over twice, clapped him on the back in approval. Was this what Lupe had to put up with? Bloated old farts who couldn't get hard without an endless jaw-cracking blow-job. I glanced at my watch as I secured my arm more firmly around his waist and started to lead him toward the exit. He handed me the keys. It was nearly an hour since I'd left Lupe. Would she be waiting for me at the corner as I'd told her to?

The Korean stood close by with a slight smirk on his lips. He followed us to the fern-decked foyer.

"Hang on, baby," the drunk slurred, lurching away from me. "Don't go away. I gotta piss like a racehorse." He stumbled into the head.

"I'll wait in the parking lot," I said to his retreating back. Asshole better come back, I thought, or I'm in deep kimchi.

The Korean and I walked outside. It was dark. The sky was full of as many stars as you can see in Los Angeles. Across the water drifted the sound of laughter from a party on a balcony overlooking the channel. He took my arm again, more firmly, and moved me toward the moored boats. He smelled like Karl Lagerfeld cologne.

"Bellflower's a nice place," I said.

He pushed me along quickly to the chain link fence at the edge of the water. I glanced back at him. He was wearing Ferragamo wing tips. The light from the restaurant and the lights from the apartment buildings seemed far away. What had Ko Won told him to do with me? Below us the expensive and beautiful sailboats strained against their moorings. Kill me? I felt pretty certain he was the guy in the Chusok mask, but it had been too dark to really examine his left hand. He was behind me. I remembered a joke.

An old guy at a retirement home asks one of the lady residents to go out boating on the lake with him the following Sunday afternoon.

"Oh, that would be very nice," she says.

They go out to the lake and get into the boat. "Up or down?" he asks her.

She rips off his clothes, rips off her clothes, and makes crazy passionate love to him. He's amazed. But pleased.

I wondered what it would be like to take my clothes off with a guy as good-looking as this Korean.

The following week the old guy asks the woman if she wants to go out to the lake again. She says yes. They go out to the lake. Get in the boat and he asks her, "Up or down?"

She looks at him, puzzled.

"Up or down?" he asks.

I glanced at the guy with the ponytail. What would it be like to have him naked, above me? The ponytail didn't mean anything. Lots of men in Los Angeles have ponytails.

"What are you talking about?" the old lady in the joke says.

"Last week I took you boating. I asked you 'up or down' and you ripped off your clothes, you ripped off my clothes, and made incredible love to me. The best I've ever had."

"Oh," she says. "I didn't have my hearing aid in. I thought you said, 'Fuck or drown.' "

What would I do if he tried to grab me? If he tried to pull me down from behind I'd throw him off balance and chop him in the neck hard enough to mess up his windpipe for a while. Why had I thought I was so smart? That I could mess around with these Korean guys? If he moved to put his other hand on me to try to push me over the fence, I'd twirl and with a roundhouse kick him in the balls. I pulled my arm away from his grasp and turned to face him. "Thanks for everything. I better get going."

He pulled a gun from a holster strapped in his armpit. He held the gun in front of my face. It was big. Even in the dark I could see it was a 9mm Beretta. It's hard to calculate the stopping power of a handgun bullet. Human reaction to an impacting bullet is complex. You have to calculate permanent crush cavity (PCC) PCC EST. =6.3×(VOLUME) 45.0 and calculate temporary stretch cavity (TSC) TSC EST.– .92×(VOLUME) 56.0, therefore one-shot stopping power equals OSS= (PCC ESTIMATE TSC ESTIMATE) 2. That Beretta could scatter my ashes out to sea.

It was the same kind of gun the guy who killed Jin Oh used. Ko Won could have told him to steal the money. Maybe Kim's position with the gang wasn't as secure as I'd imagined. They'd turned on her and moved against her family. I looked down the barrel of the Beretta. It's also a weapon favored by the police. They cost about $400. If you buy it on the street, $500. Most of the cowboys banging today go for Magnums or semiautomatics they can convert to automatics.

"You playing cops or robbers?" I whispered.

The Beretta disappeared back into its holster. He quickly withdrew a badge from a pocket inside his coat and flashed it at me.

"Show me."

He handed the badge to me. It was LAPD. It said his name was Edward Lu. *Adiós* law career. *Hasta luego* Clarence Darrow. My knees buckled, and I grabbed at the fence to hold myself up. He reached for me as I swayed.

"You're no reporter and you're stepping on an official investigation. I don't want to see you around any of these people again. They're killers. That guy with the ponytail sitting across from you, the one staring at you, he's a convicted rapist. Did time at Folsom." He dropped his arms and studied me. "You have pretty hair."

I didn't want to move away from him or for the moment to end. The moonlight caressed me, and I knew I looked platinum and pearl.

A motor started up nearby, and a boat pulled out of its slip headed south to the main channel and Mexico. I stepped back. I handed him his badge. His hands were small, and the ring finger on his left hand looked as if it had been busted. We looked at each other. I didn't know if he was a cop or not.

We walked back to the front of the restaurant without saying anything more. The drunk was pacing back and forth looking for me. I asked him where his car was. We got into his Lincoln, with a personalized plate that said HOT DDDY, and Edward Lu went back inside the Rusty Wharf.

The drunk leaned across the seat trying to fondle me, but I elbowed him and hit the gas, laying rubber out of the parking lot. We raced beneath the canopy of palms toward the corner where I'd told Lupe to wait. Under a streetlight was the old Fiat. Lupe was listening to loud Mexican rock and roll. I screeched to a halt behind her. The drunk fumbled with his pants, pulling his dick out.

"Chew on it yourself." I bolted from the car.

The Fiat roared to life, and we lickety-splitted out of the Marina.

"Oh, man, you're not going to believe what I found out," Lupe exclaimed as she drove. "That condo. Every bedroom has floor-to-ceiling mirrors. The big corner apartments like Ko Won's all have jacuzzis in the bathroom. . . ."

"You see his place?"

"No way! You think I'm gonna B and E? I'm on probation! I been talking to some girls who live there. They didn't know him—there's three hundred units in the building—but they told me they see Korean guys coming in and out all the time. They said that joint you went into's like gangster city. The guy who owns it has a rep for not cooperating with the cops."

"I met a cop in there. With Ko Won."

Lupe downshifted to make the turn onto Venice Boulevard. "Right, a cop. Was he wearing a uniform?"

"Undercover, but he showed me his badge. I'm telling you, it's the only time in my life I've ever been glad to see a cop." I didn't say anything about how good-looking he was or that I'd thought I liked it when he held me in his arms.

"He must be narcotics then," said Lupe.

I looked at her.

"Ice."

"Methamphetamine?"

Lupe nodded as she got on the freeway headed back for Koreatown. "You got it, homegirl. This chick I talked to, a pro in a four-hundred-dollar La Perla bathing suit just like I seen in *Vogue* magazine, hanging out by the pool, had a cellular phone. I asked her if she knew where I could score and then she was telling me how the Koreans are big into the ice biz." Lupe turned north toward Dorothy's and continued to chatter excitedly about the fancy call girls, the fancy Marina condos, and the fancy cars. She kept glancing with rapt pride at her stolen Rolex.

I fell silent. We passed hundreds of squalid apartments on the edge of the Pico-Union as we drove up Vermont to Koreatown. The palm trees wept in the moonlight. There were no new jobs. No new schools had been built. I am a member of the National Lawyers Guild. I had believed in equality, fraternity, and the Bill of Rights. What had the Rebellion changed? Now the city was a burned-out Stonehenge of bricks and asbestos.

Was Ko Won involved in drug dealing? It was possible, but stereotypical. So Hollywood. But why else would a narc be with him? The cop from Bellflower, if that's who he was, could have infiltrated Ko Won's group. And Kim? How did she fit in?

"Take me to get my car," I told Lupe. "I got to go talk to Dorothy now. Alone. I get the feeling she doesn't like you."

Lupe shrugged wordlessly away and pumped up the volume of the Mexican rock and roll higher.

Dorothy was in the kitchen making a meat-and-vegetable dish she told me was called *sinsollo*. She gave me a Wedgwood plate, and we carried the food out to the dining table.

I wasn't hungry. I wanted a drink. "You said you'd tell me about the Queen Min box."

"You have to know more about my country." Dorothy pushed her plate of uneaten food away. "We come here as refugees and you expect us to forget our history. For us to metamorphose into something new. No, our memories are in our blood."

She told me the story her mother had told her when she was a child of ten. Her mother, Sae Oh, was born in the late 1800s to a family of poor laborers in the capital city. When Sae was thirteen she became a servant in the royal palace, where she attracted the attention of Queen Min, who made her a chambermaid and, as she grew older, a confidante. When the Japanese invaded the country again, the royal family believed their days were numbered.

"Queen Min gave my mother a rare emerald, as large as a baby's fist, to be hidden in a place of safety until after the occupation."

"Must have been worth a fortune."

Dorothy nodded. Sae left the palace and traveled north up into the mountains as the queen had told her. She buried the emerald in a pouch of leather beneath a pine tree on the edge of a cliff. When Sae returned to the palace the queen gave her a carved box as a reward to commemorate the journey.

"The box is carved with the pictures of pine and mountains. The number of pieces of inlaid mother of pearl are the exact number of miles it took Sae to travel to the mountain."

"The box could be used as a map to find the emerald!"

Dorothy sighed. "Shortly after my mother returned to the palace, the Japanese executed Queen Min."

I didn't say anything. To me it was ancient history, but I could see from the light in Dorothy's eyes it was still a real part of her life.

"It was near this time of year, October."

Dorothy said Sae had been able to flee the palace with the carved box. She returned to her family and later married.

I asked if her mother had ever gone back to the mountains to retrieve the emerald.

Dorothy nodded her head. "She tried. I was only ten years old. My mother, nearly fifty then. She'd been involved for years in the struggle for liberation from the Japanese."

"I didn't know. . . ."

"Decades before Gandhi, the Korean people used nonviolence to try to free themselves," Dorothy said impatiently, eager to finish her story. Her mother had traveled back up to the mountain, but the area was controlled by the Japanese. "My mother was captured."

Dorothy got up from the table and went into the kitchen, where I heard her filling a kettle with water.

"Did she come home?"

"Died on the mountain."

I pushed the food around on the plate. How could we remember history if it kept vanishing in front of our eyes? Dorothy's apartment showed no trace that a violent murder had taken place there a couple of days before.

"Is the emerald still buried in Korea?" I asked.

Dorothy reentered the dining area carrying a tray with a ceramic teapot and two cups. She poured me a cup of ginseng tea. "Yes. In the North."

"The mountain's in North Korea?" I could understand that the box was valuable in and of itself. It was wood, carved. It had historical significance, but would someone steal it because it was a map? "How could anybody get in or out of North Korea?"

"My country will be reunited. It's only a matter of time." Dorothy fell silent, her head bent over the cup in front of her. "But not my time. I lived through three wars. Saw Los Angeles in flames. Soon I'll die."

"But you're in perfect health. You do Tae Kwon Do. . . ."

"I don't want to live. Too much pain. My mother, my child, my sister all taken away from me."

"You still have Kim," I argued.

Dorothy looked up at me, but steam clouded her face and I couldn't see her eyes.

A blue light was on in the *do jang* of my master, Sun Lee. It was nearly quarter to twelve on Friday night. Less than nineteen hours before I'd face Ko Won again. How was I going to break it to Dorothy that her granddaughter was tied up with a gangster? Dorothy had had enough disappointments. I hesitated for an instant in the dim doorway of the *do jang*. The advanced class of which I'd become a member ended at ten. Although the street was zoned for commercial use only, I knew Sun Lee lived in a room at the back of the *do jang*. I knocked on the door.

There was no reply but the wail of a saxophone and the warped thud of a drum machine. Was he listening to Captain Beefheart?

"It's Whitney Logan," I called.

No answer.

I was surprised that the door was unlocked. Had someone been there? Was there a problem? In the strange blue light the immaculate white walls of the *do jang* glistened like a glacier. I took my high-tops and socks off in a hurry and left them in the carved oak rack next to the front door. I felt the familiar padded floor beneath my feet. I walked down the hallway toward the back of the *do jang*. "Sun Lee?"

At the end of the hall a candle flickered, its yellow flame dancing in the dark.

"Sun Lee?" I walked past the men's dressing room, which was the first room to the left. "Tiger? Golden Tiger?"

A screaming form jumped out at me from the black recesses of the dressing room. My arm was twisted up behind my back. I lunged forward as though accepting my attacker's body weight and with a quick movement shoved back. I dropped into fighting position preparing to kick.

"You missed class this evening. First time." My teacher abruptly let go of me and bowed.

"Jesus Christ, Tiger. You scared me. I thought there was someone here."

"You need more discipline." He straightened his shirt. "You should be practicing more for your promotion to red belt."

I nodded, pleased. "I have to talk to you. I know it's late . . ."

He led me back into his room, which I'd never seen before. He flipped on the overhead light. There was a futon on the floor, a Sony tv, a Sony cd player, and a poster from a competition he'd been in in Long Beach. A teddy bear with one eye sat on the futon. Sun Lee turned off the strange music. I sat on the floor and told him everything that had happened in Koreatown, beginning with the murder of Jin. I ended by telling him about the guys I'd met with Ko Won in the Marina earlier that evening.

"You're involved with a gang, Whitney. Let the police handle it."

"The cops might already be in. I think one of the guys at the bar with Ko Won's a narc."

"He told you that?"

I nodded. "Saw his badge. Name's Edward Lu."

Golden Tiger shook his head. "They're playing with you. No narc's going to tell you who he is. Particularly if he's undercover."

"So where'd he get a badge? You don't get those in a box of Wheaties."

"Made in Hong Kong. Taiwan. Korea." The Golden Tiger grinned at me. "Isn't that why everyone fears the Koreans and the Japanese, because of their ability to make knockoffs of American goods?"

I put my head down, ashamed. A toy badge. How could I not have thought of that? I asked my teacher to tell me what he knew about the Korean gangs.

"There's five gangs. With thousands of members. Primarily in Koreatown, but also the South Bay and Diamond Bar. They're totally different from black gangs or the latinos. They're not territorial. They're influenced by the *yakuza*."

I'd heard of *yakuza*. They are Japanese gangs, organized, like the Mafia. The Golden Tiger said the Japanese occupation of Korea and the use of Korean laborers in Japan had spread the knowledge of *yakuza*.

"These Korean gangs are mostly business oriented," he said. "They deal in specific crimes—"

"Like stockbrokers?"

He nodded, then went on to tell me that the members take blood oaths. If they break the gang's bylaws they are killed. They use secret handshakes and recite poems to identify themselves. They have special tattoos. When the immigration law changed in '65, the gangs began to grow. The new kids from Korea were quick to assimilate. "The old folks wouldn't use English. The youth want to be Western." The old structure of the family began to crumble.

The gangs started at Uni High, where the Korean kids

banded together for protection against the Chinese. The Korean Killers started hanging out around Vermont and Olympic. Soon there were the American Burgers, Rainbow, and the South Bay Killers. I interrupted and asked him who belonged to the gangs.

"Kids. College students. They get recruited, get allowances, credit cards, cars."

The reason Kim dropped out of college! To work with the gang. It was good to imagine they were an equal opportunity employer. A step forward for women. We're never going to be equal until we can all commit the same crimes. "So they're not usually as old as the guys I met today?"

Golden Tiger shrugged. "They can be sixteen, twenty-five, in their mid-fifties, and all be in the same gang. There's tremendous respect for age. The older ones, the big brothers—they sponsor the younger guys and use them as eyes and ears and muscle."

"What about ice? How's that fit?"

"The gangs are in business. It might be prostitution. It might be methamphetamine. It costs hundreds of thousands of dollars to get into the ice business."

A guy I'd represented last year told me about ice. Freebase and stay high for twenty-four hours. "How would they sell it?"

"Mostly in bars. The bargirls."

I bet Kim worked in a bar before they set her up in the restaurant. "Ko Won's got a real profitable-looking business selling electronics goodies."

The Golden Tiger resettled himself on the futon, pushing a small red pillow out of his way. "Probably a totally legit business. A guy like that could front the money for the ice—"

"And then resell it for distributions! Or use his store for money laundering!" He could be using Kim's Cafe James Dean for a laundry. "He's a straight-up fucking gangster! I knew he had too many pictures of himself with politicians in his office."

"A dead giveaway," the Golden Tiger agreed. We fell silent and watched the candlelight flicker on the walls. I got up to leave.

He cracked his knuckles. "Even if that guy you met tonight is a cop you can't trust him, especially if he's a member of the Asian Gang Unit. Even other cops don't trust them. If he's real and you get in the way of a takedown . . ." He shook his head in a sad, thoughtful way.

I stood up and adjusted my purse on my shoulder. For over a year I had relied on Sun Lee to help me grow strong.

"Don't go back to Koreatown," he said.

I shrugged. I'd given my word to Dorothy and Lupe. Courtesy Integrity Perseverance Self-Control Indomitable Spirit. Those were the tenets Sun Lee had taught me in the *do jang*. "I don't have enough on these people to go to the police. They know my friend Lupe. I got her involved in this mess. I have to go back."

He chewed his lip in silent contemplation for a moment before nodding. "Every circle must be round." He accompanied me to the front door and watched me put on my shoes and socks. The Golden Tiger sank gracefully into fighting stance, stretched his arms in front of him, his hands moving like mad birds, hands moving almost faster than the eye could see, showing me how to remain fluid. Then he drew back and bowed.

He closed the door behind me. I heard him lock it, then the dead bolt slid into place. The street was quiet. It was midnight. Although I wanted to go see the Petersons who had adopted Kim, I didn't think they'd want to meet anyone new this late at night. I headed home to try to catch a few hours' beauty sleep.

With my car's high beams on, I pulled into the parking area behind my apartment. I switched off the lights and the engine and sat studying the blackness surrounding me. I thought again about the guy in the Chusok mask who'd jumped me here. He'd been about my height. Probably weighed thirty or thirty-five pounds more than I did. Black hair in a ponytail, like Edward Lu. I remembered the guy's hands on my breasts and the sound of his disgusting breathing.

The shadows didn't move. There was only the usual lethargic swish of traffic from Dickens Avenue and the sound of people drinking in apartment number 3. I went upstairs. There was a message from Harvey Kaplan reminding me my rent was overdue. I made myself a toasted peanut butter and jelly sandwich and a bourbon and Coke. I checked all the windows to make sure they were locked. I shoved my tatty black couch in front of the apartment door before climbing into the shower, where I stood for a long time with the hot water beating down on me. I set the alarm for six, made another drink, took a couple of Excedrin PMs, and slept with my gun under my pillow.

I started awake, hot and sweaty, before the alarm and dressed in the dark. I doubted the Petersons would still be living at the address that appeared on the adoption forms. No one in LA lives at the same place for more than a year. I pulled on black jeans, a black T-shirt, and tennis shoes. Splashed a drop of Chanel No. 22 on each wrist. I pushed the couch back to its usual place along the wall, grabbed a rotting banana from the kitchen, and hurried out.

The Petersons' address was in North Glendale, called the Rancho San Rafael when the Mexicans owned all the land. It's difficult to find anything left of Glendale's romantic past. After the gringo conquest, the land was subdivided. Its second history began in the early twentieth century when the Pacific Electric Railroad extended its tracks northeast from Central Los Angeles.

The house was a small hacienda plastered with stucco on a tree-lined street in the area between the Glendale City Hall and Forest Lawn Memorial Park. A white station wagon stood in the driveway. Jacaranda blossoms littered the front yard.

I glanced at my watch. It wasn't quite seven yet. From down the block I heard the distant roar of a leaf blower as a Mexican gardener cleared the sidewalk in front of another stucco house. While I was deciding whether to go up to the Petersons' door, an elderly man in a plaid flannel bathrobe came out, looked up and down the street in a proprietary way, then stooped to pick up his LA *Times* from the well-swept driveway.

I went right over to him. "Mr. Peterson?"

He straightened and looked around suspiciously at me. He was tall and thin, like a big man who'd been deflated. He was sallow and had gray eyes. He looked as if he was in poor health.

"Reverend Luke Peterson?" I smiled. I didn't know his correct title. I'd been an Episcopalian. High Church of England. He could be the Grand Pooh-Bah for all I knew about his church, the Assembly of God. I smiled some more. He smiled tentatively. I put my hand out. "I'm Whitney Logan, a lawyer and a friend of Kim's. . . ."

A sour look crossed his face. "I don't know any Kim." He turned back toward his house and started to walk away from me.

I stayed right next to him. "Your daughter."

"I don't have a daughter."

"The girl from Korea you adopted."

He picked up speed, hurrying toward his door.

"When I went to check the Superior Court records, I saw your adoption papers," I said. "Therefore, ipso facto, you're her father."

He stopped and whirled toward me. "I paid a lawyer to set it aside. I have copies!"

I shook my head. "Must be lost then," I lied. "They're not in the file."

A gray-haired woman stuck her head out the front door. "Luke, what's happening?"

"Nothing, Mother. Nothing. Go back inside."

I bounced up to the front door like a friendly puppy. "Hi, Mrs. Peterson. I'm a friend of Kim's."

"Kim?" The gray-haired woman looked staggered.

"Look, I'm sorry I seem to have gotten off on the wrong foot here. I just came to talk to you about Kim—"

"She's in trouble again, isn't she?" said the gray-haired woman. She looked as if she was going to cry.

"Could we go inside?" I asked, stepping into the doorway before she could say anything.

"We don't want to have nothing to do with her, young lady, so you just get along now," snapped the reverend.

"Kim's your daughter and God don't make no junk." I'd seen that on a bumper sticker. I wished I knew something biblical to quote. "It wouldn't be Christian to turn me away, would it?"

"Luke." The old lady glared at him. "I want to hear about Kim. You can go have a cup of decaf if you don't want to hear it." She made a tight little thin-lipped smile at me as if she was afraid her dentures would pop out of her mouth. "Yes, dear, you come right in. Don't mind him. He's always grumpy before he has his coffee."

The reverend glared back at her as he showed me rather unceremoniously into the yellow chintz living room. A tedious print of a mythic Southwest crowded with mountains and horses hung above the couch in a gilt frame. Assorted spooky Jesus pictures filled the rest of the walls. On the coffee table a silver-plated bowl held candied orange slices and red-and-white peppermints in individual cellophane wrappers. I sat down on the couch. I smelled coffee in the next room, but they didn't offer me any.

"I didn't mean to upset you," I said quickly. "Kim's not in any trouble; in fact, she's doing very well. She's expanding her business and thought you might want the opportunity to invest. . . ."

The old man put his hands up as if he didn't want to hear any more. "I knew it! I knew one day she'd try to get money out of us!"

"Her business?" gasped the woman. "She's doing well?"

"She owns a restaurant in Koreatown." I did tell the truth as often as possible just to keep things simple for myself.

"Kim owns a restaurant!" Mrs. Peterson shrieked. "Praise the Lord! You hear that, Luke? I been praying for that girl every day. Kim's doing well!"

"Couldn't be better," I agreed.

" 'Well,' hell," he snorted. "Tell her she'll never get a red cent out of me." Reverend Peterson stomped out of the room and returned with a photo album. He sat next to me on the couch and opened the album. Breathing in short, ragged breaths as if he was exhausted from so much exercise, he ruffled angrily through the pages to a picture of Kim when she was about five years old. She wore a cowgirl outfit, jeans, a printed shirt with mother-of-pearl snap buttons, red boots, and a miniature Stetson hat perched on her head. Her shiny black hair was cut in a Prince Valiant, and she was grinning broadly.

I chuckled appreciatively over the photo and nodded amiably at Mrs. Peterson.

"That's the only time Kim was doing well. And that's the

only good thing I've got to say about her." Reverend Peterson snapped the album shut and stood up impatiently.

"Luke," admonished the Reverend Mrs. with a practiced whine in her voice. "Don't talk like that. She was a precious child of God. We don't know what happened to her before we got her."

"Well, we sure know what happened after we got her, don't we?" he said. "The police calling our home nearly every night, the school principal sending us letters every week—"

"Where was her real mother?" I interrupted.

The old lady told me she'd been found near the DMZ by U.S. soldiers. No one knew who her mother was. "They brought her to us at the orphanage run by our church."

"Should have left her there," Reverend Luke snorted again at his wife.

"If we can save one soul, then our lives are blessed and have meaning," snapped her adopted mother. "Kim was a beautiful little girl. Remember when she was in first grade and the teacher wrote us that lovely note and told us she was the most well behaved child in the class?" The woman took the album from her husband and searched through it for the letter. Triumphantly she presented it to me. The faded letter was wrinkled, as though it had been perused many times. After a respectful examination I handed it back to her. I had a hard time imagining Kim as a child. I kept picturing her as I'd seen her the first time at Cafe James Dean in skintight jeans. Or nestling next to Hector Ramos, stroking his groin.

"What a wonderful act of charity on your part," I purred. "You must be very proud of her now."

"Certainly," Mrs. Peterson agreed a bit cautiously, glancing between me and her husband.

Reverend Peterson folded his bony arms across his bony

chest. An angry silence enveloped the room, smothering everything except the tick of a brass clock on the mantel above the fireplace.

"She did mention, however, that when she was fourteen you told her to leave," I prodded in a most polite tone.

"She said that? It's a damn lie!" swore Mrs. Peterson, her lips pulled back across her funky dentures so that she looked like an angry dog. "She ran away from home!"

"Tell her why if you're so eager to talk about Kim!" demanded her husband. "I'd been telling you for years that we should have shipped her back to the orphanage, but you wouldn't listen to me."

"It was so long ago, Luke," she mumbled. "It's time to forgive and forget. We won't talk about it any more." A Bible lay open on the coffee table.

"It's your fault she ran away," insisted the old man. "No wonder she ended up on the streets."

"My fault! I came home early from helping at the women's auxiliary meeting one afternoon because I wasn't feeling well. . . ."

"I'm sure you always did your best," I said.

The old man gave me a withering glance before picking up his attack on his wife. "You should have stayed home to look after her instead of gallivanting all around town."

". . . I saw a motorcycle up near the front door. I didn't know anyone who had a motorcycle. I went into the house to see what was happening. . . ."

"I told you not to let her hoodlum friends over here!" Reverend Peterson shook with anger. I thought he might pop off in front of me.

". . . I heard loud rock and roll music coming from Kim's bedroom. I walked down the hall. I called her name, but she didn't answer. I threw open the door to her bedroom. . . ."

"Go on, Mother! You're the one who always said they were nice kids."

". . . Kim was in bed with a man. They were naked. They were . . ."

"Some man!" sneered the reverend. "He jumped up and put his clothes on and ran right out the door. But Kim . . ."

". . . She just laid there, naked as a jaybird, grinning at me." The old woman shook her head as though trying to clear it of the ugly picture. "I told her there's a name for women who act like that."

"Whore!" spat Reverend Peterson.

"She jumped out of bed."

"That's when she ran away?" I asked.

The old woman looked down at the rug. "I slapped her In the face." She started to cry, and the reverend put his arm around her. "We couldn't do anything for her. Kim was wilder than a dog. Impure."

"You abandoned her! Shoved her out onto the street where anything could happen to her. She could've been killed."

Kim's adopted mother stopped snuffling long enough to say, "We didn't! We had a photo. It was old and crinkled, wrapped in silk and tied under Kim's clothes the day the soldiers found her. It had Korean writing on the back. It was a picture of a woman and a girl. The writing said the girl was Kim's mother."

"Chungmi!" I exclaimed. "The little girl in the picture was Chungmi."

They looked at me in surprise that I knew this. "Chungmi, the Shining Pearl—that was her mother's name. And the other woman was . . ." I stopped. I didn't know Dorothy's Korean name, but I was sure the other woman was Dorothy.

The reverend tried to shush his wife, but she struggled to finish her story, as if it was her last confession. "I was so angry that day. I ran to my room and got the photo. We'd never shown it to her before. I threw it in her face and told her to get out of my house."

"You didn't know if Kim had any relatives in LA and you didn't care what happened to her, did you?" I got up and slammed the door on the way out. How did they think she'd survive alone at the age of fourteen? But she had. She had the photo, and she found her way to Koreatown.

I wondered how long she'd been on the streets before she found Dorothy and how she'd managed to locate her grandmother.

I drove to Kim's apartment on San Luis Street in Koreatown, west of Vermont and up near Wilshire. It was nearly nine in the morning when I pulled up in front of her building. It was a renovated Spanish-style place, pink, probably built in the twenties, with a security system. A grocery bag full of used clothes I was going to give to the Salvation Army was in the trunk of the car. I took it out. When I saw a guy going for the door, I hurried toward the building, carrying the bag as if it was heavy. He held the door open for me and I marched in. We got on the elevator together. As soon as the man got off the elevator, I scooted out on the next floor, dumped the bag in the stairwell, and went up the stairs to the sixth floor where Kim lived.

The hall was empty. I knocked on the door. I knocked a couple of times. When no one answered, I took a thin metal file from my purse, got down on my knees, and started to work on the lock. A heavy adrenaline rush hit me. I forced myself to go slowly. I thought I felt the lock turn, so I pushed the file in more carefully as I twisted the doorknob. The door flew open.

"Hector!" The file clattered to the floor. I dropped my

purse onto the ground to hide the file. Hector Ramos stared down at me, frowning. I pushed the file under the purse, scooped it up, and stood. Hector moved toward me. I could stab him with the file if I had to.

"What are you doing?" he thundered.

"Tying my shoelace. What are you doing here? Providing maid service?" He was in his underwear and a cheesy-looking black silk robe with a dragon embroidered on it. I tried not to stare at his bikini underwear where the robe gaped open. He'd rocketed past light welterweight and was way too fat to be wearing bikinis. "I wanna see Kim."

He glanced down at my high heel pumps *sans* shoelaces. "You don't have no right to be here," he said. "I live here."

"Your name's not on the mailbox. Enjoy it while you can, Hector. Love's a beautiful thing."

He peered out into the hall. "Where's my slut sister? *La puta.*"

I juggled the purse carefully to get a better grip on the file. "At my office."

Hector howled with laughter. "Yeah, right. She's probably flat on her back on your desk right now screwing all the *mojados* she can pull off the street." He noticed his robe and tied the belt around his lumpy middle. "You here about the legal papers so I can get Joey?"

I shook my head. "Give it a rest with Joey. You think any Superior Court's gonna approve guardianship to someone who has known gang affiliations?"

Hector crossed his arms across his big chest. "I don't gangbang."

I shrugged. "I'm talking about Kim. Your bride-to-be."

"Shut your fucking mouth. You think everybody who's not white is in a gang?" He advanced toward me with his right hand forming a fist.

"Kim's not here," I guessed as I held my ground.

"I told you to shut the fuck up."

The file was about five inches long, sharpened into a point. "Where is she? Left you?"

"She went to get coffee."

"Great, then I'll come in. I could use a cup. Got business to talk to her about."

"What kind of business?"

"Girl stuff. She told me to come over."

Hector stood uncertainly in the doorway.

I pushed past him into the living room, my hand with the hidden file just inches from his gut. A dozen tall cans of Budweiser languished on the coffee table in front of the couch. "She didn't come home last night, did she?"

He didn't answer.

"There's a lot Kim hasn't told you."

He trooped into the living room and dropped onto the couch, where he'd been watching cartoons. There weren't any chairs in the living room. For a love nest it was sparsely and uncomfortably furnished.

"You're not the only man in her life. Has she told you about her thing with Ko Won?" I asked, wanting him to tell me how long she'd been gone so I could figure out where she was.

"You're full of shit! If you're going to wait here, then you keep your big mouth shut." Hector moved restlessly, as if he was thinking of getting up. "He's just a friend."

Hector looked a bit like Lupe. His eyes were wide set just like hers. "Then she must have told you he's the one who gave her the money for the restaurant," I said.

He settled back into the couch and waved his hand at me as if he was sure I didn't know my ass from a hole in the ground. "Her godmother Dorothy gave it to her!"

"Is that what Kim told you?" I grinned. "I wonder why she'd keep that a secret from you? Ko Won's your friend now too, isn't he?" I paused to see if Hector was following me.

Hector sat up and pulled the robe around himself. "I'm not gonna tell you to shut up again—"

"Dorothy's her grandmother, not her godmother. She said the people who adopted her and brought her from North Korea were dead. I saw them less than an hour ago. That she graduated from USC, but I found out by checking at the school that she never did. She told me that while she was at USC she got raped by a guy who was terrorizing the campus. She wasn't even a student there at the time. . . ."

"Maybe she got the date wrong. I'm not so good at dates myself." Hector picked up one of the Budweiser cans and shook it to see if it was empty.

"You're no good at telling time, Hector. You don't know what f-ing time it is." I ran my fingers across the dust on the coffee table. "Kim's got another crib somewhere. This isn't her home. And you're not her man." I pointed around the forlorn room. "Where are you getting the money for this pad, for Christ's sake, Hector?" I exploded. "Use your noodle."

"From my salary."

"Right! Don't you think it's a little weird that you're getting a salary for a job that doesn't exist? The sports center hasn't even begun construction yet!"

"I do PR!"

I turned and walked toward the bedroom. The bed hadn't been slept in. I flung open the closet doors. There was a black suit belonging to Hector. A pair of jeans. A dress and a skirt and blouse. Two pairs of high heels.

"Look at this, Hector. Two pairs of shoes! No woman owns only two pairs of shoes. Can't you figure it out?"

Hector stared from me to the closet and back again.

Hundreds of people were on the surrounding streets although it was only ten when I split from Hector. He told me he hadn't seen Kim since Thursday, two days ago. He didn't have any idea where she was, but I did.

It was a warm and brilliant morning. A Santa Ana blew in from the desert, burning the benevolent and blank blue sky. Hanging silk banners and washing down sidewalks, the citizens of Koreatown worked in hurried preparation for the noontime parade kicking off the celebration of Chusok. It was time for the harvest. The moon would be full at night. In some kinder, gentler time in a place where the leaves of the trees would change color and fall to the ground, the people would bring in their crops. The police were barricading the streets that ran perpendicular to Olympic.

I drove around an unmanned wooden sawhorse blocking San Marino Street and parked in front of the same blighted apartments where I'd parked the first time I'd gone to the Koreatown Civic Association. The same *salvadoreno* whistled languidly at me as I locked up my car. I hurried past him toward the community association. I was afraid it might be closed for the holiday. Here, the center of Koreatown, was the last place to check up on all the stories I'd been told about Kim before I went to find her. That meant I had to see Lee Joon again. She didn't like me. I was the foreigner.

Children's voices in high-pitched song rang out from the association building as I hurried toward it. Inside, the hall was full of kids, from toddlers to those in their teens, dressed in splendid costumes of red, cobalt blue, and emerald green silk. They wore satin caps and sashes of the most radiant yellow. Converse high-tops and blue jeans peeked from beneath their floor-length robes. Some of the older teens tried to get the excited little kids into a line based upon height. I recognized one of the organizers as the sulky dancer I'd seen at my first visit. She was stunning in a crimson robe with long gold sleeves. Her damaged skin was covered nicely with makeup, and she wore thick black eyeliner to highlight her delicate almond eyes.

"Hey, Roger Rabbit. Gonna be in the parade?" I asked.

The girl recognized me and nodded, flushed with pride. "Today I do a traditional dance. I'm the one who taught the little kids."

I asked her where Lee Joon was.

She pointed down the hall toward the art gallery. "There. With the old ones."

The art gallery was hung with sheets dyed a brilliant saffron. Draped in black robes that covered them completely, the silent old ones wore the strange pink Chusok masks identical to the one worn by the guy who'd attacked me. I knew I wouldn't be able to leave Koreatown without seeing him again.

Dozens of yellow and gold chrysanthemums were scattered across the shiny black floor. The old people trod barefoot across them so that their ancient yellow feet were caked with pollen and petals. They turned their backs to me, gathered into a circle, and began to dance. I stood inside the door. I was a pale fleck at the edge of the tapestry they were weaving. The room filled with their chorus of piercing shrill Mongolian cries. I couldn't understand a thing. I couldn't tell which one was Lee Joon or whether they were men or women. They moved gracefully, weightless, like ghosts. The leering, mocking masks turned again and again to inspect me as the circle wove slowly past me.

The music faded away, and the dancers spun to a slow arrhythmic conclusion. One of the figures broke away from the group and clapped its hands above its head. The group broke out in excited and well-pleased laughter, removing their masks and calling noisily to each other in Hangul. Lee Joon rushed up to me with her mask in her hand.

"What are you doing here? I don't think you come because you're a fan of Korean music and dance," she said. She looked annoyed to see me again.

"I have to talk to you. A few questions about Kim."

"I'm busy. Parade start soon. We dance in parade." She turned to rejoin her group.

"It'll just take a minute."

With her hands on her hips Lee Joon glared at me. "This is a special day for us. Don't try to push in here."

I told Lee Joon that Dorothy had sent me.

Lee Joon shook her hands dismissively at me. "She could have told you everything you want to know about Kim." Lee Joon looked impatiently around toward the other dancers, who were beginning to straggle out of the room. "Why should I help Dorothy? I never liked her. What's she to me?"

"The sister of your best friend, Jin." I took a few steps in the direction of the door. "I'll leave if you don't want to know what happened to Jin. I was the last person who saw her."

Lee Joon looked stunned for a moment, then she moved me to the far side of the gallery. The old ones finished hanging their masks on the saffron-covered walls and went out into the hall with the children. I heard the old people singing, then above them the voices of the children joining in.

"What do you know about Jin?" Lee Joon asked in a worried whisper. "Tell me!"

"Not so fast. I need answers to some questions first." I told her I thought she'd locked me in the steam room at the baths. "It's not too late for me to report it to the police." I shoved my forearm in her face and showed her where I'd been burned.

"That explains why Kim was there!" exclaimed Lee Joon after a quick inspection of my pink flesh. "She never goes in evening. Says she's too busy at the restaurant."

"Kim!" Of course. She'd known about the Queen Min box. The *kye* money. She kept Hector hooked up with the sports center to provide some multicultural brown camouflage for whatever bunko crime or phony scam she and Ko Won were running. Lee Joon watched me expectantly. I felt mean, jerked around. "Jin's dead. Killed last Tuesday."

"*Ahnee, ahnee!* No, no!" Lee Joon screamed as she swayed, starting to collapse. I reached for her. She hit me in the chest with both of her tiny balled-up fists. I grabbed her wrists with my right hand and put my other arm around her, pulling her toward me. I hoped no one had heard her. I'd hate to have anyone find me like this. What would they think I was doing? I made shushing noises.

"You lie!" She tried to wriggle out of my grasp.

"No. *Ahnee.*" I shook her roughly. Too rough for an old lady. "You know it's true. You said so yourself."

She went limp in my arms, nodding miserably and mumbling Jin's name. She began to sob, so I held her next to me and felt her trembling body. They'd known each other for nearly half their lives. They'd been friends for longer than I'd been alive. I thought of Lupe. How long would she be my friend?

"What happened?" Lee Joon cried.

I whispered in her ear that I'd seen a man in a mask steal the *kye* money and then shoot Jin. Lee Joon moaned as she shoved me away. Her face was streaked with mascara, and wet, dark liner seeped into the maze of wrinkles around her eyes. "That's why you ask questions about Kim. Kim in this somehow, isn't she? She's no good."

"You know who Chungmi is?"

"Kim's mother." Lee Joon wiped her eyes with the sleeve of her costume. "Oh, Jin, my poor Jin . . . ," she kept repeating.

"And you know who Chungmi's mother was?"

She stepped back, erect with trembling dignity. "Why not just ask who told me?" Her face brightened with cruel pleasure. She must have known this story for a long time. "Nancy Johnson. Jin told her years ago when they played cards every day. Stupid to tell Nancy Johnson anything. She tell everyone. Even Chu Chu Park."

"Everyone's always known?" I groaned. I ran my fingers nervously through my hair. I knew Kim had been lying to me, but Dorothy?

"We never told Jin or Dorothy or Kim that we knew. Best to give some respect to their family."

I stared at the Chusok masks hanging on the walls. They stared back blankly at me. Damn, I'd liked Dorothy. I'd thought she was the kind of little old lady I'd like to be one day. I asked Lee Joon if she knew how Kim had found Dorothy in Koreatown. I repeated what the minister and his wife had told me about kicking Kim out of their home.

Lee Joon nodded. "She came here, the civic association, when she was fourteen. I was volunteer at the front desk. She couldn't speak any Hangul. Only English. She was a skinny girl, but already had a bosom. Said she was hungry. That her mother was dead. She said some church had brought her here, but they treat her bad so she ran away."

"Did you try to find the people she'd lived with? Or call the authorities to help her?"

Lee Joon shrugged. "Best for Korean girl to live in Koreatown. Then she showed me the picture she had. It was Dorothy!"

"You knew Dorothy?"

"In those days everyone knew everyone. Not like now." Lee Joon told me she took Kim over to the apartment building where Dorothy and Jin lived and Kim stayed there with them, sometimes with Dorothy and sometimes with Jin, until she was nearly eighteen years old.

I asked her what Kim had been like after she left her grandmother and great-aunt.

"Like every other bargirl." Lee Joon seemed delighted to dog Kim. "Work three or four years at bar on Olympic."

I took my hand out of my coat pocket. I'd been told by a juror after my first jury trial that it made me look insincere. I almost got the guy I represented convicted on solicitation because I'd addressed the jury with my hand in my suit pocket the whole time and they didn't like that. "Dorothy told me Kim had always worked in the restaurant before she became the owner. Why would she lie to me?"

Lee Joon examined the mask in her hands before answering. "You don't understand how important family is. Maybe you don't have one. . . ."

Yeah, I have one. If you want to call it that. Two parents, never divorced. One child. Three bedrooms. Three baths. Living room, den, formal dining room. We move among the rooms without speaking.

"Worst thing in the world to bring shame upon your family," Lee Joon was saying. "No one's going to say Kim's a bargirl. Even though everybody knows it. Knows she sleeps with a lot of men. Take their money. Be big shot with gangsters."

Lee Joon put on the Chusok mask. "Go home. Leave Koreatown for Koreans." She walked out into the hall and disappeared among the clouds of yellow silk.

I ran out of the building to get my car but saw it would be impossible to drive to Dorothy's. Thousands of people waiting for the parade to begin lined the curbs and clogged the streets. I called the office to find out where Lupe was, to warn her in case Hector decided to go take his beat-up *macho* shit out on her. She didn't answer. I pushed in the code for the message machine.

"Whitney." It was the Golden Tiger. "There's no Edward Lu with the LAPD. I called a buddy of mine who's a hacker, able to bust into practically any computer system. . . ."

I slammed the phone down and jogged north across Olympic toward Dorothy's apartment. I was mad as hell. She'd known all along about Kim but couldn't admit her own flesh stole from her. Or would kill for what she wanted. Dorothy had almost gotten me killed because she wanted to preserve the fiction of her family.

Lupe's Fiat was parked in front of Dorothy's apartment building. What was she doing here? I took the stairs two at a time and ran down the landing. I pounded on the door. Did Lupe believe there was something more for her here in Koreatown? What could it be? I leaned against the wall catching my breath as I waited for one of them to answer. I felt sick all the way through. What had been driving me all along was the shame that Lupe had seen my cowardice in Dogtown. Now I'd put her in another fucked-up situation.

Lupe opened the door with a cup of steaming chrysanthemum tea in her hand. She handed it to me, then stood aside. The radio was playing "Autumn Leaves," and I saw Dorothy dressed in a white suit and sitting on the couch.

"What are you doing here?" I gasped at her.

Lupe went back into the living room without saying anything. She sat down on the couch next to Dorothy and put her arm around her. Dorothy clutched a white handkerchief in one hand and waved it feebly at me. She'd been crying. I glanced at Lupe with alarm. What had she been up to?

"I wear white today because I am mourning Jin. . . ." Dorothy's voice trailed off, and I thought she was going to cry again.

I put the tea down on the dining table, too angry to feel sorry for her. "Stop it. You could have saved us all a lot of grief if you'd told the truth about Kim from the beginning."

"I'm sorry," mumbled Dorothy. She twisted the handkerchief and looked down at her lap.

"Sorry! I've been chased, beaten up, almost raped . . ."

"Leave her alone, Whitney, she's an old lady. She's worn out," Lupe growled. "Whatever she did, she did to try to keep her family together."

"Keep her family together! What a load of bullshit! Jin was family too. She was killed, right here in this room. It wouldn't have happened if you'd faced the facts about Kim a long time ago, Dorothy."

"Kim didn't have anything to do with it!" exclaimed Dorothy.

"Don't lie to me. Stop lying to yourself. You'll never get

your daughter back," I yelled. "You don't even know for certain that Kim's your blood. She was a failure in school, a liar, a bargirl, a whore . . ."

Dorothy's eyes begged me to stop saying ugly things about her granddaughter.

"Everything was there in the open for everyone in town to see." I smacked the table. "I was the only one who couldn't see what was going on. Did she ask you for money? The Queen Min box?"

"I told her she'd get the box after Jin and I died. . . ." Dorothy put her head into her hands.

"Go on," I said. "All of it. You owe it to me now."

"She knew the box was part of our family, our history. I tried to give her whatever she wanted. Jin said I spoiled her. Kim heard Jin tell me not to give her the box and to stop giving her money. Kim said I didn't love her. She said I left her mother to die in a whorehouse," Dorothy cried. "I told Kim that if Jin died before I did, she could have the box."

"Jesus fucking Christ, this is your idea of family?" I moaned.

Lupe put her arm more protectively around Dorothy. "Shut up! Stop being such a moron, Whitney. If anything ever happened to your parents, you'd do the same thing."

I heard myself laugh in a loud, ugly explosion. "Place the lives of other people in danger? Have someone killed?"

Lupe let go of Dorothy and stared up at me defiantly. "If anything happened to Joey, I'd do whatever was necessary. Lie, cheat, steal. Why do you think I worked the streets?"

"Because you didn't finish school," I snapped. "Because you're poor. You never heard of deferred gratification. Because—"

"You act like you were raised by wolves," Lupe said angrily. "Your family's the most important thing in the world. To be with your family, to support your family."

I imagined my mother and father sitting in the living room back in Maryland, not speaking to each other. It was almost two and a half years since I'd been back there.

Dorothy sat up. A bit of color returned to her cheeks. She took Lupe's hand and I saw her squeeze it. "I stopped wanting to live after I realized Kim had planned it all. When the man spoke to Jin, I knew he wasn't Korean. He had to be one of Kim's friends."

Lupe nodded her head at Dorothy in understanding. "My grandmother's the same way. Only speaks Spanish. Doesn't know anybody who's not Mexican."

I dropped down in the chair next to the couch and looked Dorothy in the face. "I can't believe it. You knew from the moment you hired me. You were afraid if you called the police they'd be able to figure it out. I was supposed to screw things up so none of your friends would know what happened."

Dorothy took a sip of tea. "I had to. She's my family. Lupe understands what that means."

Lupe squeezed Dorothy's hand.

We all sat there without saying anything. I remembered an afternoon when I was a freshman in college. I'd been invited to dinner at the house of one of my sorority sisters. As she drove me down an oak-lined street I glanced into the living room of a large brick house. A beautiful blond little girl about eight years old sat in a red velvet chair. Her legs dangled over the edge of the chair without touching the ground. She held a large picture book, and on either side of her stood her parents, Mom and Dad, who leaned over her with rapt attention and boundless love as she read aloud from the book. I began to cry and turned away so the girl driving the car wouldn't see. How I wanted my family to be just like that. At dinner my sorority sister's mother served me crab cakes, roast chicken with fresh peas, and strawberry shortcake. I thought they were a perfect family too. Her father never made it home, and later I heard my "sister" and her mother arguing in the kitchen about money. The little girl in the red velvet chair? She was probably being fucked by her father.

Dorothy disengaged herself from Lupe and poured herself more tea. "There is something you can do that the police can't."

Snatching my purse from the floor where I'd tossed it next to the chair, I stood up, shaking my head angrily. "Let's go, Lupe."

"Bring my granddaughter home to me."

"That's a laugh. Why should I do anything else for you?"

Dorothy smoothed the white silk jacket she wore. "Lupe's told me about you. You want to make the world a better place. Deep down you believe people are good. Find Kim. Tell her I forgive her. No matter what she'd done or how far away she tries to go, she is still the daughter of my daughter."

"That really pulls my heartstrings," I said. "I'm outta here. Come on, Lupe."

Lupe glanced at Dorothy but didn't move.

I hesitated. "Lupe?"

I must be a bonehead. It was all so tender. The warm connection between Lupe and Dorothy. A swelling crescendo of violins. I stood in stupid contemplation of Lupe's dogged love for her family. I felt subhuman because I didn't love my family.

Dorothy turned from Lupe to me. "I'm giving your friend Lupe five thousand dollars for her son, Joey. Half now, half when you find Kim and convince her to come home."

I glanced at Lupe. Her eyes were bright with excitement and hunger. If I didn't agree, she'd try to find Kim herself. She'd get killed. "We want cash."

Dorothy nodded.

Lupe got up. "Don't worry, Dorothy. We'll bring her back to you."

I stomped out of Dorothy's apartment with Lupe following. The sound of a marching band came from over on Olympic. I glanced at my watch. It was just past noon. The Chusok parade had begun.

"I just wanted to get the fuck out of Koreatown," I raged. "I can't believe you'd cut a deal with her behind my back."

"Go back to the office, then. I'll handle things myself. I shoulda known it. You're just a *gabacha*. No *alma*. Emotionally constipated. You hate being white and you don't got no soul."

"*Chíngate*, homegirl. I got my feet on the street. And no matter what kind of sissy you think I am, I'm not letting that old lady or you screw me out of the money. I've earned it. I put my ass on the line for her. And I've helped you plenty, so don't be giving me any bullshit now about white and brown, or black and yellow. Let's just talk about the green."

"What an honest moral revelation," said Lupe. "You're gonna go for the dough. You're not just a goody-two-shoes crusader after all."

Did she know I was doing this for her? "Yeah, I feel like a whole person. Indignant and greedy."

Lupe nodded at me. "Great. I want to see how you pull this off, O great white liberal, fixer of all that is wrong. Shouldn't be too hard. We just find Kim and tell her Dorothy wants her to come home. And I can't wait to see Hector! Tell him his *amorcito*'s a murderer. That's hot! That must be a real turn on, sleeping with the criminally insane. I'll give you a third of it, just like you were gonna give me."

"From now on we're fifty-fifty on everything."

"Sixty-forty," said Lupe. "Dorothy gave the money to me. I've got a kid." She stared defiantly at me, waiting to see if I was going to give her a bad time about Joey. I didn't. I told her Ko Won was using Kim's restaurant for some kind of money laundering. "That guy I told you about from the bar in the Marina, the one who said he's a cop—"

"Your new boyfriend!" crowed Lupe. "Whitney's in love! With a pig. Maybe we can knock this thing off by dinnertime and you can go out to sup *con tu novio*—"

"I'm pretty certain I recognized his hands."

"His hands?" Lupe howled. "You been jacking off thinking about what he can do to you with his hands? You do jack off, don't you?"

I shook my head impatiently. "I think he's the guy who tried to rape me. Since I've been studying Tae Kwon Do I got into looking at people's hands. His are a bit small, ring finger on his left hand's crooked like it's been broken. The first two knuckles of his right hand are callused like he always tries to lead a punch with them. He's the guy who killed Jin."

"Holy shit," gasped Lupe. "Why didn't you say so sooner? Let's wrap this up. We'll tell Kim she better go make peace with her grandmother because the cops are closing in on Ko Won's gang. Then we're gone. *Adiós* Koreatown."

"Fifty-fifty. I got a gun."

Lupe turned toward Olympic as the sound of the parade drew closer. The Santa Ana blasted the street, and the rough wind pulled at Lupe's long black hair. She smoothed it back from her face and stared off into the distance. Finally she nodded, "Ok, girl, you got a deal. *Vámonos.*" She shuffled impatiently from one foot to the other, eager for us to be on our way.

I grabbed her by the arm. "I wanted to tell you. You've been a real inspiration to me, Lupe. These strong family values. I never told you this, but I come from a dysfunctional family. There, I feel good sharing that with you." I let go of her. "And I'd feel even better if you'd give me my share of the money now."

Lupe frowned for an instant, not knowing if I was serious. Then she opened her purse, flashed $2,500 in hundred dollar bills, and slapped half of them into my hand. "I suggest you use yours for some psychotherapy. I'm gonna buy Joey some clothes and get me a real Chanel belt." She grinned. I wondered if there was more money that she hadn't told me about.

I said we should go to Ko Won's store. Although he was probably riding a big float in the parade, someone there would know where he was. I was pretty sure Kim would be with him. We could give his office a quick toss while he was gone. I told Lupe I'd already been to see Hector that morning, and Kim hadn't been with him. "Come on, we gotta walk."

Lupe looked at me as though I had proposed something truly insane, totally revolutionary. Bananas. Walking in Los Angeles.

The street was busy with stragglers rushing to catch the parade. The closer we got to Olympic the louder became the sound of music and clashing drums. At Olympic the crowd was four and five deep lining the boulevard. It was nearly all Korean with a sprinking of Salvadorans and Mexicans, who clumped in their own small groups, pretending to be oblivious to the Koreans standing next to them. The latinos had probably looted some of the very merchants who were paying for the bands and floats in the parade. Lupe and I ran across Olympic between a group of dancing children and a marching drum band. We pushed our way through the crowd and down the block to Ko Won's store.

The store was open. A clerk at the front counter was conducting a busy sale of video cassettes and film to tardy parade-goers in straw hats and paper visors imprinted with the name of Ko Won's store. Lupe and I slipped down one of the aisles while the clerk was busy. We went back to the office where we'd first met Ko Won. The door was locked, but I knocked insistently on it.

Ko Won's voice asked something in Korean.

"I'm looking for Kim," I said.

I heard an office chair rolling across the floor, then footsteps. Ko Won opened the door. Kim sat in his office in a tailored black suit with no blouse under the jacket, strands of pearls covering her breasts. She smoked indulgently while holding a vcr remote control in her other hand. She glanced away from the video screen she was watching and looked over at us.

"Your grandmother told us to bring you home," I announced.

Kim laughed, then said something in Korean to Ko Won. He laughed. "Relax," he said to us. "It's a holiday. We were just giving thanks for how good the year's been and remembering those who've been so helpful to us."

"Come here," Kim said to us. "I think you'll enjoy the video we're watching."

Lupe looked questioningly at me. I wished I'd gone back to the car for my gun. I looked at Ko Won in his elegant tapered suit. If he was wearing a gun I couldn't see it. He moved back over to his desk and leaned protectively against it. That told me he had one in the top drawer.

I walked over to stand beside Kim. I looked at the video.

On the screen Kim, in a black merry widow and black thigh-high vinyl boots with stiletto heels, faced the camera as she stood straddling a fat man who lay on his back on the floor of a crummy room. Her exquisite butt was toward his face. The faceless man pulled at his penis.

Kim touched the remote control so sound filled the room. We heard the man's moaning and panting. I glanced quickly over at Ko Won and wondered if he was the man in the video. He looked as if he was enjoying the show very much. I stared back at Kim in the video. She crouched and moved back as if she was going to sit on the man's face, but before she got down she swirled her pelvis up and away from him. He moaned more. Next to me, Kim touched the remote so the sound went up louder.

Lupe walked over, stood beside me, and studied the video. I didn't look at her, but I could feel her next to me as she shifted restlessly. Did Lupe do scenes like this? She'd never actually told me what she did on the street. I'd guessed from her knowledgeability of the S&M happenings at the Church of the Big Mother that she did. It was, I supposed, all pretty standard. High heels, soft little whips, pretend spankings.

In the video Kim turned to face the man. The camera zoomed in on her as she squatted over the prostrate man. She spread her vagina with her fingers. Her muff was dark black, the hair straight and silky. Her labia were nearly crimson. A stream of urine ran out and down onto the face of the man below her.

Lupe shook her head as though she was disgusted but not surprised by Kim. "Figures," Lupe said. "I knew she was a real skeezer."

The man's ragged breathing on the video soundtrack sounded as if he'd been pushed over the edge into ecstasy. He began to babble, to talk fast and crazy, incoherent words. I couldn't make out anything he was saying. He sounded as if he was loaded.

The camera pulled back to reveal his face.

It was Hector Ramos!

Kim burst into laughter.

"You filthy fucking whore," Lupe swore. She jumped at Kim. *"Pinchi puta, hija de perra, con tu culo viejo . . ."*

Kim bolted from her chair. Lupe swung at her. Kim's right arm came up fast, blocking the punch. Ko Won shoved his chair away from the desk, where he'd taken a seat. Lupe stepped in closer to Kim, trying to grab her by the neck. Kim slapped Lupe as hard as she could. Lupe staggered backward into the desk. Blood trickled from the corner of her mouth. She pushed herself up and threw herself at Kim, ripping at the pearls around Kim's neck. One of the strands broke, and pearls rained across the floor. Lupe clung to her, digging her fingers into Kim's throat. Kim grabbed Lupe's arm with both hands and smashed it down on the edge of the desk. Lupe screamed, grabbing her arm to her chest and doubling over in pain.

Ko Won stood up from the desk.

I leapt toward Kim, planted myself solidly on my left foot and with a roundhouse kicked harder than I'd ever kicked the training bag at the *do jang*. I caught her in the ribs, and I heard something crack and give way beneath my foot.

Ko Won ripped open the top drawer of the desk. He pulled out a gun. I picked up the chair Kim had been sitting in and swung it in his direction. It didn't sail easily over the desk the way you'd expect it to in a movie, but it hit him and threw him off balance. Lupe flung herself against the wall, grabbing for the light switch near the door. The overhead light went out. The evil video flickered in the dark. A shot went off. Kim shoved Lupe aside and bolted from the room.

I ran for the door too, but tripped over the upended trash can and went sprawling. As I got to my feet I saw Kim running down the main aisle of the store and out onto the street.

16

I ran out the front door. A float fashioned of red carnations rolled down Olympic Boulevard. Cheers and applause greeted the princesses on it. They were dressed in long gold-and-pink silk dresses like the ones Jin and Dorothy had been wearing the morning I first came to Koreatown. Old women and children watching from the sidewalk waved flags in the air.

Lupe came careening out the door right behind me. "That fucking bitch. Where'd she go?"

I looked up and down the crowded sidewalk. Had I lost Kim in the swelling crowd? Ko Won emerged from the store talking angrily into a cellular phone and scanning the swarming street. A drunk and lost-looking *salvadoreno* bumped into Ko Won, who shoved him angrily away with his free hand. Then Ko Won spotted us. He barked into the phone.

Lupe grabbed my arm. She shoved me toward the street and started to run.

Was Ko Won calling some of his men? Fifty yards away

I saw Kim running east through the crowd. I jerked free of Lupe and sprinted after Kim.

A marching drum corps of black kids from Watts pranced ahead of the float. They stopped, quickstepped, broke and danced while the drums pounded. The Koreans stared at them in silence. I pushed past Mexican families with teenage kids in Guns n' Roses T-shirts; past Korean women in navy tailored pantsuits and sensible jewelry; past Salvadorans with their princess daughters in bright lacy dresses, which stood out stiffly from their thin brown legs; past an old Buddhist nun with a long gray robe and a shaved head.

I ran the way I do on the track at the high school near my apartment. Shoulders loose, hands curled in soft fists, my breathing easy and regular. Kim was forty yards in front of me, running as fast as she could, as I closed the distance between us. I was nearly behind her. She'd kicked off her shoes and she must have been completely hyped on adrenaline, because I knew I'd hurt her when I kicked her. She wove through the crowd, cutting to the right then to the left. Over the pounding drums I thought I could hear Lupe's labored breathing as she struggled to keep up with me. I quickly glanced around at her. Her hair flew wildly and her face was etched with pain.

I slammed into a young Korean guy in black jeans and a yellow polo shirt and we both went down. Apologizing, he tried to help me up, but I was already on my feet and running after Kim again. People clustered around carts selling dolls and food. All along the street many people wore Chusok masks, and thousands more of the weird pink masks swung from poles carried by vendors. Lupe was caught in the crowd far behind me, losing ground, and I left her to struggle through for herself.

Kim glanced back over her shoulder. I was less than ninety feet behind her. Kim burst into a sprint, angling for the end of the block where a Tae Kwon Do team was putting on a demonstration in the middle of the intersection. Everyone on the team wore white uniforms sashed with colorful belts denoting his or her individual rank in their school. A select corps of black belts were in hand to hand combat while the less experienced belts moved back and forth in a choreography of advance and retreat punctuated by loud fierce cries. Kim looked toward the intersection. I jumped toward the curb, thinking she was going to try to run across Olympic between the battling martial arts students.

Kim veered instead to the right at the end of the block and sprinted through the crowd toward a side street. I hurdled over an ice chest and sent a family scattering as I raced after her. They jumped up, yelling at me. Kim disappeared down the side street and into a two-story building hung with a scarlet-and-yellow banner with writing in Hangul, English, and Spanish.

—Welcome to Koreatown—
—Korea—Land of the Morning Calm—
—Bienvenidos a Koreatown—

I charged after her into the building. Inside there was a glass-domed atrium full of people in both regular clothes and traditional robes. The center of the atrium was open, and a wooden stage had been erected there. On the empty stage was a long table covered with white paper and oranges, bananas, apples, peaches. Half a watermelon wrapped in cellophane lay next to a sheaf of green leaves. A microphone stood at the edge of the stage. I searched the milling crowd quickly from where I stood near the entrance. I didn't see Kim.

I made my way into the happy swarm as a guy in a green t-shirt walked up to the mike and tapped it. The tapping sound echoed through the atrium. People stopped talking and drew closer to the stage. After a moment a line of women dressed in identical sky blue gowns marched up onto the stage carrying drums and a wooden musical instrument that looked like a Balinese gamalong. The women sat down on the stage and began to play. The crowd, many of them carrying Panasonic video equipment, surged closer to tape the ceremony.

I searched through the crowd again. I saw Lupe come in the door, stop and look around. She gave the room her defiant once-over. She saw me and began to move through the revelers toward me. There were several hundred people, mostly Korean, but also some latinos and a few whites and blacks. The Koreans were dressed up in good suits and party dresses. I spotted Kim at the far end of the stage breathing hard and with her hand on her ribs where I'd kicked her. She was sweating and wiping at her face with her other hand. She wasn't looking in my direction.

I slipped farther back to the edge of the crowd where the atrium was bounded by bamboo trees with yellowing leaves and began to move slowly toward her. Lupe tried to get through the mass to follow me.

Three more Korean women in the blue robes came through a path that cleared for them in the crowd. They carried a long knotted white cloth above their heads. They were heavily made up with thick foundation powdered with white rice powder. They had painted their eyebrows black, arching up to their temples, and their eyes were also lined with black. Their mouths were crimson. They passed near me. I turned away so Kim wouldn't see me if she was watching their entrance. Cymbals crashed.

An old man in a white gown and a black high hat and blue shoes marched behind the women. He carried a maroon-colored umbrella over his head. A series of frightening bird cries tore through the air. One of the old women put down her drum and whirled to the center of the stage. I realized the cries were coming from her. The dancers on stage swayed with their eyes closed. I moved toward Kim. A Korean guy in a dark suit danced toward the stage waving dollar bills in each hand. He quickly put the money on the stage, which I now understood was an altar.

I edged closer to where Kim stared transfixed at the altar. I wondered what meaning, if any, the old ceremonies had for her. Hadn't she wanted to leave her culture and ties to the past behind? Was she amused by what she saw now? Disgusted? The lowest class, the *ch'onmin*, had been butchers, monks, slaves, serfs, actors, and shamans. This spiritual circus was taking place in a mall. Kim's face was flushed but radiant, almost peaceful. Her right hand moved slowly up to caress the remaining strand of pearls she wore. She closed her eyes and bowed her head for a moment, her lips forming silent words. Then Kim opened her eyes and darted forward and tossed her strand of pearls on the altar.

I pushed toward her.

Glasses of drink passed among the musicians. Another dancer got to her feet and began to twirl around and around in place. She made a dizzying number of revolutions, then dropped to her knees and bowed her head to the floor twice. A third female shaman jumped up, grabbed the microphone from the edge of the stage, and began exhorting the unknown with guttural cries.

A white woman in the audience began to dance in place to the beat of the drums. The Koreans surrounding her pointed at her and laughed. The musicians offered each other more booze. A woman from the audience rushed forward carrying a bottle of Cutty Sark and waved it around before setting it on the stage. The singer sang with vibrato increasing in tempo and urgency.

I crept to within yards of Kim. She looked away from the stage, still flushed and mesmerized, and over in my direction. Her face was a serene island in the excited crowd. I'd never seen her look so gentle or innocent. I stepped toward her. She seemed surprised to see me, as though she'd forgotten where she was. An old woman handed a girl a hundred dollar bill to put on the platform for her. The horde shoved forward, many with cash in their hands.

I crouched behind a couple headed to the stage with their money and ran around the bamboo trees. Kim stepped back from the altar. I saw her looking in wild confusion around the atrium for me. Another woman shaman with a red bandanna tied around her head got up and began to dance. Her blue robe twirled around her legs. She lifted her bare foot slowly, her arms extended outward. The drummers joined together in feverish syncopation to carry the dancer on her journey.

I came from behind the trees and toward Kim. She ran for a flight of stairs at the far end of the hall.

I was nearly close enough to reach out and grab her when she twisted away, hurtling into a dimly lit hall that led toward the back of the building. She'd been here before. She shoved open the back door, and for an instant I saw the immaculate blue sky off to the east. Then she was gone. The door slammed shut.

I opened the door.

In the large parking lot behind the building a village had been constructed of plywood painted the color of clay. Roofs colored like tiles of many intricate designs topped the houses. It looked like a movie set. I didn't see Kim. I stood panting among the artificial houses.

In front of me hundreds of cobalt blue tiles raised diagonally against each other formed a gate in front of the largest house. I went through it and into the house. Sliding walls made of heavy ivory-colored paper divided the house into two rooms. The first room was furnished with the simplest essentials: a couple of small tables and some chests for clothing and bedding.

I went into the second room.

Kim stood facing the wall. She was holding her side. Her breathing was so ragged I was sure I'd cracked her rib.

"This house, this is a re-creation of a Korean village from the last century," she wheezed painfully. "This is my history. This is where I come from. Tonight there'll be a party here for Chusok. Food. Dancing—"

I put my hand up to stop her. I wasn't interested in the *National Geographic* tour. "Dorothy asked me to come get you."

"Whitney!" I heard Lupe yell. I could tell from the sound of her voice that she was just outside. "Where are you?"

Kim glanced at the door. We both heard Lupe's high heels as she came through the open portal and through the empty first room.

"In these old houses they built fires under the wooden floors, pipes carried the heated smoke from the fires and heated the whole house." Kim looked around the room as though trying to memorize it. Then her eyes traveled slowly over me. She was sizing me up, measuring the distance between us. "Always watch your opponent's eyes," the Golden Tiger says. "In your opponent's eyes you can see every move he's going to make." There wasn't anywhere left for Kim to run.

I took a step toward her. "She wants you to come home."

"*Ondol.* The heating was called *ondol.*"

Lupe shoved open the partially closed rice-paper door and stepped into the room with us. Her white silk blouse had come untucked, and her skirt was ripped from trying to run in it.

"We slept on the floors of our houses," Kim whispered.

Lupe struggled to catch her breath. "You got the bitch!" she crowed to me.

As she wheeled to face Lupe, Kim's features rearranged themselves into a mocking mask. She looked more like herself now. Cunning and quick. "Love your outfit," Kim sneered at her. "Loved it every time I've seen it on you. You must make a fortune when you wear that on the streets."

Lupe ripped off the jacket of her gray flannel suit and threw it down on the floor. She put her hands on her hips, vogued and jerked her chin up at Kim. "Try looking this good, whore-dog."

"Any day, sweetheart. Any day." Tossing back her long velvet hair Kim pursed her lips and blew a kiss at Lupe as she strutted toward her.

"I was born sexy," Lupe purred. "You had to learn it from your whore mother."

I stepped in between them, trying to separate them.

Kim leaned forward quickly, grabbed me by the shoulders, and kissed me. She pushed her tongue into my mouth and guided my hand down onto her breast. "I can take care of your girlfriend here better than you can," she taunted Lupe.

I shoved her away. I spit on the floor and wiped my mouth with the back of my hand.

"That figures. She tastes as rotten as she looks," Lupe said as she moved away, tucking her blouse in. "Yeah, Whitney, you're right. I don't have to compete with a piece of shit like her." Wiping at her sweating face Lupe wouldn't look at me, but she glared at Kim. "She knows you sent the guy who killed Jin. And she wants you to come home anyway."

"Dorothy?" For a split second Kim's eyes shifted away from us and toward the far wall.

I followed her gaze, but didn't say anything. There was a sliding panel there. An escape route? The room was dead silent except for our uneven breathing.

"Dorothy thinks I had something to do with Auntie Jin getting killed!" Kim's voice wavered toward theatrical hysteria.

"She's known all along," said Lupe.

"She's crazy! She's always thought I was trying to take advantage of her."

"Weren't you, Kim? I come from a pretty fucked-up family, but I can't imagine killing any of them. You stole seventy-five thousand dollars from her, but why did Jin have to die? I'm sure Dorothy would have given you the money. Why didn't you just ask her for it?"

"I did." Kim waved her hand angrily as if this was all Dorothy's fault, as if Dorothy deserved whatever happened for being stubborn.

Lupe shook her head. "Why didn't you ask your friend Ko Won for it? Guess your worn-out *caja* just ain't worth it."

Kim folded her arms across her chest. The top button of her jacket had come undone, and her ivory breasts glistened with sweat.

"What's it about, Kim? Money laundering?" I prodded. "I think the restaurant was opened with money from Ko and you gave him the *kye* money to put into a drug lab 'cause you couldn't go into that kind of business on your own. He makes money from ice or whatever the fuck it is and pushes cash through your restaurant. I bet he's not kicking back to you like he promised."

"Yeah," said Lupe, laughing. "You're probably making less than when you were a bargirl."

Kim moved closer to me. "Cafe James Dean's a real restaurant."

"And I'm Ivana Trump," I said. "You should go home and make your peace with Dorothy before you get busted. The cops are right behind us."

"You're a lot of laughs, blondie," Kim hooted.

Lupe picked her jacket up off the floor and dusted it off. "I'll wait for you outside. It stinks in here. I need some fresh air."

I nodded, "Yeah. We'll be out in a sec. I'm sure when I explain things to Kim she'll want to come with us."

"Your grandmother paid us to find you," Lupe said. "A nice pile of real cash. Now I got the money and you can kiss my ass." She tossed her jacket over her shoulder and, with one last poisonous look at Kim, strode out.

Kim and I stared at each other. Her eyes flashed resentment at me.

"What happened to the Queen Min box?" I asked. I could feel that my face was still red, my lips slimy and venomous where she'd touched me.

Kim waved her hand dismissively at me. "That piece of junk."

"It's a map to a treasure."

"Bullshit. The old stories don't mean anything anymore."

I'd never know if the box was real or not. Kim could have sold it to a collector or thrown it out. History has always been negotiable. "Dorothy's not gonna press charges against you, but I saw Ko Won out at the Marina the other night. A cop was there," I said. "Undercover."

Kim smirked. "Oh, really? What'd he look like?"

"Long black hair in a ponytail. Green eyes. Good-looking."

Kim turned toward the sliding paper wall. "Good-looking. You hear that, Eddie?"

The wall panel slid open.

Edward Lu stepped into the room.

I looked back and forth between them. Ko Won must have called him from his cellular telephone as Lupe and I raced out of the electronics store. Kim knew where she was going when she ran out of Ko Won's. To meet Eddie. They were all in the same gang, but I didn't have much time to savor the satisfaction of being right.

Eddie looked me up and down. He was in the same sharp black suit I'd seen him in at the bar. He was packing. Why hadn't I brought the frigging gun? That's what it's for, isn't it?

"Meet my old man, Eddie. Actually, you've met him before."

I looked at Eddie. "Yeah, at the Rusty Wharf in the Marina."

Kim laughed. "Before that."

I nodded my head in sick confirmation of what I'd suspected, but I couldn't speak.

"At your place," Kim prodded.

He *was* the guy in the Chusok mask! Anger rushed from the pit of my stomach to my head. I wanted to throw myself on him. I wanted to kill him. "You tried to rape me!"

"Where do you suppose I got that idea?" smiled Eddie. If he'd been the slightest bit wary of me when I fought back against him outside my apartment building, he didn't show it now. It must have been a fluke that I'd been able to deck him. Or had he let me hurt him to make me overconfident and foolish?

I turned and stared at Kim with dumb animal hatred. "You rotten cunt!"

Eddie snickered.

"Shut up, Eddie," snapped Kim.

"Why'd you tell him to do that?"

Kim shrugged. "Thought it would scare you off."

"Maybe you'd like it," Eddie suggested.

I glanced toward the door. How would I get out of here? The Golden Tiger says there's no shame in running away from a fight. "Does your boyfriend here know about Hector? That you're doing the nasty with him?"

"Who do you think shot that video?" laughed Eddie. He seemed like a guy who had fun wherever he went.

"Hey, Eddie." I looked from Kim to Eddie. He dressed good. He was handsome. "How much of the old ladies' seventy-five grand did you get?"

I watched him watch Kim. Maybe he was in love with her. I shouldn't forget the romantic angle. Maybe Kim did have a pussy that was better than any other on earth.

"The whole thing?" I asked. "I think if you're going to kill someone, you should get the whole thing."

"You told me it was twenty-five thousand," he said to Kim.

"It was." Kim moved closer to him. "She's lying!"

"You must have taken out fifty after Dorothy brought the money home from the bank," I said to Kim. "She told you to kill her auntie Jin too, didn't she? Bet she gave you a key so you could just walk into the old ladies' apartment."

Kim shot a wild look over at me. "I never told him to kill her! You think I would have taken you there if I'd known that's what he was going to do? I didn't even know he was going to be there then!" She whirled toward Eddie again. "Asshole, you were only supposed to scare them!"

"You stupid bitch!" Eddie snarled. "You know I'm gonna waste anybody gets in my way."

"Nobody's gonna buy that I told someone to kill my auntie."

How nice it would have been to believe her that she didn't want Jin dead, but I knew it was true. I grinned reassuringly at her. "That's right, Kim. You're gonna put on a pink dress, cry in front of the jury, and you're gonna walk right out of that courtroom as innocent as the day you were born.

"Murder," I said, shaking my head at Eddie. "While in the commission of a felony. That's special circumstances. You're looking at the death penalty. That's so cool: you fry, and Kim goes shopping. Right on, sister." I gave her a thumbs-up. "And you, Eddie, trying to impersonate a cop. Man, that's so old."

"Fuck you. I was a cop," Eddie said rather petulantly.

"Sure. Let me guess. Asian Gang Unit." I laughed. "In your dreams. I've checked on it. LAPD personnel never heard of you."

"Internal Affairs busted me on some chickenshit charge. That's why my name doesn't show up." He picked a piece of lint off his immaculate suit. "Pure chickenshit."

"Right." I yawned. "I'm sure lots of your fellow officers will come forward to testify as to your fine character. They'll be pushing each other out of the way to get to the witness stand."

Eddie shook his finger in my face. "You wanna do the job right, you gotta go shake hands with people IAD say are dirty. Then they say you're part of organized crime."

"Weren't you?"

Eddie moved away, now restless and angry. "They think we're all gooks. Who do you think the chiefs are? All white, all fucking flatheads who were in 'Nam or Korea. We all look alike to them. Just gooks."

Maybe he had been a cop, once upon a time. Going up against Internal Affairs is like being court-martialed. And he could make a lot more money with Ko Won than with the LAPD. Not to mention being presented with such splendid opportunities as stealing *kye* money from a group of old ladies. "Did Kim tell you that while you were busy packing for your trip to Death Row she was fucking Ko Won?"

Eddie looked from me to Kim, but he didn't look very surprised. "Were you?"

"No." Kim tossed her beautiful long black hair. I imagined them together, her hair cascading over him as it had over Hector Ramos in the video.

"You wouldn't lie to me, would you?" he asked. "I wouldn't like that."

Kim put her hand on his arm and smiled. "You know I wouldn't, honey."

"Good." Eddie stroked her hair. He let it run through his caressing fingers. "So where were you last night?"

"You weren't on the job banging Hector," I said. "I went to the apartment. He said you hadn't been home all night." I felt a little sorry for Hector in his lonely love shack. "You must have been with Ko Won."

"Eddie, baby, that's not true."

Eddie took Kim's hand off his arm and grabbed her wrist. "Ko told me. If you're lying about that, you're lying about how much money there was."

I inched away toward the door. "What happened to the Queen Min box? The big Queen Min emerald?"

"Emerald?" Eddie glanced quickly at me.

"She's talking shit, Eddie." Kim whined.

"I wondered why it was so goddamn important to you to keep that piece of junk," Eddie snarled.

"There's a map carved on it," I added. "Tells where the emerald is." I swallowed the hard lump in my throat so I could tell the big lie. "Jin taught Kim how to read the map. Jin was the only one who knew how."

"I been watching you." He grabbed Kim's hair and jerked her face close to his. "Right outside the door while you were sucking Ko's dick last night. You fucking lying bitch. You're history."

Eddie pulled out his gun.

"Come on, Eddie, don't joke around," Kim said, trying to move backward toward the ivory paper wall. "You and me, forever, you said so. We share everything."

I heard the sound of the parade passing by on Olympic. "Yeah, I think this has gone far enough," I said. "Let's all—"

"Shut up," Eddie said. "Down on your knees, white girl."

I crouched into a fighting position, ready to strike out if he got any closer to me.

Eddie turned with a quick roundhouse and kicked me so fast I couldn't block it. I flew backward, but I got back up. Kim tried to run past him toward the door. He grabbed her and threw her sprawling to the ground. He pointed the gun at us. "On the floor, both of you."

I got down on the floor.

"Eddie, baby. What about all our plans?" Kim whimpered.

"Whore. Think you can steal from me. Tell me to kill your auntie. You wanted to be in business, well, this is business." He jerked the gun at her and shoved her toward the wall.

Kim got to her knees. "Eddie . . ."

He pushed her head down until it was bowing on the floor.

My heart was pounding. He was only inches away from me.

"Eddie . . . ," Kim moaned.

"Business is business." He put the gun to the back of her head. I heard firecrackers exploding outside as the parade passed by. Eddie pulled the trigger, and everything turned red.

He came toward me. Everything started to shimmer around the edges. A dead silence fell about me, and in it I heard the voice not of the Golden Tiger but of my father.

"Whitney?" he whispered. "Whitney?" My bedroom door creaked slowly open. My father walked across the room to my bed. I was afraid to move. Couldn't protect myself. He pulled down the blanket. He bent over me. His hand hovered inches from my vagina. . . .

Then I saw the Golden Tiger appear, his white uniform whipping the air as he kicked and punched, hiding everything in the past from me. "Whitney!" I heard the Golden Tiger shout as his image faded. "Now, Whitney, now!"

I rolled and grabbed Eddie around the knees, knocking him off balance. Falling, he tried to hit me with the gun. I grabbed his wrist, shoving the gun upward and toward his chest. It went off. It clattered to the floor. Eddie fell to the ground.

I lay on the floor trying to catch my breath. Eddie's face was next to mine. He stared at me. There was a bullet hole the size of a tangerine where his cheek had been. His one remaining eye flickered closed. Blood ran from his mouth. I got to my knees, then to both feet. I picked the gun up from the floor. I wiped it off with my t-shirt. I put the gun back in Eddie's hand and closed his fingers around it.

I walked through the open doorway into the larger of the two rooms. An antique chest of walnut lined with cedar and with brass fittings stood in the center of the room. A typed index card explained in English that the chest was called a *jang* and that the etchings on the brass fittings were symbols of long life.

I walked back through the blue gate out into the streets of the paper-and-wood village. Later I would learn from Dorothy that such gates are for good luck. Lupe stood at a corner under a wooden pole that held a lantern. I glanced at my watch. Everything had happened in the paper village in less than ten minutes. *"Vamos."*

"Where's Kim? What happened?"

I wanted a drink. "Well, she's not going to be marrying your brother."

"I heard shots."

"It was only firecrackers. The parade. Come on, let's go."

Lupe started for the house where Kim and Eddie lay.

"She's dead," I said.

"You . . . ?" asked Lupe as she turned back to where I stood.

"One of Ko Won's guys killed her. The one who said he's a cop. He's in there too. They killed each other."

Lupe looked at me, searching my face. I had never lied to her before, but I wasn't going to tell her what I'd done. Had I wanted Eddie to kill Kim? In that instant I had. I felt her minute inspection, and I didn't blink. I made my eyes soft, innocent.

"I guess they didn't trust her anymore," I said. "Too ambitious. Trying to play too many people against each other. . . ." I stopped, looking away from her to the austere and silent parchment houses. "I'm sorry about the money."

Lupe sighed. She studied my face again. Her eyes were dark brown, almost black. Deep as wells. I don't know what she saw in my face at that moment. "Yeah, ok. I guess I'll have to live without a Chanel belt."

She waited to see if I'd say anything more, but I didn't.

"You could still do that tv show with the sex goddess," she offered. "It would be a good way to get your name known. I can help you with your image." She grinned, but looked away as though she understood the solitude I needed to quiet the rage in my soul.

We walked down the artificial street. The paper houses were bleached white by the noon sun and shimmered nascent in the hot light. We walked back through the building and the bamboo atrium in silence. Other dancers were on the stage. We walked through the happy, noisy crowd of Koreans and Mexicans and Central Americans. We opened the door and stepped out onto the holiday street.

The uneasy truce quiet that had settled over the city in the last months was punctuated by music. I would go tell Dorothy Oh her granddaughter would not be coming home. The Queen Min box was lost. The *kye* money was probably gone, but she would have the Shining Pearl restaurant. There would be people who wanted soul food. They would sit at tables together to eat and laugh and drink.

The Santa Ana wind blasted down the street, tugged at the brilliant banner hanging over the building, and ripped loose one of the ropes holding it. The banner drooped, the words crumpled upon themselves and disappeared.

NO JUSTICE
NO PEACE